CASH MONEY CONTENT

MURDERVILLE 2

THE EPIDEMIC

FROM THE MINDS OF

ASHLEY & JAQUAVIS

Murderville 2
The Epidemic

Copyright © 2012 by Ashley & JaQuavis

Cash Money Content™ and all associated logos are trademarks of Cash Money Content LLC.

First Trade Paperback Edition: July 2012

Book Layout: Peng Olaguera/ISPN

Cover Design: Oddball Dsgn

For further information log onto www.CashMoneyContent.com

Library of Congress Control Number: 2011931199

ISBN: 978-1-936399-07-9 pbk

ISBN: 978-1-936399-08-6 ebook

10 9 8 7 6 5 4

Printed in the United States

MURDERVILLE

PREVIOUSLY IN MURDERVILLE 1

"TELL ME WHERE THE MONEY AT, BITCH!" the goon said as he circled the girl who sat bound to the wood chair. The beauty just sat there and cried in agony, the ropes were tied so tightly that they stopped her circulation. The masked goon grew frustrated and struck her across the temple with the butt of his gun, splitting her flesh open. Blood trickled down her face as she remained silent but cringed in pain. "Tell me! Where does Po keep the money?!" he screamed as he ripped the ski mask off his head, tired of waiting for a response. He knew that the money was somewhere in the house because he had been following her drug-dealing boyfriend for two weeks. He witnessed him enter the house with his street money, only to exit empty-handed. He knew that the stash was inside the house somewhere. The woman just cried in pain and never answered the intruder's questions, frustrating him to the brink of rage.

"Yo, if you don't tell me where the stash at . . . I'm going to blow your brains all over your pretty little wall," the goon said as he pointed the gun at the young woman's head. He waited for a response, only to get nothing from her except more tears. The goon knew that he didn't have a lot of time, and he had already searched the house from top to bottom and came up with nothing. He slapped the girl, taking her silence as disrespect. He put his gun in his waist and wrapped his hands around the girl's neck and squeezed with all his might. He watched as her face turned blush red. She squirmed but there wasn't much she could do because of the ropes restraining her limbs. The goon thought about how she had blatantly ignored all of his questions, and he wanted to see her die. In his twisted mind, it would be payback for undermining his authority. He continued to squeeze her throat until the squirming stopped and her eyes stared into space . . . at nothing. She was dead.

The goon loosened his grip, letting her chin fall into her chest. He breathed heavily and stepped back from the woman's lifeless body. He took one more look around the room and noticed a plaque on the wall. It was a high school diploma. It read: "Michigan School for the Deaf" and was awarded to Scarlett Jones. That's when it began to make sense to the goon. *She couldn't answer my questions . . . because she was deaf. She didn't even hear me,* he thought as he was overwhelmed with guilt. He quickly fled from the house empty-handed, leaving the twenty-two-year-old beauty to sleep forever.

* * *

James "Po" Taylor drove down the highway and yawned as he glanced down at the clock on his dashboard. He hated that he was coming home so late, but it was for a good reason. He had picked up all the money he was owed in the streets. He finally had enough paper saved to buy the house he had promised his longtime girlfriend, Scarlett. He was deeply in love with her and had known her since she was a child. Although she was deaf, they had no problem communicating because Po had learned sign language years ago. He smiled as he thought about her beautiful face. He knew that he could finally give her what she deserved, and that was a beautiful house and a way out of the ghetto. He pulled into their driveway and grabbed the duffle bag full of money.

Po entered the house and reached for the light switch. He flicked it on and off repeatedly and smiled. He expected Scarlett to come from the den where she usually watched television until he came home. He saw the flickering of the television coming from the den and heard the news being telecasted. *She must have fallen asleep,* he thought to himself as he began to take off his coat. He hung it up and reached into his pocket for the ring that he had bought her earlier that day. He couldn't wait until the morning to tell her that they were moving and decided to wake her up. Little did he know, Scarlett would never wake up.

He walked into the den and noticed that she wasn't there. He then went upstairs, and his heart dropped when he noticed the way the house was torn up. It was as if a tornado ran through it. The bed was flipped over, and the drawers were pulled out and emptied onto the floor.

"Scarlett!" Po yelled as he frantically rushed to the other room. As he burst into the room, he saw the love of his life bound to a chair. "No!" he yelled as he raced to her and dropped to his knees in front of her. He unloosened the ropes to release her and tears began to fall as he noticed she wasn't moving. Her lips were dark purple, a far cry from the blush red they usually were. "Please, God, no. Please!" he pleaded as she fell into his arms. He rocked back and forth with his love in his arms. Tears flowed as he begged God to somehow make Scarlett wake up. He looked down at her and rubbed his hand over her face to close her eyelids. He then knew that she was gone forever.

The sun's beams crept through the blinds and shined on A'shai and Liberty's faces as they lay next to each other. The hospital-issued pager sounded off and began to vibrate, making it dance across the nightstand. The sound woke a sleeping Liberty, and she opened her eyes and couldn't believe her ears. It was the sound that they had been waiting on for an entire year. Liberty's body felt so weak. She could barely lift her head, but she managed to smile as joy overcame her.

"Shai, Shai, baby, wake up. We have a heart," she whispered faintly as she rubbed Shai's cheek with the back of her hand. "Shai?" she called again, noticing that his skin was cold to the touch. "Baby, wake up," she called as she managed to prop herself up. She nudged him with all the might that she had, but he didn't move. She didn't know at that point, but all along she had thought he was having a glass of cognac when in actuality he had been sipping on an old Creole drink called Black Tea. He had slowly ingested it as he told her the story of their lives, wanting to die with his soul mate. A'shai had been dying before her eyes, and she didn't even know it. His "special drink" caused a slow death and showed his commitment to his love for her. If she couldn't live, then he no longer wanted to, so he chose to die with her so they could forever be together.

Liberty continued to shake A'shai, but it was to no avail. She noticed that he wasn't breathing, and it all hit her like a ton of bricks. She mustered all her strength and grabbed the phone to call 911.

"Nine-one-one. What is your emergency?" the operator asked.

"Somebody please help. Shai isn't breathing. Oh God . . . He's not breathing!" she said, not even caring about her own health or the heart pager. Her time was also ticking, and if she didn't get to the hospital she would also die, but at that point, she didn't care. She was ready to meet A'shai on the other side.

Tears began to run down her face as the harsh reality set in. She collapsed on his chest on the brink of her own demise.

Liberty saw a bright white light, and she smiled, knowing that she was about to meet A'shai and they could finally be happy together. No more pain and no more of life's ills. She was ready to go to the afterlife. She saw a little boy standing in front of the bright light. As she looked closer, she saw it was A'shai as a young boy. He smiled from ear to ear and called her name.

"Liberty," he said in a playful tone. "Liberty," he repeated as he reached out his hand for her. Liberty knew that she was approaching death and rather than being scared . . . she was happy. She began to walk toward him, but for some reason she could not get any closer.

"Liberty," the paramedic called as he stood over her.

"No," Liberty whispered as she slowly shook her head. "No . . . Let me go with him." The paramedics scurried to save her life, something that she did not want. Liberty tried to tell the paramedic to let her die, but she was too weak to get another word out. An oxygen mask was placed over her mouth as she tried to mouth that she didn't want to be saved. She overheard the other paramedic talking.

"What happened to the guy that was with her?" one of paramedics asked.

"He was DOA. We had to call in the coroner."

ONE MONTH LATER

Po stood over the grave of his lost love and gently placed a bouquet of flowers on the grave. He rubbed his hand across her tombstone and bowed his head as he prayed for God to take care of his woman. Guilt overwhelmed him as he thought about how he had put Scarlett in harm's way. A single tear streamed down his cheek as he knelt down and shook his head. "Whoever did this to you . . . They are going to pay. I promise. You . . ." his voice began to crack. "You didn't deserve this, baby," he continued. Po stood up and began to walk to his car. He felt his phone vibrate on his hip. He looked at the caller ID and noticed that it was his right-hand man, Rocko.

"Hello," he said as he placed the phone to his ear.

"Yo, I know where the kid at that ran in your spot," Rocko said with the hostility showing in his voice.

"Word?" Po asked as he clenched his jaws and his heart began to speed up. He had been waiting for a break for two weeks, and his man had finally found one. Po had put fifty thousand on the goon's head, and it had paid off quickly. The streets had spoken.

"Yep. I'm in front of the kid's mother's house right now. Niggas is saying that he skipped town because he knew that you would be looking for him."

"So, let's bring him back into town. You already know how we going to do that, right?" Po said as he felt his trigger finger begin to itch.

"Say no more," Rocko said just before he hung up the phone. Without saying it, Po had just ordered the goon's mother to be killed and he would find out the logistics later. He had to return to the hospital and pick up Scarlett's belongings and sign a few papers since he was her only family. Scarlett's parents were killed in a car crash, so Po was all she had. He also had to sign off on the donor papers. Scarlett always expressed that she wanted to be an organ donor when she died, and Po had kept her wishes. As fate would have it, someone with the same rare blood type as Scarlett needed her heart. The organ was immediately removed from her chest moments after she was pronounced dead. It was one of the hardest decisions Po had to make, but he knew that Scarlett would have wanted it that way. For some strange reason, something in his gut wanted to know where the love of his life's special heart had ended up. Nevertheless, he would never know. It was against the hospital's policies so all he could do was wonder.

Liberty walked into the hospital to see the surgeon that performed the heart transplant. She had been released from the hospital only a month prior and was instructed to return that day to get a checkup. Although she had a new heart, it was still broken. It would forever be empty, and A'shai was the only man who could fill the space. She felt the soreness of the stitches that rested on the left side of her chest, which would always be a constant reminder of the reason A'shai committed suicide. *If only he had waited . . . then we would be together right now,* she thought. She kept replaying the night that he drank the Black Tea that had eventually sealed his fate.

Her life had been a blur over the past couple of weeks. Burying A'shai, going back into the home that they once shared, and living alone. She felt like her life would never be normal again. A'shai had enough money stashed away so that wasn't a problem. She had a nice home and every material thing that she could want, but all of that was meaningless without her knight in shining armor. Liberty went to get checked by the doctor and after getting her prescription she was on her way back out. She headed out the door, and it seemed like everything began to happen in slow motion. She saw a young man coming toward her in a black hoodie, and then a tinted truck slowed down behind him. The only thing she saw was the back window roll down, and it felt like her heart dropped to her stomach. The sinister face of Samad appeared. A'shai's bullets hadn't been enough to take his life. He had been looking for Liberty for years, and today was the day that he had finally caught up with her. It was as if she had seen a ghost. A'shai's bullets hadn't been enough to take his life. Since that day, Samad sought out revenge and vowed to kill A'shai and Liberty. He sat in the back seat and looked at her with pure hatred and crazed intentions.

Liberty saw another masked man stick his body out of the window while holding an AK-47 assault rifle. She froze in fear, her mouth dropped and her legs began to shake. She could see the goon point the gun directly at her and she braced herself, preparing for her death. Her life flashed before her eyes and she dropped her purse and waited for the gunshot that would end it all . . .

ONE

RAT TAT TAT TAT TAT TAT TAT

The sound of the assault rifle thundered through the village, and panic ripped through Liberty's chest as she was startled from her sleep.

"Get up! Get up now, girls!" her mother whispered frantically as she shook Liberty and her cousin, Dalia, in urgency.

Liberty's eyes darted around the thatched hut home as her father guarded the door. In his trembling hands he held a hunting rifle, the only weapon he owned. Seven bullets were all he had been able to afford when he had gone to market. A week's worth of ammunition. One shot for every day to catch his family's dinner. Instead, he was preparing to use seven bullets against seventy men. It was hardly enough. He was about to fight an unmatched bout . . . an unwinnable war. As much as he wanted to run he had to stand his ground. His impending death was near, but he prayed that his actions would be enough to spare his family. He squared his shoulders in an attempt to appear strong, but he was afraid and his fear was like an infection that spread to his heart, sealing his family's inevitable fate. He was sick with silent grief as he anticipated the torture to come.

"Mama, what is happening?" Liberty yelled in confusion, eyes wide, heart rattled, as gunshots rang out loudly. The sound of boisterous men grew increasingly louder as the caravan of violence grew near. Their whoops and hollers were barbaric as they screamed out their war cries, full of pure adrenaline as they announced their presence.

"It's the rebels! They have come," her father revealed.

"My mother!" Dalia screamed as she darted toward the door.

"No! No! You can't go out there. They will kill you!" Liberty said as she grabbed her cousin's hand.

"They will hurt her!" Dalia cried as the thought of her widowed mother facing the rebels alone caused her to tremble.

"Enough, girls. That's enough! No one is going anywhere. We have to be quiet. We have to be still. You have to be brave." Liberty's father kissed his wife on the forehead as she gripped his forearms with shaky hands. Her terror crippled her as pools of tears formed and the dreams of tomorrow washed away in streams that flowed down her cheeks.

"But my mother?" Dalia insisted with big, pleading eyes.

"She is in God's hands now. It is up to a higher power to keep her safe. It is my responsibility to keep you three safe.

There isn't much time," he said as his eyes darted toward the door. He gripped the gun so tightly that the palms of his dark hands lost all color and his fingertips throbbed. His breaths were short, shallow. He was suffocating in silent affliction as he stared at his doomed family. His gut told him that this would be the last time he would ever be in the presence of his wife and child. He fought the emotion that threatened to spill from his eyes, and his pride remained intact. He kept his tears at bay and prepared to put up the fight of his life to save his family.

"I love you," her mother whispered. Liberty looked into her father's eyes as he stared into her mother's face. In him she saw undeniable grief. Even at the tender age of ten she recognized his sadness and her soul bled as her heart became heavy with uncertainty. The madness surrounding her filled her with trepidation, and she could hear her pulse racing as her heart galloped with intensity. She could see her father mourning her very own death before it even occurred.

"Father?" Liberty said as a lump filled her throat.

"Be brave," he repeated as he kissed her, and then Dalia. His lips were ice cold, and although it was a gesture he did every day, this kiss felt final. Liberty knew that it might be the last show of affection she would ever receive from her father, and she cherished it. She closed her eyes and locked the brief, yet intimate moment into her memory. When she finally looked up, she saw her father's back as he headed over to the door.

"Under the bed, now . . . hurry!" her mother insisted as she ushered the girls to their knees. "We have to hide."

They waited . . . waited for death as they huddled together, hiding, while their eyes focused on the rickety door that separated safety from destruction.

The screams that began to fill the air caused the girls to sob uncontrollably.

Liberty gripped Dalia's hand so tightly that her fingers were numb, and she closed her eyes, squeezing them tightly, while wishing that it were a horrible dream. They all knew the threat that the rebels posed. Everyone knew. When the rebels came they destroyed everything in their paths, leaving nothing but mutilated bodies and fatherless children in their wake. A rebel invasion symbolized the end . . . extinction . . . and it was right outside Liberty's door.

The rebels invaded her home mercilessly, chopping down the door with bullets, turning it into Swiss cheese. The sparks from their weapons were like flashes of lightning that illuminated the darkened hut.

Rat tat tat tat! Rat tat tat tat!

The cadence of the guns matched the pace of Liberty's heart as horror caused her breath to catch in her throat. She wanted to close her eyes, but she was too afraid to blink. Her young eyes witnessed mayhem, and for the first time in her young life she realized that the devil was real. The evil she saw in the sweaty, blood-covered rebels as they raided her home was all the proof she needed. They weren't men of God. These men marched with Lucifer's army.

Liberty's father aimed his old, rusted gun and fired, hitting the first man that came through his door. "Aghh!" her father roared as he stood his ground, killing three members of the regime without hesitation. He pushed the men all the way out of his home, not wanting them to discover his family inside. There was no time to think. He acted out of instinct and fought with all of his strength until he no longer could. His efforts soon proved futile. He was outnumbered. The few rebels that he managed to kill were easily replaced. They came like roaches, one after the other, relentless in their pursuit of murder and power. The rebel regime was too strong and large. There were too many rebels to count . . . too many to fight . . . too many to remain fearless, and as he looked into the eyes of one of the men, the ruthlessness that he saw caused his fingertips to grow ice cold. He was staring into an empty shell, a dark soul whose only intention was bloodshed.

The world seemed to move in slow motion as Liberty watched her father aim his gun and wrap his finger around the trigger, but before he could let off another shot he was fired upon, the bullets lifting him clean off the ground as his body jerked . . . left, then right . . . right, then left. He landed with a thud, murdered in cold blood right in front of his home for the entire village to see. His dead eyes fell upon Liberty as a blood river flowed beneath him. The intensity of emotion that she felt overwhelmed her. Her chest was so heavy with sorrow that it caved in. No child should have to bear witness to such atrocity. In that moment she was scarred forever. Liberty had never been so full of fear in all of her life, and she couldn't stop the gasp that escaped her lips.

Her mother quickly put her hand over Liberty's mouth,

but it was too late. Liberty's cry was like a speck of blood in a pool full of sharks. Her cry had been heard. The rebels ransacked the hut, destroying everything. It wasn't long before they flipped over the bed, discovering their hiding spot.

"No!" her mother roared as she instinctively jumped up to protect Liberty and Dalia.

"What do we have here?" one of the rebels taunted, speaking slowly as he circled her like a predator stalking his prey.

"Please. Don't hurt us," her mother spoke, her voice so fragile that it broke with every word.

The man smiled in amusement as he stepped behind her and gripped her neck, applying pressure as he bent her over.

"No!" her mother screamed as she tried to fight. "No, please!"

The rebel ripped the thin fabric of her skirt and forced her against the wall as he roughly spread her legs. The retched scent of his breath filled her nostrils as she screamed in protest. His hands were not her husband's hands, and they violated her in the worst way. The sweat that dripped from his brow felt like acid on her back as he entered her, defiling her womanhood, filling every hole of her body with shame as he thrust wildly.

"No!!!"

Dalia cowered near Liberty as they watched the rape. Their small bodies were paralyzed in agony as they witnessed the unspeakable act of sin. Their screams mixed with the pleading that erupted from Liberty's mother. The young girls hugged each other, and Dalia whispered, "Cover your eyes, Liberty."

The girls closed their eyes and held hands until the screams became whimpers and the whimpers became moans of a woman hanging onto her last breaths. When the moans stopped Liberty knew that so had life. Life as she knew it had ceased to exist and tears flowed nonstop down her face. The rebels hovered like rabid dogs as they salivated over the young girls. The fronts of their army fatigues rose in sexual heat as they marked their next victims.

The men wanted them, and as they approached, the girls wished for death.

"Enough!" a voice bellowed from behind the mob of men. Trembling, the girls clung to each other, arms intertwined desperately as if they had the strength to stay connected that way forever.

They watched in trepidation as the men parted and one of the senior rebels stepped forward. The thud of his heavy combat boots beat the dirt floor, resounding like an African drum, providing the soundtrack to the massacre he had brought upon the village. "Go rally the others. Make sure every hut has been searched. Take anything of value," the man ordered without ever taking his eyes off of the girls.

Dalia and Liberty resisted as he snatched them to their feet. Their tiny fists did little to stop him from imposing his will. He eyed the young girls. They were equally beautiful, but could not have been more opposite than day and night. Dalia's skin was dark, rich like velvet, sweet like chocolate, and smooth like the earth's finest silk, while Liberty's skin was bright like the faintest color in an artist's palette. She was exquisitely unique. She was a trophy. He grinned as he thought of the position of power he held. He was second in command in the rebel regime and always got first pick of the spoils of war. He stepped toward the girls, causing them to huddle together fearfully. He roughly gripped Liberty's arm, and Dahlia erupted in rage. She had always been the stronger of the two, and she kicked the rebel directly between his legs, causing him to buckle.

"Run, Liberty!" Dalia yelled.

Liberty took off with Dalia on her heels. The bush was only a hundred yards away. If they could make it into the jungle Liberty knew that they could escape. It was their backyard, the place that they played in every day. She could easily hide there and survive for days if she had to. All they had to do was make it into the bush.

Liberty's lungs burned as she yelled, "Run, Dahlia!" Her bare feet hit the dirt so hard that they bled, but she kept running. She didn't look back until she heard her cousin scream.

"Li-be-rty!!!" Dahlia's shrill voice cut through the air like lightning cut through the sky, causing Liberty to halt instantly. She turned back with tears streaming down her face, and her heart fell into her stomach.

Dahlia had been caught.

Indecision pulsed through Liberty as her eyes quickly scanned her village. Bodies lay everywhere . . . women, men, children . . . It was a complete massacre. So much blood stained the dirt it appeared as if it had rained down upon the earth. She ran toward Dahlia, but before she could get to her, Dahlia was forced into the back of a Jeep.

"Liberty!" Dahlia screamed.

"Dahlia!" Liberty yelled back, sobbing as she watched the vehicle begin to drive away. "Dahlia, don't leave me!" Liberty stopped running as she reached her home. Her father's corpse still lay in the middle of the village, and his eyes were opened wide as if his soul could still see the tyranny around him.

"What did they do?" she sobbed. Her father's hands had been chopped from his body. His lips kissed by the blade of a machete. The men had completely mutilated him. Liberty's knees gave out, and she leaned over onto her father's chest. She sobbed so loudly that it caused all eyes to focus on her. Racked with emptiness, she held on to his bloody remains. In the blink of an eye she had been transported to hell.

"Wake up, Daddy! Please! Help me!" she cried. Her eyes told her that he was gone, but her heart wouldn't allow her to let go. A mob of men surrounded her, and she stood to her feet in terror. They grabbed at her body. Groped her and snatched at the thin fabric of her clothes. She tried to fight through the maze of taunting men, but they overpowered her.

Liberty was tossed back and forth, from man to man, as they violently played with her.

They pushed her so hard that she fell to the ground as she wept, her face falling hopelessly in her hands.

Out of nowhere a young voice yelled in protest. "No, leave her alone. Let me have her!"

"No . . . no!! No!! . . ."

"No . . . no . . ."

Po walked over to Liberty and gently awakened her out of her troubled sleep.

"Yo . . . yo, ma, wake up. It's just a dream," he said as he brushed the hair out of her face and sat beside her on the bed.

Liberty looked around the ratty motel and shook her head, bringing herself back to the present. She wasn't in Sierra Leone. She was in Detroit, Michigan, hiding out with a man that she didn't know. A man who had saved her from Samad's bullets. After the hospital shooting he had ushered her into his car and raced away from Samad's shooters.

I must have fallen asleep, she thought as she put her hands over her face and groaned in frustration. Liberty's heart raced, and the horror she felt was as fresh as it had been so many years ago. She sat up and breathed deeply as she closed her eyes. Her hands went to her clammy face as she shook her head. "It wasn't a dream. It was a memory," she replied in a solemn whisper as she wiped the tear that slid down her face.

"What?" Po replied with a lost expression on his face.

Liberty shook her head in dismissal and waved her hand. "Nothing. You wouldn't understand," she replied. She remembered the pain as if it had happened yesterday. It had been a long time since she had dreamt of Sierra Leone, but A'shai's death had thrust her right back into mourning, jogging memories of yesterday's past.

"I'll tell you what I don't understand," Po stated as he peered out of the motel window, cautiously surveying his surroundings. "Why does someone like you have bullets flying at you in broad daylight? Fuck is that, nigga?"

Liberty looked up at Po. How could she explain her life to a complete stranger? Samad had purchased her. Technically, she was his property, but she wouldn't dare speak the truth. There was no simplifying where she had come from, and Liberty didn't feel like she owed him any explanations.

"What type of shit *you* into?" Po questioned, while staring at her intensely.

"What type of shit are *you* into?" Liberty shot back defensively, feigning ignorance. "How do you know those bullets weren't meant for you?"

Po thought about his current predicament. He had just lost the love of his life behind his own street dealings so he knew very well that the gunfire at the hospital could have been aimed at him. As he looked at the delicate woman before him he surmised that she was too innocent to be the target of such wrath. Her eyes pierced his as they stared at each other in uncertainty. A tense silence infected the air as her chest heaved up and down in fear. Po could sense her trepidation. Despite the fact that Liberty tried to appear strong, he knew that she was afraid. Her trembling fingertips gave her away, and Po was immediately filled with remorse. *I almost got her killed too,* he thought.

"So you didn't recognize any of the mu'fuckas? You have no idea who those men were today?" he grilled for good measure.

Liberty paused as she thought about telling the truth, but she didn't trust the man in front of her. He was a stranger who couldn't possibly understand her struggle. "No," she answered flatly, but inside she was horrified that Samad was lurking somewhere, preying upon her and threatening her very existence. Liberty wasn't strong enough to face Samad. *I'd be dead right now if he hadn't pushed me out of the way of those bullets,* she thought as she eyed Po. Liberty had narrowly escaped Samad's clutches. She refused to give him another chance to end her life. She would run for the rest of her days if she had to.

Po walked toward her and sat on the double bed directly across from her. He rested his elbows on his knees and intertwined his fingers, resting his head against his forefingers while in deep thought.

"Look, we just got to lay low for the night. I don't know what's going on, but we need to let this shit die down. In the morning we can go our separate ways," he instructed.

"In the morning? I need to leave now," Liberty said urgently, anxious to put as much distance as possible between her and Samad. There was no way that she could let Samad find her. She would live her days in paranoia, watching over her shoulder, because if Samad ever caught her, he would kill her. She stood and headed for the door, but before she could open it all the way, Po's firm hand closed it.

"That wasn't a suggestion, sweetheart," he said sternly. "Get comfortable." The steely look in his eyes let Liberty know that the terms he had laid out before her were non-negotiable. She folded her arms with a sigh of frustration and rolled her eyes as she marched over to the bed. She sat back against the grungy headboard and grabbed the remote control to turn on the TV.

Po paced the room on guard as his mind raced. For years he had moved so carefully. Every move had been meticulously calculated. He had prized himself on being strategic in the streets and suddenly felt as if everything was falling apart. With the death of Scarlett, his entire world had changed. The money that he hustled for years to save seemed worthless now that she was gone. Detroit no longer felt like home. Everything around Po reminded him of Scarlett, and now that niggas were gunning for his head he knew that it was time to go. He could no longer decipher his friends from his foes. With bullets flying in broad daylight, things in Detroit were about to get reckless, and after avenging Scarlett's murder he planned to blow like the wind.

He peered out of the curtains one more time before grabbing the remote out of Liberty's hands and changing the channel.

"Hey, I was watching that," she protested.

"Now we're watching this," Po replied as he settled on the news station. Liberty's eyes widened when she saw images of the hospital pop up on the screen. "I need to know what they know."

Liberty's heart thundered inside of her chest as she listened to the details of the news report. She hoped that her identity didn't come into question, and she breathed a sigh of relief when the segment finally passed. No details about herself or Samad were released, and the police had no suspects.

Po clenched his jaws in frustration and looked back at Liberty. "Just hang tight until morning. Once I'm sure we weren't followed you can go home."

"Where's that?" she whispered back, barely audible. The only home that Liberty had ever known was with A'shai. Wherever he was, that was where she wanted to be. Living without him would prove impossible. He was her reason for breathing, and now that he no longer could, she felt lost.

Po could see the sorrow hanging from Liberty's shoulders. Sadness clung to her like a coat to a rack as she stared blankly at the space in front of her. She was caught up in the memory of what was and what could never be. Stuck in love with a ghost so she couldn't move forward. She didn't even know what her next move should be. Now that Samad had found her, Detroit was no longer an option. She had more than enough money to start her life over somewhere else. A'shai had ensured that they were set up. He had taken care of her most of their lives, and even in death he still watched over her. The first chance Liberty got she was going to empty A'shai's safe and piece her life together as best as she could.

"What's your name?" he asked.

Liberty looked up at him, and he could see her heartbreak.

Po didn't know what could have possibly happened to a girl so beautiful, but he knew from jump that her story was deep. Her sorrowful eyes told a tale that her lips would never confess, and the things that she had screamed out in her sleep held too much emotion to be conjured up by the sandman. Her skin was like porcelain, delicate and pale, while her hair was thick and fell in layers around her face. For the first time since their chaotic, fateful meeting, he realized how uniquely gorgeous she was.

"Liberty," she replied.

"Look, Liberty, I don't mean to come off so harsh. I'm just cautious, and I would rather move smart than fast. I don't know what happened outside of the hospital today, but I do know that I would rather be safe than sorry. I tend to be bad luck for beautiful women," he said with a charismatic smirk. "I just lost someone who was very dear to me. I don't need any more bodies on my heart. We don't know each other, but please, just do me a favor and sit tight. A'ight, ma?"

Liberty nodded her head in agreement. "What's your name?" she asked.

"I'm Po."

She extended her hand and almost lost her breath when her heart skipped a beat as he shook it.

"Thank you," she said.

"For what?" he answered.

"For caring about what happens to me. A lot of niggas would have just sent me on my way. Although I don't appreciate being stuck here until morning, I can appreciate a genuine person when I meet one. I haven't run into a lot of them in my lifetime. So thanks."

Po put two fingers to his forehead and nodded his head in salute before he turned his focus back to the television. No other words were spoken that night. They both were dealing with their own issues, nursing wounds that were so similar that it was irony at its finest. They were mourning the loss of love, but neither of them spoke about it. Instead, they suffered silently while keeping up a composed exterior to fool the world.

Liberty turned her back to Po and mumbled, "First thing in the morning I'm kissing Detroit good-bye."

Her words caught Po's attention, and he asked, "What you running from?"

"The past," she answered simply. Exhausted and still adjusting to the new heart in her chest, Liberty quickly dozed off.

When Po was sure that she was asleep he finally allowed himself to relax. He pulled his gun off his hip, clicked off his safety, and chambered a round into the head before placing it on the nightstand next to him. If anything did pop off in the middle of the night he wouldn't be caught off guard. Po would wake up blasting, no questions asked; the same way that he slept every night. He was never at peace, and it was the one thing he hated most about his chosen hood profession.

Po's paranoia forced him to look outside of the curtains once more and put the security chain on the door before retiring for the night. He walked past Liberty and saw goose bumps forming on her bare arms. He pulled the cover over her body, and then noticed the Greyhound bus ticket that she clasped tightly in her hand. He removed it and put it on the nightstand next to her, and then surrendered to his own bed, falling into a restless sleep.

By the time Po awoke the next morning Liberty was long gone. Off to catch that bus Po supposed as he looked around while shaking his head. *Bitch was hardheaded,* he thought. He quickly dismissed Liberty from his thoughts before peeking cautiously out the door. Seeing that the coast was clear he concealed his pistol on his waistline and headed to his car. The quicker he kissed the city of Detroit good-bye the better off he would be.

Po pulled up to the home he had shared with Scarlett and instantly a knot formed in his stomach. Every time he stepped a foot inside, he was tormented by the memory of her death. He could still see her body tied to the chair in which she was tortured. The horrible memory ate away at his conscience, and he was overwhelmed just at the sight of the place.

"Let me hurry up and get the fuck out of here," Po mumbled as he reluctantly got out of his car and headed up the walkway. Distracted by grief but eerily aware of his surroundings he froze when he got to his door. The hairs on the back of his neck stood straight up as his internal alarm sounded. Pulling the 9 millimeter off his hip was second nature, and he flicked the safety off, ready to dead something . . . anything . . . anyone . . . on sight.

Like a thief in the night he moved with stealth as he

fearlessly entered, but when he saw the state of his house he realized that the intruders were long gone. Couch cushions were cut in half, furniture was turned over, hardwood floor boards were ripped up. Everything was completely ransacked, but Po knew that this was no random break-in. Whoever had come had been looking for something specific, and as Po raced down to his basement he prayed they hadn't found it. He rushed over to the laundry room and pulled open his electrical panel.

"Fuck!" he yelled. He hit the concrete wall so hard that he instantly regretted it as his hand exploded with pain. "Fuck! Fuck! Fuck!" he shouted, half out of pain and half out of anger. The quarter million that he had saved up for Scarlett and him was gone. The safe that he had installed behind his electrical panel lay wide open. The only thing left inside was a white piece of paper. He frowned in confusion as he nursed his aching hand, then reached inside to grab the note.

If you want your belongings back bring the girl to me.

"That lying bitch!" he yelled through clenched teeth as he thought of Liberty. He punched at the air in frustration. It had taken him a long time to stack that much money. It was his only way out. It didn't matter what he had to do to get it back. He had to go get it. He was too close to his exit to let a major setback like this put him back at square one.

Liberty's entire body went numb as she stared down at the elaborate headstone that decorated A'shai's grave. She knew that it was foolish to be there. Her actions right now were reckless and completely predictable, but she couldn't leave town without visiting him one last time. His absence in her life was so surreal. Even when they had been apart she could still feel him. His presence had always been prevalent in her life. Their spirits were always connected. This was the first time she had ever felt separated from him. She could no longer feel A'shai. She was so blinded by the pain of his death that there was no room to feel the love that he had left behind. A part of Liberty was mad at A'shai for deciding his own fate. His act was so selfless that in the end it had backfired, leaving her bitter and lonely without any hope for love in her future.

"I wanted you to live for both of us, Shai, not die with me," she whispered. "I will love you forever, A'shai Montgomery. You gave me life."

She kissed her fingertips and traced the letters in his name before walking away, her heart grieving, but her face silently solemn.

She got into the cab that awaited curbside and gave the driver directions to the home she once shared with A'shai. She hadn't been back since the dreadful night that A'shai had taken his own life. She was too afraid of what she may see or the way that she would feel when she stepped inside. Liberty had avoided their home, but now she couldn't any longer. She needed A'shai's money to survive.

"That'll be forty bucks even," the cabdriver announced as the car came to a halt.

Liberty looked up but quickly ducked back down when she saw the familiar faces walking out of the house.

"Please drive away," she instructed. "Now! Hurry!" she urged as she slumped low in her seat.

"Look, lady, I don't need no shit. Do you have my $40 or not?"

Liberty reached into her handbag and pulled out two twenty-dollar bills and tossed them in the front seat. "Now drive this car!" she whispered harshly.

The cabdriver eased away from the curb reluctantly while Liberty lay concealed in the backseat. She peeked out of the rearview mirror carefully and fear gripped her as she saw Samad's goons carrying bags out of the house in which A'shai had stored his hard-hustled cash. Everything that she needed was in those bags. She may as well have been dead, because being broke was the next best thing. She couldn't hide for long in her current predicament. *Oh my God, oh my God, oh my God. He's going to find me,* she thought frantically. Liberty went into her hobo bag and pulled out the small wad of money that she had on her. She flipped through the small bills frantically, realizing that she only had a few hundred bucks. The rest of her financial worth had been inside of that house, which was now under surveillance by Samad. Her hope sank as her eyes met the cabdriver's in the rearview mirror.

"You want to tell me where I'm driving to?" he asked obnoxiously.

Liberty wiped the tears from her face. She was tired of wallowing in her own weakness. For as long as she could remember she had been the victim. Victim to the rebels, victim to Ezekiel, to the drug cartels, to Abia, then Samad . . . It was time to say enough. She wouldn't be a victim anymore. *If I give up then Shai died for nothing . . . all of this is for nothing. I have to live for him,* she thought. Liberty took a deep breath and held her head up high. She was a fighter, and she was going to use everything she had to survive.

"The bus station."

Liberty was about to start her life over as a hunted woman, but she would make Samad chase her to the ends of the earth to catch her. She was just trying to live.

TWO

PO PACED BACK AND FORTH AS HE clenched his jaws tightly, obviously outraged. Rocko sat on the couch inside of his trap house watching his right-hand man try to figure out the next move. The chain of events had just rocked Po's world, and he knew that he couldn't just take the loss. He had lost close to $250,000 of straight drug money. There was no recouping that. He stacked that money up a thousand dollars at a time, anticipating the day that he could retire. He had lost the love of his life over that money, and now, in a blink of an eye, it was all gone.

"Everything is gone?" Rocko asked, already knowing the answer to the question.

Po slowly nodded his head while giving Rocko the coldest stare. He then reached into his Levi denims and looked at the note for the tenth time.

If you want your belongings back bring the girl to me.

Beneath the message was an address in Los Angeles. Po couldn't believe what he was looking at. He knew that whoever the man was, he meant business.

"That mu'fucka took everything I had. All the money is gone. Every single dime. I have no money to go back to my connect with, nothing in the bank, and no product. Shit is all bad, bruh," Po said as he shook his head in defeat.

"So, let's just go grab the bitch up and serve her to the nigga on a platter," Rocko said as he gripped his handgun tightly in his right palm. His short dreads were neatly twisted and rested against his jet-black skin. His short physique was toned and muscular. Rocko wasn't too much of a hustler; he left that up to Po. He was an enforcer . . . a shooter. His game was murder. He had no remorse for any life he took, but was as loyal as they came. He had been running with Po since they were young boys.

"Shit is just fucked up. I saved her from the nigga at the hospital, and now I'm thinking about delivering her to him. I don't know, fam," Po said as he looked over at his friend. Rocko's face instantly frowned up; Po wasn't acting like himself. Rocko stood up and shook his head from side to side in disbelief.

"What's wrong? You acting like you soft on the broad or something," Rocko said, trying to figure out what was stopping Po from feeding Liberty to the wolves.

"It's not that," Po said as he dropped his head. He mumbled under his breath, "She reminds me of . . ." Po kept seeing Liberty, and then his slain girlfriend. Although they didn't resemble each other physically in the slightest, Liberty reminded him of Scarlett. There was something about her eyes. Po quickly shook the notion and thought about his stash being gone. He then took a deep breath. "We have to go get her," Po said as he started to devise a plan.

"Where is she? Do you know where she lives?" Rocko asked.

"No, but she left a bus ticket for today on the nightstand at the motel. She's taking the next thing smoking out of the city. Let's go. Hurry!" Po said as he shot for the door. Rocko followed closely behind, and just like that, they were gone.

Liberty sat on the outside bench, waiting for her bus. She had a one-way ticket to Arizona. She didn't know what would be waiting for her when she got there, but she still was heading west. She only had the money that A'shai had put in a bank account for her, which was a tad under ten thousand dollars. Samad's goons had cleared out the safe with the big money, so she would have to spend wisely to avoid going broke. Ten racks wouldn't last forever, but she hoped that it was enough to help her start over. She was headed toward a new beginning while running from her past.

Liberty looked at her watch and noticed that she had three-and-a-half more hours before her departure. Her heart pounded and pain shot through her chest as she nervously looked around, hoping to God Samad wouldn't find her. "Come on, come on, come on," she whispered as she glanced at her watch again while anxiously tapping her foot on the ground. Just as she lifted her head, she noticed a tinted black truck pull in front of the bus station. The passenger window came down, and Liberty was frozen in fear as she closed her eyes and took a deep breath. When she opened them back up, she saw a face appear, looking directly at her. It was Po.

"Need a ride?" he asked as he glanced at his side mirror, and then back at Liberty. Although Liberty barely knew Po, she was actually glad to see him. Knowing that Samad and his goons could have popped up on her at any moment had her paranoid. Liberty returned the smile and looked around.

"What are you doing here?" she asked.

"I'm here to come get you. You just dipped out on me. I wanted to make sure you were okay." Po said. "Where are you headed exactly?"

"Arizona," she answered as she looked down at her ticket.

"What's in Arizona?" he asked with a frown.

"Nothing, but that's kinda the point. You know?" she replied. Liberty was seeking solace and going to a discreet town in the middle of nowhere was right up her alley.

"I need a road trip anyway. Get in," Po said as he hit his unlock button.

"Are you serious?" she asked in disbelief.

"I'm here, aren't I?" he replied as he stepped out of the car and walked over to her. He picked up her duffle bag and headed back to his car.

Just before opening his trunk, he looked at Liberty. "Come on, it'll be fine." Liberty couldn't help but smile as she stood up and shook her head.

"Okay, let's do it," she said as she headed to the passenger side and got in. After loading her bag in the trunk, Po joined Liberty in the car and slowly guided the car away from the curb. Although Po felt slightly guilty about deceiving Liberty, he knew it was all business. He was not about to get into the unfinished business that Samad and Liberty had going on. He just wanted his money: nothing more . . . nothing less.

Po left Rocko behind; this was something he had to do by himself. The way Samad's people moved, he knew that he was feeding Liberty to the wolves and he wanted the blood to be only on his hands. As Cash Money's latest hit lightly pumped through the speakers, they merged onto the highway and headed west.

"Why are you doing this?" Liberty said as she pulled off the hair tie that held her ponytail and let her hair flow onto her shoulders. Po briefly looked over at Liberty and couldn't help but notice her beauty and flawless skin. He focused back on the road, reminding himself that this was a business trip.

"I don't know why I'm doing this. That's a good question," he responded. So many thoughts ran through Po's mind as he tried to ignore his conscience. He was literally trading someone's life for money. He tried to convince himself that it was just business, but there was something about Liberty that drew him to her.

Liberty reached into her purse and pulled out a Lauryn Hill CD, her favorite. She then looked at Po for approval, and he grinned and nodded his head. She slipped the disc in and the melodic sounds filled the car as they listened closely to the lyricist. Two hours passed and not one word was spoken between the two of them. It seemed as if Lauryn Hill soothed them, making the ride easy and comfortable.

Liberty turned down the music. "So, Po . . . tell me about yourself. At least we can keep each other entertained. It's a very long car ride," she said.

"Well, what do you want to know?" Po asked as he kept his eyes on the road.

"What do you want to tell me?" Liberty responded as she turned her body and folded her legs Indian-style. She looked directly at him.

"I'm twenty-five. No kids, no family."

"Girlfriend?" Liberty asked, as she raised an eyebrow.

Po glanced at her out of the corner of his eye as he gripped the steering wheel with one hand. "That's a long story," he said.

"I'll just bet it is," Liberty replied with a small smile.

Liberty could tell that Po wasn't open to discussing his personal relationships so she quickly switched the subject and one small conversation led to hours of debating, questions, and good times. They talked so much that the hours seemed to zoom by and they were across country before they knew it.

Ten hours later they were entering the state of Colorado. Po began to get heavy eyelids so they stopped at a hotel to get rest. He suggested that they sleep in the same room "so he could protect her," and she agreed. She felt secure with him, but what Po was disguising as protection was really peace of mind for himself. He wanted to keep a close eye on the key to his money, which was Liberty. There was no way he was letting her out of his sight.

The conversation didn't stop when they got in the room. They sat up all night and talked about everything under the sun, and both Po and Liberty felt a connection to each other—like a force was bringing them together. They eventually fell asleep with their clothes on and both had sweet dreams.

THREE

THE BEAMS OF THE MORNING LIGHT CREPT through the blinds of the hotel room. Po slowly opened his eyes and felt the weight of a body on his chest. He looked down to see Liberty peacefully sleeping on him. They had fallen asleep while talking into the wee hours of the morning. Po slowly cracked a smile as he admired her natural beauty, then a sudden wave of guilt overcame him as the smile quickly faded from his face. This was the part of the game that he hated. The treachery, the betrayal, the hidden agendas. His hand was being forced to set up a woman he barely knew. Her life for cold cash didn't seem like an even exchange, but it was what it was at that point. It was too late to turn back.

"What the fuck am I doing?" he said to himself as he stared at Liberty. He took a deep breath and closed his eyes. Painful images of a slain Scarlett appeared in his mind. He missed her so much and having a woman close to him reminded him of the times they had shared. Tears formed in his eye and a single drop cascaded down his cheek. The wound was still fresh, and he missed her so much.

Po slowly slid from underneath Liberty and stood up. Liberty was sound asleep and seemed so innocent. He wiped his tear away and headed toward the shower. They were only a few states over from Los Angeles. He knew that the unique circumstances would soon be over, he would get his money back, and he would never see Liberty again.

Po made his way over to the shower and stripped. He turned on the shower and stepped in, letting the hot water cascade down his toned body. At that point the tears began to flow freely as the burden of not having anybody in his corner sunk in. Scarlett was his only family, and now that she was gone, he felt alone in this world. Rocko was there, but there was nothing like a woman's companionship.

"Scarlett," he cried out as he banged on the wall, trying to release the pain that was building from within. He wanted his girl back.

After ten minutes, Po eventually regained his composure and turned off the water. He grabbed a towel and wrapped it around his lower half as he headed out of the bathroom. His heart dropped when he looked at the bed. There was no one there. Liberty had left. He panicked. With Liberty gone so was his chance of getting his stash back.

"Fuck!" he yelled as he punched the wall in frustration. He ran to the door and looked out and saw that his car was no longer parked out front. He slammed the door closed and clenched his jaws in bitterness. He had just driven halfway across the country for nothing. He plopped down on the bed and shook his head in defeat. Life had been dealing him a losing hand lately, and his luck had gone from bad to worse in the blink of an eye.

Hearing someone slowly opening the door he quickly reached for his gun that he placed under the pillow the night before. His heartbeat slowed, and he aimed carefully at the door like it was second nature. It was times like this he was built for. He closed one eye so that he could shoot with precision, and Liberty came into his line of fire while holding two boxes from the diner up the road.

"Oh my—" she said as she froze in her tracks and stared down the barrel of a gun. Po lowered his gun and took a deep breath.

"I just went to get some breakfast. I wanted to surprise you," Liberty said as she stood there confused.

"Look, I'm tripping. The shootout has my nerves on edge. I apologize, ma. Sit down. Relax," Po said as put his gun back under the pillow, stood up, and grabbed his clothes from on top of the dresser. Liberty turned around and faced the door so that Po could get dressed without her watching.

"I didn't know I was coming back into a war zone," Liberty said playfully as she tried to ease the tension.

"I apologize. Shit's just crazy right now," Po explained as he finished dressing. He walked over to Liberty and gently turned her around. "So, what's in the box?" he asked as he grinned. Liberty reluctantly returned the smile and sat at the small table in the corner.

"I hope you like omelets," she said as she placed a box in front of her and then one across the table for Po.

"Actually, I do," Po answered as he took a seat directly across from her. They managed to share the small table and have breakfast together. Po's heart still was pumping, but he did little to let it show. The more he looked at Liberty, the more he wanted to tell her the truth about where they were headed. He wasn't into rescuing damsels in distress. He was basically escorting her to her own demise.

After they finished up their food, Po looked down at his watch. "We have to stay on track. Are you ready to hit the road?"

"Yeah, just let me shower and I'll be ready," Liberty said as she stood up and walked over to the closet. She pulled her duffle bag from it and put it on the bed. As she began to pull out her clothes she peeked over at Po who seemed to be in deep thought.

"Okay, close your eyes. I have to get undressed," Liberty said playfully while she held her blouse close to her chest.

"Okay, I got you," Po said as he smiled and closed his eyes.

Liberty walked over to Po and waved her hand in front of his face to make sure he couldn't see.

"I promise you I can't see a thing," he confirmed as he crossed his arms and sat back in the chair.

"Scout's honor?" she said.

"I ain't no Boy Scout, ma," he replied with a laugh. "I got you. Go ahead and get undressed."

Liberty quickly slipped out of her clothes, exposing her slim frame and plump buttocks. Her smooth, fair skin looked as if it were dipped in a pot of honey. She was beautiful and

41

was the type of woman that dwelled in the dreams of men. Po couldn't help himself but peek just a little. He slightly opened his right eye and was astonished by her physique. Her clothes didn't tell the story of her body. She was slim, but her breasts were perky while her hips were wide. Her backside was perfectly sculpted and hung like two teardrops. Po had to open his other eye so he could get a good view.

Beautiful, he thought to himself as she stood completely naked and headed to the bathroom. His eyes were glued to her body, and he was mesmerized. Just before Liberty entered the bathroom, she slightly turned her head and locked eyes with Po. Po couldn't take his eyes off of her. He had got caught looking, but he couldn't bring himself to take his eyes away from the beauty queen. Po's eyes drifted to the scar on her chest. It was the only imperfection on her body.

Liberty looked down at it too and placed a hand over the incision site. She turned crimson red as embarrassment filled her, and she hurriedly disappeared into the bathroom. Po didn't know that he wasn't only the only person that thought she was one of the most beautiful women he had ever seen: the world did also. Wars had started over her, and soon another one would be ignited.

The following night the sound of the engine humming and the vibration of the car ride rocked Liberty to sleep. Po made his way through the clear highways while thinking about his next move after he got his money back from Samad. He looked over at Liberty and took a deep breath as they neared the destination. He had managed to enter California while she was sleeping, so she had no idea that they were in Samad's neck of the woods. He had driven all through the day and night to end the fiasco as soon as possible. Liberty never even realized that they crossed the California state line hours before. Samad's residence was about ten miles away according to the navigational system.

The sun was just rising and his heart began to beat faster and faster as he approached the residence. He wanted to just turn around and not give Liberty up to Samad, but he had to remind himself that it was business. The thought of Po walking into a trap filled his mind, but he knew that he had to take his chances. He had to at least attempt to get his money back. It was either that or start from scratch and risk going to jail or dying in the streets while peddling drugs. He wasn't trying to see that life again. Po clenched his jaws as he looked over at Liberty who was in a peaceful slumber. She rested her head gently against the window as he pulled up to the twelve-foot steel gates of Samad's estate.

He noticed the extravagant estate sat on acres of land. It was simply amazing. It was definitely fit for a kingpin that hustled at the highest level of the game. Po's eyes focused on the two guards standing at the gates, each with a shotgun in hand. The estate was heavily guarded, and Po knew that the only type of business that required such extreme measures of security was the drug business. He was dealing with a kingpin.

As soon as Po pulled up, the two Arab guards raised their weapons and approached the car. Po rolled down his window. The guard leaned down and glared menacingly at him.

"Samad is expecting me," Po said as he looked the guard square in the eye.

"We know," the guard mumbled as he glanced over to the passenger seat and saw Liberty asleep. The guard pulled the walkie-talkie from his hip and said, "They have arrived." He then gave the other guard a signal, and their access was granted. Po rolled up his window and proceeded down the long driveway that led to the mansion. Liberty began to squirm, and Po looked over at her beautiful face and the guilt sank in.

"I'm sorry," he whispered as he shook his head.

"Sorry for what?" she said as she smiled and stretched her arms out. She focused on what was ahead, and her smile instantly was wiped from her face. She saw a house that would never be erased from her memory. It was Samad's place. A place where she had experienced so much misery . . . so much pain.

"No, no, no. Please don't take me here," she pleaded. Po looked over at her and saw the tears forming in her eyes.

"I have to. I'm so sorry," Po said as he looked away and continued to pull up to the house.

"Please turn around! Please!" Liberty begged as the tears began to flow. Her limbs began to shake, and she realized that she had been tricked by Po. "I thought you were different!" she yelled as she looked at the door handle and thought about jumping out and taking her chances. However, Po had the child locks on. As Liberty tugged on the door and pleaded with Po, tears streamed down her face, and Po shook his head in disappointment as he never once looked over at her.

He pulled up to the house where three more Arab guards were waiting and a slender man wearing a Hugh Hefner-like robe over his slacks stood.

"Nooo. Please, please don't do this. He's going to kill me!" Liberty screamed as she grabbed Po by the collar of his shirt. She began to tug on him violently, scratching his neck. Po clenched his jaws and took the pain; he still wouldn't look over at her. He knew he deserved the scratches so he took it like a man.

As he pulled up and stopped he merely whispered, "I'm sorry." He dropped his head while unlocking the door. Immediately Samad's goons opened the door and dragged her out while she kicked and screamed for dear life. Samad stood and watched with a smirk on his face. The goons held Liberty up and stood her right in front of him. His eyes assaulted her body as he stared her up and down. Liberty lowered her head in submission.

"Welcome home," he said calmly as he took a puff of his cigar and walked toward Po's car. The goons dragged Liberty inside the mansion, and Po watched as she faded into the house, pleading for her life.

"I see you are a smart businessman and took me up on my offer," Samad said smoothly as he stood in front of the driver-side door.

"Where's my money?" Po asked as he cut straight to the chase.

Samad put two fingers in his mouth and whistled. Seconds later, a man came out of the house with a duffle bag in his hand. He walked over to Po's backseat and opened the door. He tossed the bag in and immediately headed back to the house.

"It's all there, plus a bonus. One hundred grand to be exact," Samad said smugly. Po reached back and unzipped the bag and began to flip through the bills. He saw nothing but rubber-banded Franklin faces and was instantly relieved.

"Good business. I'm gone. But can I ask you one thing," Po said as he put his car in reverse.

"What's that?" Samad asked just before he puffed his cigar.

"What are you going to do with her?"

"Do you want to know the truth?" Samad asked as he stepped closer to the car.

Po nodded, not really sure if he wanted to hear what Samad was going to say.

Samad closed his eyes and slightly grinned as if he was envisioning his sweetest memory. He took his time before he spoke, wanting to be as accurate and as vivid as humanly possible.

"First, I'm going to torture her for hours . . . slowly. I want her to feel death without experiencing it. It will be so beautiful. So painful. Then, once she has learned her lesson, I am going to make her my wife," he said. His words were so passionate that you would have thought he was describing an immaculate painting. Samad's obsession with Liberty

46

was evident. Po could tell that he had been waiting for years to exact revenge on her.

Po didn't know what to say after that. He immediately saw in Samad's eyes that he was a monster. Samad was practically drooling over the opportunity to punish Liberty. Po's stomach turned as he noticed the slight erection that showed through Samad's slacks. He was a man of power with a sick obsession for women. The glint of insanity in his eyes revealed his demonic intentions for Liberty. He would have no mercy on her, and Po was horrified that he had contributed to such madness. Vomit warmed the back of his throat as he thought of Liberty, but it was too late to change his mind. What was done was done. Po shook his head, disgusted, and then rolled up his window. He turned his car around and pulled away with a heavy heart. As he sped down the driveway, passing the guards at the gate, he hit his steering wheel in frustration, nearly hit the landscaping crew that was coming in as he zoomed by.

Po didn't want to give Liberty up, but it was a done deal. He had to do what he had to do.

Liberty lay naked on the bed with each of her limbs bound to a bedpost. A tightly tied handkerchief muffled her mouth while her eyes darted around the bedroom. Samad had purposely left Liberty tied up for hours to torture her more. It was the waiting that drove her insane. She felt as though she were sitting on death row. The actual time spent anticipating the horrific event that was fated to occur was just as painful as the punishment itself. Samad understood this, and it gave him extreme satisfaction. He was inside of her psyche, and her mental anguish gave him great pleasure.

Liberty's eyes shot to the door when she heard someone enter: it was Samad.

"Well, you have finally returned home, Liberty. I have waited for this day for too long. I once told you that you belonged to me. I meant that with every fiber of my being," he said as he stood over her and looked at her body and watched her squirm in terror. He reached down and ran his fingers up her body, sending horrific chills racing up Liberty's spine. Her tears flowed freely as she closed her eyes and cringed at his touch.

"I'm going to teach you a lesson about leaving me," he threatened. He walked over to his closet and pulled out a long leather whip. He had planned this moment for years, and it literally made his dick hard thinking about what he was about to do. He walked over to Liberty while grinning and slowly twirled the whip. Liberty's muffled screams didn't affect Samad at all as he thought about the pain he was about to inflict. He opened his robe with his free hand and whipped out his slightly erect penis. He then aimed it at Liberty's face and began to urinate on her. She closed her eyes and twisted her body to avoid the pungent stream of piss, but it was to no avail. The urine got into her eyes and splashed all over her face. He shook his penis tauntingly as he continued to piss over her whole body while laughing in repulsive pleasure. Once he got done he grabbed the whip and began to strike her with all his might. He hit her all over her body, leaving red marks with each lashing. Samad struck her repeatedly, and this was only the beginning. He was determined to make her suffer in the worst way.

Po paced his hotel room and waited for the knock at the door. He asked Rocko to fly out to him. It had only been twelve hours since he had dropped off Liberty, and she was the only thing that was on his mind. A knock on the door alerted Po. He grabbed his pistol from the dresser, then made his way over to the door and looked through the peephole. When he saw that it was Rocko he lowered his gun and unlocked the door.

"Rocko," he said in relief as he looked at his right-hand man who stood there.

"I can't believe you are going to do this," Rocko said as he stepped inside and shook his head in disbelief.

"I have to do something. This shit is going to eat at me, bro," Po said as he closed the door behind Rocko. "There's something about that girl, man. It's like I see Scarlett in her. I'm telling you. Shit seems crazy, but she reminds me of her. You with me or what?" Po said as he peeked out the window with the gun in his palm.

"I'm here, ain't I? I might not agree with the play you about to put down, but I'm with you 100 percent. Believe that," Rocko responded as he picked up Po's extra gun and cocked it back, putting a bullet in the chamber.

"Say no more," Po said as he thought long and hard about what he was going to do.

Samad had given Liberty oral sex for three hours straight while she still was bound, but there was nothing gentle about his touch. He sucked and nibbled and licked on her roughly. Eating her womanhood for so long made her raw. He was absolutely obsessed with her.

The stench of urine and blood filled the air. Samad was sweating at the point of exhaustion as he pleased himself, all while he was torturing Liberty. By now, she could sob no more. She had cried her eyes out and was basically numb to the torment. She stared blankly into space as Samad rose and maneuvered himself into a missionary position over Liberty. He entered her vaginal cave and slowly stroked her as he kissed her forehead passionately. He began to have sex with her, and as he looked down at Liberty it was as if she wasn't even there. Samad began to pound away as he threw his head back in pleasure. Liberty didn't even blink as her mind drifted to her lost love . . . A'shai. She got lost in his gaze as she pictured his face staring into hers. Once upon a time he would have bust down the door to save her from the torture she was enduring, but he was no longer around to protect her. Still the thought of him brought her mental relief.

Samad felt a climax approaching as he began to pump feverishly and aggressively. Sweat dripped from his forehead and onto Liberty's naked body as a glob of semen shot inside of her. Samad smiled and looked down at her. He saw a single tear slide down her cheek, but the blank stare she wore never left her face. He chuckled, and then spit into her face, degrading her as if she were nothing. He slid out of her and stood up.

"After I shower, the next phase will begin," he said as he

looked at her with disgust before walking to the attached bathroom.

Po and Rocko sat in the front of the van wearing workers' clothes and doctors' masks. They looked like two lawn workers, but they weren't there to chop any grass. Po looked in the back of the van at the two Mexicans tied up, sitting back to back. Rocko had duct taped their mouths, hands, and feet so that Po's plan would go smoothly. Impersonating the help was the best idea Po could come up with to sneak into Samad's residence. Remembering the crazed look in Samad's eyes, Po knew that he had to move swiftly if he wanted to keep Liberty out of harm's way. Usually, he would never jump into someone's business while putting his own life on the line, but there was something special about Liberty. He just had not been able to put his finger on what it was exactly.

Po kept his head low as he tried to avoid eye contact with the two guards standing at the gate. He threw up his hand, and the guard granted him access as he talked to the other guard. Little did the guards know, they had just let two goons into Samad's home. Po slowly pulled into the gate and couldn't believe that his plan had worked. He drove up to the front entrance and looked over at Rocko. Rocko's eyes held no fear. In fact, Rocko had a small grin on his face as he cocked his gun back. Po shook his head at his man. He knew that Rocko lived for days like this. Rocko loved to live life on the edge, and this was right up his alley . . . that gangster shit.

Liquid splashing in Liberty's face woke her from her troubled sleep. She was still tied up from the day before, and she squirmed trying to turn her face away from Samad urinating on her again.

"Wake up, Sleeping Beauty," Samad said as he finished relieving himself on Liberty. He had been getting pure enjoyment from torturing her, and he planned on a full day of doing the same thing. He even let most of his security take the day off so the screams wouldn't be heard by them. He wanted complete privacy for his torture session with Liberty. He was determined to make the day a gruesome one for her. One that she would remember the next time she thought about running away from him.

Liberty breathed heavily as the urine dripped into her eyes and nose. The vomit that erupted from her was trapped between the gag in her mouth and the back of her throat, causing her to choke violently. Samad laughed as he dropped his robe and climbed onto the bed. He was going insane, and Liberty would suffer severely from his madness. At that point, Liberty just wanted to die. She thought about reuniting with A'shai in the afterlife, which brought her a small measure of comfort. Tears streamed down her face as she closed her eyes and thought about her lost love. She knew that if A'shai were alive, Samad wouldn't have touched her. She felt so lonely without her protector and best friend. Even in death, he was the love of her life.

"I am going to fuck you like a whore is supposed to be fucked," Samad said as he began to stroke his penis. He forcefully spread her butt cheeks and spit in her anus.

Liberty cringed at his touch and closed her eyes. She began to pray. She didn't even want help at this point: Liberty was praying for a speedy death. She didn't want to endure what Samad had in store for her. She knew he wanted to cause her as much pain as he could. Liberty began to break down and cry, knowing that she was helpless.

Po and Rocko easily slipped through the back patio and entered the luxurious home. Both gripped their pistols in their hands, ready to shoot whatever got in their way.

"Damn. This shit laid the fuck out," Rocko said as he crept in and looked around alongside Po. Samad's mansion had marble floors and tall pillars. He was swimming in money, and Rocko instantly knew they were dealing with a major player of some sort. He had never seen anything so extravagant. Little did they know, they were trespassing into the home of the most successful kingpin on the West Coast.

"Shh," Po said as he put his index finger to his lip. "Do you hear that?" he asked as he looked up the large staircase, which was made of porcelain. He heard muffled screams. Po quickly headed toward the stairs, and Rocko followed closely. They slowly crept up. The screams got louder the closer they got to the door. Po stood outside the door, and his heart pounded, not knowing what was waiting on the opposite side of the door. The sound of skin slapping against skin filled the air. He carefully cracked the door open and witnessed Samad sodomizing a defenseless Liberty. He entered the room and crept up behind Samad who was pounding away. The sight broke his heart. Po was as tough as they came, but the sight of rape disgusted him.

Followed closely by Rocko, Po gently pressed the barrel of his gun to the back of Samad's head. Samad jumped up, and Rocko followed up with a strike across his face, knocking him off the bed. Rocko stood over him and pointed the gun at his head. Po called the shots and like a trained pit bull, Rocko barked. It was second nature to him to be a goon.

"You sick fuck!" Po yelled as he began to untie Liberty. The horrendous stench of urine invaded his nostrils, and he frowned as he looked at Liberty's battered body. She resembled a slave on a plantation with all the whip marks across her back and legs.

"Do you know who the fuck I am?" Samad screamed as he looked down the barrel of Rocko's gun.

Po released Liberty of all the ties, and she quickly pulled the handkerchief from her mouth. She stood up, but collapsed, not having any strength in her legs to hold up her weight. Po caught her before she hit the ground and whispered in her ear. "Everything is going to be okay," he said as he slowly helped her to her feet.

"This is no business of yours!" Samad yelled out as hatred burned inside of him.

"Shut the fuck up," Po screamed as rage filled his body. He sat Liberty on the bed and rushed over to Samad who was attempting to stand up, striking him across the temple with the butt of his gun. The blow was so powerful it sent Samad flying to the floor again. His back hit the marble so hard that it knocked the wind out of him. Blood leaked from Samad's mouth as he writhed, weakly turning onto his side.

"Please, look. Let's make a deal. I can change your life. What's the cost to let me go?" Samad said.

Po and Rocko weren't playing. Samad recognized the look in their eyes and knew it oh too well. They had come to kill.

"You think you can buy your way out of this? Huh? Look at her. Look what you did to her," Po said as he glanced over at Liberty's battered body. He quickly walked to Samad's closet and grabbed a robe. He then covered Liberty and whispered in her ear. "Turn your head, okay?" he said. She nodded her head in agreement as she sniffled and covered herself with the robe.

"You can't buy your way out of this one, homeboy. You are a piece of shit. Do you know that?" Po said as he looked down at Samad. "Men like you make me sick. How could you hurt a woman like that, huh? You can't be a man if you can bring yourself to do something like this," Po said as he slowly began to pace the floor. Scarlett filled his thoughts as he pictured how she had been bound and beaten severely before her murder.

"What we do to niggas like this, Rocko?" Po asked as he grinned and looked at his right-hand man.

"First, I'ma shoot this nasty mu'fucka's dick off, and then stuff it down his throat," Rocko said as he kept his gun pointed at Samad.

"You a crazy mu'fucka, Rock, you know that?" Po said as he chuckled at his right hand.

"Look, I have a million dollars' worth of pure unstepped on cocaine in my safe. It's all yours if you let me go. It's behind the picture on the wall," Samad nodded desperately toward the original Picasso in the room. "You seem like a businessman. Let's make a deal. I know you are not going to let this filthy bitch come between you and money, right?" Samad pleaded as he unleashed a nervous laugh.

"Oh yeah?" Po asked said as his eyes lit up.

"That's right. You can have it all," Samad said as he sweated profusely.

"That's a nice deal. But I got an even better one for you," Po said as he put his gun in his waist and began to rub his hands together.

Samad smiled and it seemed as if a ton of bricks were just lifted from his shoulders. "I knew you were a smart man," he said as he slowly sat up and wiped the blood from his mouth. "What's the deal?" he asked.

"You're going to give me the combo to the safe, and I am going to skip the torture and let Rocko put you to sleep with two shots to the head," Po said as he nodded to Rock. Rocko then pointed the gun toward Samad's exposed penis.

"Now, what is the safe combo? If you lie or take too long to answer, my man's going to shoot off your dick, playboy," Po stated.

"Whoa, whoa, whoa. Think about this. I have guards outside. If they hear any gunshots, they are going to come up here guns blazing. I have twenty men on staff. So think about it. Your two guns up against my twenty. That's not good odds," Samad was quick to point out.

"Well, I want to introduce you to my friend. His name is 'Silencer,'" Po said as he dug into his gardener jumpsuit and pulled out a screw-on silencer. He then tossed it to Rocko who twisted it on the tip of his gun, then immediately pointed the gun back at Samad's crotch.

"What's the combo?" Po asked calmly as he walked up to Samad and looked down at him. Samad hesitated and didn't say a word as he and Po locked eyes. That's when Po looked at Rocko and gave him a nod and almost immediately Rocko blew Samad's dick off. Samad squealed in pain as he saw his bloody crotch and a piece of his penis blown off. He squirmed like a fish as he began to shake feverishly.

Po looked over at Liberty, and she looked at him. "Are you okay?" he asked. She nodded her head yes and looked at Samad squirm in complete agony.

"I want to watch," she said as she turned her body toward Samad.

"Looks like you got a gangster on your hands," Rocko said as he smiled at Po, and then looked at Liberty. Po returned the smile before focusing his attention back on Samad.

"Now, I'm going to ask you again. Next shot is going to blow your balls clean off," Po promised as he watched Samad cry like a baby.

"Agh. Oh, Allah!" Samad said as he panted heavily. "Eight, fourteen, twenty-six. That's the combo," he cried as he applied pressure to his crotch trying to stop the profuse bleeding.

Po went over to the painting and took it off the wall.

Just like Samad said, there was a huge hidden safe behind the painting. Po put the combo in, and it opened, exposing plastic-wrapped bricks of cocaine. Each one of the bricks had a stamp on it that read "epidemic." His face lit up like a kid's in the candy store. He looked at Rocko and smiled. Rocko then pointed his gun at Samad's head and prepared to pull the trigger, rocking him to sleep forever.

"Hold up!" Po yelled as he walked over to Liberty. He looked at Rocko and signaled for him to toss him the gun. Po then handed it to Liberty. "You want to do the honors?" he asked her.

Liberty hesitantly took the gun and stood up. With a shaky hand, she walked over to Samad and looked down at him with hateful eyes. He began to slip out of consciousness because of the blood loss. Po slipped behind Liberty and helped her point the gun and steady her aim.

"Now, you want to hold it with two hands and get a firm grip. Close your eyes or you will never forget the look in his eyes after this is done and over. That look stays with you forever. Believe me," he instructed.

"I want to see. I *want* to remember," Liberty said, just before she closed one eye and slightly raised the gun.

"Oh shit. Li'l ma got some spunk," Rocko said in surprise as he stepped to the side.

"I got you. Just pull the trigger when you're ready," Po slowly whispered into her ear. Just as the words slid out of his mouth, Liberty squeezed. Matter of fact, she squeezed until the clip was empty, filling Samad's body full of holes. To say 3-Swiss cheese was an understatement.

Once the bullets were gone, she dropped the gun and stared at Samad's corpse, never blinking as tears ran down her cheeks. Po looked over at Rocko and threw his head in the direction of the safe. Rocko went into the closet and grabbed a piece of Samad's luggage and began to empty the safe. In the process of saving Liberty, they had stumbled upon a come-up.

FOUR

HYSTERICAL, LIBERTY FELL INTO PO'S ARMS, BURYING her head into his chest as he held her shaking body close. She broke down completely. Po hugged her tightly and consoled her as she crumbled in his arms. Rocko looked at Po in shock as he watched Po handle Liberty gently. Rocko had never seen Po's soft side with anyone but Scarlett, so to see him treat Liberty with such care was odd.

"How could you bring me back here!" she cried as she gripped his jacket collar and sobbed uncontrollably. She hit him in the face, slapping him with the sole ounce of strength she had left. "I trusted you!" she screamed angrily. In a mixture of rage and relief she clung to him, jerking his collar as she spoke. "You brought me back to him!"

Po took her smacks because he knew that he deserved them. "I'm sorry. Let me get you out of here."

Liberty pulled away from him, but her wobbly legs gave

out beneath her. Samad had beaten and raped her badly. Her body was weak.

"Don't touch me!" she shouted. "You lied to me!"

"I can't believe we did all this shit for a bitch," Rocko mumbled in disbelief as he watched the scene unfold. In all the years he had known Po, Po had never put a play down over a woman. Po was motivated by money, so to kick in a man's door, guns blazing over this one girl was uncharacteristic of him.

Po shot Rocko a look that told Rocko to hold his peace, then knelt down to console Liberty. He knew that she didn't trust him. She had every right to doubt him, but she had to let that go so that he could get her away from the murder scene.

"Let me get you out of here. I'm not going to hurt you. You can stay here with the nigga body or you can let me help you," Po said in a low but serious tone. Liberty's entire frame shook from fear and pain. Her once-flawless skin was marred black and blue from the beatings she had endured.

"Fine, just get me away from here," Liberty said, giving in as she glanced at Samad's corpse. Even in death the sight of him sent chills down her spine. Po scooped her up off her feet and carried her fragile body over to the bed. Liberty turned her face into Po's broad chest to avoid staring at Samad's lifeless body. "There's so much blood," she whispered.

Po turned her face toward his. "Just look at me, a'ight?"

"Yo, it's time to roll, fam," Rocko stated.

"I'm gon' get you out of here, ma," Po promised as he opened up the armoire and removed a crisp white business shirt off of one of Samad's racks. He wrapped it around her body, moving swiftly as he helped her button it up. He picked her up again and headed out of the room. Rocko gave Po a skeptical glance, and Po's firm stare was all it took to get Rocko on board. The pair had been rocking with each other since the sandbox. Rocko wouldn't question Po's decision.

"Fuck it, let's roll," Rocko said as he led the way toward the front entrance with his gun drawn and trigger finger ready.

Just before they exited Samad's mansion, Liberty spoke. "Wait. The office upstairs. The bricks you took out of that safe are peanuts compared to what he keeps locked in that room."

Rocko stepped outside and looked around in paranoia. "Yo, we don't got time for this shit, fam. Let's get out of this mu'fucka."

Liberty gripped Po's neck and whispered, "Trust me. It's worth your while."

Po headed upstairs with Liberty in his arms without hesitation.

"Fuck! What's with him and this bitch?" Rocko mumbled under his breath before following.

"Go right; it's the last door at the very end of the hall," Liberty instructed.

Po followed her lead and entered the room. Liberty climbed out of his arms and weakly headed toward the walk-in closet.

"Yo, Po! We don't got time—"

Po put his hand to Rocko's chest, cutting him off. "Five minutes, fam, and we out of here." His eyes followed Liberty the entire time he spoke.

Liberty stopped in front of the large glass showcase that contained the urns and her eyes burned with tears. "I'm sorry no one could save you," she whispered, acknowledging the forgotten souls in the urns, the women that Samad had made disappear before her. Po walked up behind her. "We've got to go, ma."

"No one even knows that they're dead. No one even cares," Liberty stated.

Po's eyes diverted to the showcase of urns. "What are you talking about, Liberty?"

"If you hadn't come back, I would be inside one of these urns by the morning," she said as a tear glided down her face.

Rocko shifted uncomfortably in his stance as Po's eyes widened at Liberty's revelation.

"Let's go," he insisted as he grabbed her arm.

"Wait. I'm not leaving here until I get what's owed to me," she said. "Move the display, please."

Po looked at Rocko and nodded his head. Rocko hesitantly pushed the glass display aside, revealing the door that it concealed behind. Liberty had always known the door was there, but Samad had instilled so much fear inside of her that it was only in his death that she had the courage to open it.

She quickly opened the door and turned toward Rocko. "I think this was worth the risk, don't you?"

Rocko and Po stepped into the large room and both their eyes widened in surprise. Greed filled them as they looked at the treasure to which Liberty had led them.

Liberty was right. There were more bricks of cocaine than they could count. They lay stacked neatly against the back wall. Bank bricks of plastic-wrapped money were piled on a steel table and an arsenal of automatic guns hung from the walls. They had hit the ghetto lottery. The value of what lay inside of this hidden room was more than what Po would have ever attained in his entire life.

"Damn," Rocko whispered.

"I told you," Liberty said with a smirk as she exited the room and headed back toward the office.

Rocko turned to Po. "Yo, shorty a keeper," he said jokingly.

"Let's bag this shit up and get out of here," Po said before he went after Liberty. When he found her, Liberty was rifling through Samad's desk drawers, her hands frantically searching until they landed on a black book. She handed it to Po.

"What's this?" he asked, taking it in his hands and flipping through the pages.

"It's his ledger. Every time he would conduct business, he would record it in this journal. Names, dates, locations, amounts. It's all there," Liberty informed him. "You can have it all. The drugs, the guns, the contacts. All I want is a portion of the money. I've been passed around from owner to owner, man to man, since I was a kid. I appreciate you coming back for me, but I don't want to feel like I owe you. I don't want to be indebted to you or anybody else ever again. I just want my freedom."

Liberty spoke with such passion that Po couldn't help but wonder what her eyes had seen in her lifetime. The pain from which she spoke he knew nothing about, but he could tell that it was deep rooted.

"You don't owe me shit, ma. I came back because . . ." he paused as he realized that he didn't even know why he had come to her rescue, and before he could come up with an answer Rocko interrupted them.

"I'ma need more bags, fam. There's so much shit in here we gonna live like kings, baby. We on now."

They snuck out of the house and coasted right past the guards in the van. After dumping the van and the lawn workers, who would soon be able to untie themselves, around the corner, they got into Po's car and headed out. Liberty had just closed a horrible chapter in her life, but little did she know, she was about to start a new one.

Rocko and Po stayed up all night counting dead presidents. They were high off life. The money was good, but they both knew the potential flip from the coke and guns was far greater. The penthouse suite of the West Hollywood hotel they chose gave them the perfect view of the glittering city below. It was 4 A.M., and the city was winding down, but Po and Rocko had never felt more alive. Po's life had taken a turn for the worse when he had lost Scarlett, but meeting

Liberty seemed like a silver lining around the dark cloud that hovered over him.

"How we gon' get this shit back home?" Rocko asked.

"Shit, for me, this is home, at least for now," Po stated. "Ain't shit in the D for me, fam. Too many memories there. Without Scar . . ." Po's words trailed off as he thought of the murder of his first love. A vice grip of pain captured his heart, and he took a deep breath to ease the grief. "I'm not going back," he concluded.

"Fuck it. We'll bring the hustle to Hollywood," Rocko cracked, letting Po know he was down for the ride. "For the record, bro . . . Scarlett's death ain't on you. It's a part of the game, and the fuck boy that called that play is grieving just as hard over his own mama right now."

"His mama ain't enough. I want his head, and that's one trigger that I have to pull personally," Po stated, tension pulsing through his jaws as he grit his teeth in fury.

Rocko nodded in understanding, then motioned toward the master bedroom where Liberty was sleeping.

"And what about her?" Rocko asked.

Po's thoughts drifted from Scarlett to Liberty. "What about her? She's just some chick. I put shorty in a tight spot, so I helped her out. That's it. The only thing I'm focused on is getting this money. In the morning, I'm gon' give her a third of this paper, and the bird can fly," Po replied nonchalantly as he tapped one of the banded stacks of bills on the table before throwing it into the pile. "Meanwhile, this little black book is my key to a new empire."

The sun crept over the city washing away the sins of

the night. The floor-to-ceiling windows let in the light as Po leaned against the glass, peering out over the city. Rocko lay sprawled across the sofa. Fatigue had been his undertaker hours before, but Po couldn't rest. His mind was full of money schemes as he plotted his next move. L.A. was new stomping grounds for him, and he would be the new kid on the block, but with Samad's book in hand, he had an obvious advantage over the competition. As he looked back into the room where Liberty slept he couldn't help but think of Scarlett. The emotional roller coaster he was on took him through hills of grief, loops of anger, and dips of resentment. He was more than ready to get off this ride of mental anguish, and money was the perfect distraction.

Rocko groaned behind him as he arose from his sleep. "You still up, bro?" he asked.

"Couldn't sleep," Po replied. "We can't keep this shit here. It's time to get busy, fam. I need you to find a place where we can set up shop out here. This is too much work to keep where I sleep. Store it somewhere safe. Somewhere low-key."

Rocko nodded. He opened the closet and found a bell-man's cart inside. He began to load the duffel bags on top. Just before he exited the room, Po stopped him.

"Yo, Rocko," he shouted.

Rocko paused midstep and turned to Po, looking him dead in the eyes.

"Spend that bread slow, fam. Don't draw no unneces-sary attention to yourself. If the nigga Samad is as large as

I think he was, we might encounter some problems. That's a murder that we don't have to be tied to if we play it smart, understand?"

Rocko nodded in agreement. "I got you," he said, before leaving the room.

Po turned toward the room where Liberty slept and went to her bedside, then he sat in the chair across the room and leaned forward, resting his elbows against his knees. Po didn't know what to do with Liberty next. Yes, he had saved her, but he wasn't trying to be her savior. He knew that it was time for them to part ways, and he hoped that the money he had set aside for her was severance enough. He was so absorbed in his thoughts that he didn't notice Liberty wake up.

"How long have you been sitting there?" she asked as she sat up in the bed, resting her sore back against the headboard. She winced as she felt the effects of Samad's vicious hand.

"Not long," Po answered as he stood and walked over to her. He grabbed a pillow and put it behind her back, then he sat on the edge of the bed and looked at her. She was the definition of beauty, good by nature with a heart so pure that it had been abused many times. Po didn't understand how someone could bring her harm. Being in her presence warmed his cold heart, and he could not fathom why. Po never changed up for anyone, but he felt differently toward Liberty. Being around her was like putting a Band-Aid over his wounded heart. She was healing to him, without even knowing it. But because his fiancée had just died, he felt disloyal for finding relief in Liberty. He couldn't explain his connection to her, but he would be lying to himself to say that one didn't exist. If he felt nothing for her, he would have left her for dead. It wasn't sexual or even a love thing. Her spirit was good . . . like Scarlett's had been. She reminded him of what he had lost. If anything, he wanted friendship from her.

"How you feel?" Po asked.

"I hurt all over," Liberty replied. "But it doesn't matter now. He's gone, and he can't hurt me ever again. I don't have to be afraid anymore, and I owe that to you."

"I'm the reason why you're lying here like this in the first place. I should have never taken you back there. I'm sorry, ma. You were just a face standing in the way of me and my paper, but once I got to know you, I couldn't just leave you there. That shit ate at me," Po replied. "I apologize to you, Liberty."

Liberty didn't reply. She didn't know how to feel toward him. Her anger was so prevalent, but so was her gratitude. Not even A'shai had been successful when it came to killing Samad. Po had done that, and he had done so on her behalf. That had to count for something.

Po leaned over, noticing the still fresh scar that lay across her chest. He looked at her as he reached to touch it.

"Can I?" he asked.

Liberty looked down at her scar in confusion, then back up at Po. She unbuttoned her shirt some and lifted her neck to allow him access.

The warmth of his fingertips kissed her skin like rays

from the sun as she closed her eyes and took a deep, timid breath. Po's fingers trembled as he traced the slightly bubbled scar.

"I had a bad heart," she explained. "I had a transplant."

Emotion built in Po's eyes, and as he looked at Liberty he saw Scarlett's face. He pulled his hands back as if he had touched a hot stove, then stood uncomfortably to his feet.

"We split the money last night three ways. You have more than enough to take care of yourself," Po said before he walked out of the room. He went into the bathroom and leaned over the sink as he gripped the sides. Scarlett's face was a constant in his brain as he thought of Liberty's scar.

Could she have Scar's heart? he thought. He shook the notion from his head, knowing that it was too big of a coincidence to be true. Liberty's demeanor was so similar to Scarlett's, however, that he couldn't help but compare the two. The death of his fiancée had done a number on him, and he knew that he couldn't jump headfirst into the game while in such a vulnerable state. *Get it together,* he thought. He exhaled loudly and exited the bathroom to find Liberty standing outside the door, duffel bag hanging from her arm.

"I'm out of here," she said. "Thank you again." She kissed his cheek, then weakly limped toward the door. Liberty was barely able to stand, and it looked as if the weight of the duffel bag would cause her to fall over. She needed medical attention and time to heal, but what she wanted most was to run as far away from L.A. as she possibly could. When she felt safe then she would stop and tend to her wounds.

"Where are you headed?" Po asked.

Liberty paused in uncertainty as she thought of an answer. The money in her hands was a passport to opportunity. It was possible for her to go anywhere and do anything she pleased. It was enough to purchase her security, but still she felt lost. Without A'shai, she felt lonely. Without love, she felt hopeless.

"I don't know," she replied. "I've never made a decision like this before. Someone else always decided for me. My destiny has never been in my own hands."

Saying it aloud made her realize just how much of a captive she had been. Liberty was a caged bird. She had never flown on her own, and the thought of doing so now terrified her.

"Well, now's your chance, shorty. If you ever need anything, don't hesitate to call," Po said. "After the goldmine you led me to, you have a friend on the West Coast for life."

Liberty smiled and nodded her head, somewhat sad that they were about to part ways.

"I don't even know what to do first," Liberty admitted. "What do I do? Where do I go? I don't even know where home is. I'm just . . ."

"Lost," he finished for her.

Liberty nodded and peered at him with a bashful smile.

"Then take some time to think about it. You can stay here for awhile. The suite is paid up for the next couple of weeks. You're welcome to collect your thoughts here, ma,"

Po said. "You will barely see me. All I need the room for is to sleep and eat. The rest of my time will be spent getting acquainted with the streets of L.A."

"Really?" she asked.

Po took the duffel bag off her shoulders. "Really, Liberty. I would enjoy the company, and besides, I need somebody to help me count all the money I'm about to make."

"Now that I can do!" she said with a laugh.

Po grabbed her hand and pulled her over to the hotel safe. He stuffed her money inside and turned his head.

"Enter a combination. You're the only one who will have access to your money. I want you to feel completely comfortable," Po said as he looked her in the eyes. "From the way you talk, it seems like you've fallen victim to a lot of people. I'm not one of them. You're good here."

His words tugged at Liberty, and she wondered where this man had come from. He seemed noble and protective, the way that A'shai had been. Liberty entered a combination, then turned to Po.

"Thank you," she said.

Po nodded his head, and then retreated to the second bedroom, his head spinning. Liberty had no idea what her presence did to Po. He couldn't allow her to walk out of his life right now. He didn't know her well; shit, hardly at all, but the way that she made him feel was too familiar to say good-bye to—at least not yet. He lived in a world where he had seen his street dreams become nightmares, and he had lost the one person that he had ever loved. Then Liberty

happened into his existence, and in her face he saw opti-
mism, in her smile he recognized hope. Something told him
that she had been through enough tribulations to last two
lifetimes, but she was still standing. He needed her to teach
him how to piece his life back together. How to superglue
his shattered soul.

FIVE

PO SAT STARING AT THE BRICKS OF cocaine that were neatly stacked in the storage unit.

"What's the plan?" Rocko asked.

"I've got some shit lined up with some real heavy buyers. I've got a meeting tomorrow night with a nigga out of Arizona, so I need you to be on point for this one. You're my eyes and ears, fam. We were getting money back home, but the shit we about to dive into is on a whole 'nother level," Po said.

"No doubt," Rocko replied. "You sure you don't want to take the work back to Detroit? We know how the game goes back home."

Po shook his head in discord. "I already told you, Detroit is my rearview, my nigga. L.A. is where it's at for me right now. You can put a few plays down back home if you want. Get your money, Rock, but I'd rather not touch it."

Rocko nodded. "Understood."

"Meet me tonight at the hotel at 9 o'clock," Po said. "Don't be late."

Liberty leaned against the door frame as she watched Po rack his .45 and stash it in the holster that sat on his hip. His face was stern, focused, and on the task at hand as he mentally prepared himself for the meeting in store. Black jacket, dark denims, and Polo boots gave him a hood swagger. His fitted hat sat low on his head, almost completely concealing his eyes.

KNOCK KNOCK!

Liberty jumped at the unexpected noise.

"It's just Rocko," Po said as he walked over to the door.

"You ready?" Rocko greeted.

"You got the shit?" Po asked.

"Everything's good," Rocko confirmed.

Po turned to Liberty who stood nearby hugging herself. "Lock the door behind me. I'll be back late, so if anybody comes knocking before then, you blow holes through the door, a'ight?"

Liberty's eyes widened in alarm.

Po walked over to the table and grabbed the gun that lay atop of it. He cocked the pistol and approached Liberty. He stepped close to her and held the gun up to her face.

"This switch is the safety. All you got to do is click it, point, and pull the trigger. Red means dead," he instructed as he showed her in thirty seconds how to defend herself.

She looked like a deer caught in headlights. Why was he preparing her for this? Did he have enemies that she didn't know about? Was staying in L.A. with him a mistake? A million questions ran through her mind in that moment, and he sensed her fear.

"Look, I don't know what I'm getting myself into. No one even knows where to find me, but you can never be too safe. This is chess not checkers, Liberty, and if you're gonna be around I need you to be on point. If something doesn't feel right, don't hesitate. You shoot first, ask questions later," he said sternly.

She nodded and the way her brow creased in uncertainty was so familiar to Po. For a brief second he saw Scarlett in her. Their mannerisms were so similar that it overwhelmed him sometimes. The way she pursed her lips when in deep thought, the way she swept her hair from her face . . . It was all things that Scarlett used to do. Out of instinct he kissed Liberty's forehead, then walked out of the door, leaving Rocko looking perplexed.

Rocko looked at Liberty briefly, then tapped the door. "Lock up," he said before catching up to Po.

"What was that?" Rocko asked.

"What was what, nigga? We're just friends. I need shorty to know how to move though," Po said.

Rocko heard what Po was saying, but his actions were telling a completely different story. "I thought she was supposed to leave town yesterday," Rocko said.

"Nah, I'ma keep her around for awhile. She didn't have nowhere to go. Now we gon' keep talking about Liberty, or you want to focus on getting this money, nigga?" Po cracked. "You acting like you interested. You want me to hook you up or something, mu'fucka?"

"Hell, yeah," Rocko joked. "Shorty nice . . ."

Po shook his head as they got his car from the valet and pulled off into the night. There were only two things on his mind: power and money. Everything else was irrelevant.

Po pulled up to the address where he was supposed to meet the buyer and frowned in confusion when he noticed it was a crowded restaurant.

"What the fuck is this? This can't be the right spot," Rocko said as he looked at the fancy patrons entering the West Hollywood establishment.

Po pulled out the throw-away cell phone he purchased for the occasion and checked the text message to confirm the address.

"This is it," Po said. Knowing that he couldn't carry thirty bricks into a busy restaurant Po shook his head in frustration. "We've got to leave it in the car."

"What?" Rocko exclaimed. "Nigga, you can go inside to meet this nigga. I'll stay and watch the work. That's a lot of shit to leave in the trunk."

"Nigga, I value my life more than I value that weight. I need you watching what's moving around me. You got the burner, right?" Po asked.

"I don't leave home without it," Rocko stated arrogantly.

Po and Rocko exited the car, handing the keys to the valet. Po pulled out five $100 bills and placed them into the kid's hand.

"You watch my car. No one comes near it. Don't take your eyes off of it, understand?"

"Yes, sir," the kid said excitedly as he stuffed the money into his pocket.

Po and Rocko entered the restaurant. They were immediately greeted by the maître d'.

"Gentlemen, this way."

Po and Rocko both wore the screw face as they maneuvered through the crowd. They stuck out like sore thumbs. The other patrons were donned in upscale apparel, while Po and Rocko were hooded out.

They were escorted to a private section of the restaurant where an older black gentleman sat conversing with a vixen by his side.

"Gentlemen, this is Mr. Blue," the maître d' introduced. He pulled out chairs for Po and Rocko. "Can I take your drink orders?"

Po waved his hand in dismissal and sat down across from Mr. Blue, eyeing him and briefly admiring his beautiful companion before addressing the issue at hand.

"This isn't quite what I was expecting," Po stated, clearly uncomfortable in the public setting.

"What did you think? That we would meet in a dark alley at midnight?" Mr. Blue countered as he sat back in his chair. "This is a different league, Po. You're a long way from Seven Mile."

"What, nigga?" Rocko said, getting defensive as he reached in his waistline.

"Before you even draw on me, Whitney here will have your gut full of lead," Mr. Blue stated.

Po placed his hand over Rocko's to stop the gunfight

before it began. "We're good on this side. Let's just get down to business. How do you know my name and where I'm from?"

Mr. Blue chuckled and reached into his jacket to retrieve three cigars. He passed one to Rocko and Po, then lit his own. He inhaled deeply, taking his time to savor the taste before exhaling.

"As I said before, this is a different league, Po. I know you got my information from Samad's records, and I also know that you are responsible for his untimely demise. A man that can kill Samad with such ease is a man worth looking up. That's a man that I need to know," Mr. Blue said. "What *you* didn't know is that Samad's home security cameras run twenty-four hours a day. I got the tapes so that I could find out who I was dealing with." Mr. Blue slid the tapes across the table to Po. "These are the only copies, no duplicates were made. No one can tie you to Samad's murder. I hope that this gesture will get our new business relationship off to a good start."

Po accepted the tapes and nodded his head.

"At this level, business is discussed among allies around dinner. If you had contacted anyone else in that book and showed up looking unpolished, they would not have dealt with you. This is a business just as much as Wall Street. We don't deal in duffel bags and one-dollar bills. This is a billion-dollar industry, Po, so you must act accordingly. In the future, bring your wife not your goon and leave the street gear for the runners on the block," Mr. Blue schooled.

"Understood. My price is $18k. It's nonnegotiable, but

I think you'll find that it's very reasonable," Po stated, purposefully setting his price lower than what Samad had noted in his book.

"Indeed it is," Mr. Blue replied. "I need fifty. I have to start light to ensure that the product you have is of the same quality that I'm used to."

"That's understandable. My man Rocko will make the drop for me. Get used to seeing his face. He's the only person I'll ever send to conduct business on my behalf," Po stated. "I'll have your order ready tomorrow morning. I will text you the time and location where the exchange will be made."

"Good business," Mr. Blue said.

Po and Rocko rose from their seats, and Mr. Blue raised his hands in protest.

"Stay! Eat!" Mr. Blue offered.

Rocko glanced at Po who shook his head. "Next time," he assured. Po reached his hand across the table and sealed the deal with a firm handshake before he and Rocko walked out of the restaurant. They both were feeling on top of the world from their first flip. Each knew that this was simply the beginning. They had hustled from the bottom and now were major players at the top of the game. Life was good.

Po entered the hotel room announcing his presence. "Yo, Liberty, I'm back!" he said as he placed his gun on the table near the entryway. He removed his jacket as he made his way into the suite.

"I'm in the bathroom. I'll be right out!" she announced.

Her voice cracked slightly as if she had been crying. Po walked over to the door, which was slightly cracked. He peered through the door to see Liberty standing with her back to her mirror and her head turned so that she could see the many bruises that covered her back. She sniffed and wiped the tears from her face. Po knocked lightly and pushed open the door just as she slid the hotel robe over her shoulders, covering her injuries.

She turned to him, embarrassed, as she closed the robe tightly, gripping it around her body.

"Are you okay?" he asked.

"I'm fine," Liberty answered quickly. "How did it go?"

"Everything's good, ma. Don't worry yourself with that," Po replied. "Come here." He pulled her hand toward the tub and sat her down on the edge as he drew her a bath.

"You don't have to . . ." she protested.

Po checked the temperature of the water and ignored her. He stood up and before he walked out he said, "Get in and relax. I'll be right back."

Liberty crossed her arms across her chest and watched him leave the room before she stepped into the water. Po came back a few moments later with a champagne flute in his hand.

"You went a little overboard with the bubbles, didn't you?" she asked with a laugh as she blew a handful of suds his way.

"Just like a woman. Complaining even when a nigga try to do something nice," he said with a smirk.

She smiled as he got on his knees beside the large Jacuzzi

tub. He grabbed the sponge beside the tub and dipped it into the water before gently washing the bruises on her back. She winced from his touch and closed her eyes as she brought her knees to her chest. Po frowned as he noticed the healed scars that covered Liberty's body. "These aren't fresh scars," he whispered as he touched them, tracing them gently. "How long was that nigga beating you?" he asked angrily.

"I got those scars long before Samad ever met me," Liberty whispered in reply. She sipped the champagne, and then let her head hang onto her chest as Po washed her neck.

"Who hurt you, Liberty?" he asked.

"Everyone I have ever met, except you and . . ."

Her words drifted off into silence. She was unable to bring herself to say his name.

"And who?" Po asked.

"A'shai. He was my everything, and now that he's gone, I have nothing left," she said.

He could feel the emptiness behind her words and knew exactly how she felt, because her loss matched his own. He stood and held out a large towel for her, turning his head as she stepped into it. She wrapped it snugly under each arm then made her way into the living area. Po sat her on the couch and handed her the glass of champagne.

"A'shai killed himself because he wanted to die with me. We were supposed to be together forever, through anything. Nothing could tear us apart, not a war, not Samad, not even death, but then the doctors found me a new heart.

So now I'm here, and he's dead. You don't know the guilt I feel for being the one to live," Liberty said.

"Do you know whose heart you have?" he asked, unable to help himself.

Liberty shook her head and replied, "No, and I know that getting this second chance is a gift, but without A'shai, it feels more like a curse."

Out of all the people that Scarlett's heart could have gone to, Po had the nagging feeling that it was beating strongly, two feet away from him inside of Liberty's chest. He looked at her and made a mental note to get the answer to the question he sought. If his suspicions were indeed true, there was no way he was ever letting Liberty leave his life. That organ was the last piece of Scarlett he had left, and it didn't help that he was astounded by Liberty's aura. She was delicate like a rare flower, and the winds of life had blown at her so hard that it had wilted her spirit. Po could see that Liberty was hurting. He empathized with her on a level so profound that their chance meeting now felt as if it had been written in the stars all along.

Po put his hand on Liberty's chest and felt the rhythm of life pulsing through her.

THUMP THUMP

THUMP THUMP

He held his breath as the beat of his own heart synced with hers.

THUMP THUMP

THUMP THUMP

"It's not a curse, ma, believe that," he said. He cleared

his throat, feeling as though things were getting too thick between them, and stood up. "It's late. You should get some sleep. We have a long day tomorrow."

Liberty stood to her feet. "What's happening tomorrow?" she asked.

"We go shopping. I need you to come to business meetings with me from now on. You'll need fancy dresses and makeup, the whole nine. You think you can handle that for me?" he asked.

"Of course I can," she answered sweetly.

"Good. Besides, it's time we blow some of this money," he said with a charming smile.

Liberty smiled and nodded her head in excitement. "Good night."

"Sleep well, ma," he replied as he turned to the window and peered out over the illuminated city. Po sighed deeply as he poured himself a shot of cognac, and he shook his head to clear his thoughts. He could feel himself meandering down a slippery slope. The easy route was right before him, and it didn't include Liberty, but he always had a hard head. He liked to do things the hard way, and although it felt wrong to keep Liberty nearby, at the same time it felt right. *What the fuck am I getting myself into?* Was the last thought that crossed his mind before he retired for the night.

SIX

LIBERTY AWOKE TO THE SOUND OF ROCKO and Po talking out on the terrace, but when she stepped out to join them all conversation ceased.

"Hey, Rocko. Good morning, Po," she greeted.

"What's good, lady?" Rocko spoke, quickly coming to the realization that Po was feeling her, even if he wouldn't admit it to himself just yet. The fact that Liberty was still around gave away Po's feelings toward her. He had never cuffed a chick the way that he was now. Po was soft on Liberty. He turned back to Po, suddenly feeling like the third wheel. "I'ma shake, fam. While you *shopping* for the big meetings and shit, I'll be going to get a handle on the street shit. Let these West Coast niggas know there's a new administration in town."

"I can dig it," Po stated. "I've got another meeting tonight. We'll link back up in the A.M."

The two men embraced and locked hands before Rocko

departed. Just as Rocko was leaving the penthouse, the concierge walked inside. Behind him was a maid with a table of food.

"You can put it on the terrace," Po instructed. "Did you get that other thing I requested?" he asked as he turned toward the concierge.

"Of course, sir," the man said. He snapped his fingers and another woman came inside the suite carrying a garment bag. "Hermès dress," the concierge said as he turned to Liberty. "Size six looks about right. Shoes and handbag to match."

Po tipped the concierge generously for the trouble and waited until everyone left the room.

"You want to join me for breakfast, ma?" he asked.

"Hermès?" Liberty said. "You didn't have to do that, Po."

"We gon' do a lot more of that. It's nothing. Don't worry about it," he replied as he placed his hand on the small of her back and led her to her chair.

The two sat down and conversed over a smorgasbord of food. The more Liberty spoke, the more Po grew to like her. There was so much more to her than what met the eye. He let her vent about A'shai, listening attentively as she described the loss she felt. Little did she know that he was feeling his own strife as well. He shared little about himself. He had learned long ago that it was better to listen than to speak.

"Tell me about the scars," Po said, more as a demand than a request. "When I asked you about them last night you were vague. What could you have possibly done to make someone hurt you like that?"

Liberty's back stiffened, and she grew uncomfortable as visions of Sierra Leone flooded her mind. Her journey to independence had been a long one; one that she would rather not recount. The intense stare that Po gave her spoke volumes. He wasn't going to let her brush the subject under the rug.

"I'm from Sierra Leone," she finally said. "I was forced to the U.S. on a human trafficking ship, then sold into prostitution. Eventually I was purchased by Samad. I was his property until A'shai rescued me from it all."

Po put his fork down in disbelief. At the most he had suspected an abusive boyfriend. He would have never pieced together such a complicated past, and now that he had heard the truth he felt bad for forcing her to share it. Sympathy emanated from him.

"Don't look at me like that. That is the exact reason I never tell anyone. You shouldn't judge," she whispered.

"I never would, Liberty. I know nothing about the world that you come from. I only know that I am sorry that you had to go through so much," he said. "If you ever need to talk, I'm willing to listen."

It was as if a burden had been lifted from Liberty's chest. The floodgates were open, and as she started to tell him more about her past she felt a sense of relief. The shallow world of money schemes that Po lived in seemed so easy compared to the hardships that she had been forced to endure. The only bright spot in her life was also her darkest memory. Her eyes sparkled each time she spoke of A'shai, but quickly clouded over, threatening to rain tears of heartbreak. Po found himself admiring her now more than ever. She was a phenomenal person. He had never encountered anyone like her. They spent the next two hours talking, neither growing tired of the conversation.

"I'm damaged goods," she said to him with a smile.

"You're perfectly flawed, ma. You're a beautiful woman, but your story is what makes you special. Don't be ashamed of it," he replied.

Liberty lowered her head and cleared her throat. "We better get going."

They stood, and Po wrapped his arm around her shoulder, pulling her close to him. "Let's go get your wardrobe up, shorty," he said. "I'ma show you how to play with this money."

Po and Liberty ripped through Rodeo Drive, lightening the mood with shopping and laughter. Po didn't care how much he spent, because he knew that he had a money tree in his possession. There was a lot more where that came from. Thanks to Liberty he was connected so a shopping spree was the least he could do to show his appreciation. The pair became fast friends as they spent the day together. Po had always been so serious, so standoffish when it came to dealing with the world, but with Liberty, he was relaxed. To his own surprise, he trusted her. With Liberty, he didn't feel the need to keep his guard up. What took years for people to earn—his trust—she had claimed overnight. Liberty didn't know it, but she had Po's full attention. The magnetic attraction that she had once shared with A'shai she was building with Po without even trying.

* * *

In his natural element, Rocko took to the streets like a duck did to water. He had no problem leaving the corporate shit to Po; Rocko was a goon and thrived best in his own environment: the hood. In L.A., the drug game was run differently than in Detroit. Everything was gang-affiliated, and Rocko knew that there would be smoke as soon as word got out that out-of-towners were setting up shop. A shooter at heart, Rocko didn't care if he was intruding on someone else's block. He didn't need a gang of mu'fuckas behind him to take over. He and Po had done it solo for years. The only alliances they needed were Smith & Wesson.

"You ready to go? This meeting is very important. I can't be late," Po called through the door as he checked his watch before stuffing his hand in his Ferragamo slacks. Po cleaned up nicely. From first glance one would have never guessed his hood occupation. The high-end threads hung perfectly on his broad shoulders, and with Liberty by his side he would be easily accepted into this new circle of power.

Liberty stepped out of the room, and the sight of her took Po's breath away. Her beauty radiated as she stood in front of him. The wine-colored Caroline Herrera dress hugged the contours of her body. The silk fabric matched the softness of her skin, and for the first time Po was speechless in her presence.

Liberty was seasoned when it came to men, and she

could see the approval in Po's eyes. She blushed and said, "You clean up well, handsome."

"Thanks," he replied with a bashful smile. He guided her out of the hotel and toward the driver that he had hired for the night.

"All of this for a meeting?" she asked.

"I'm not on no extra shit, ma. It's needed, trust me," Po replied.

The two greeted the driver, and then climbed inside, headed toward their destination.

The city streets were a blur in her window as they flew down them, headed to Malibu. Liberty didn't know what to expect, how she was supposed to act, what she was getting herself into. She just hoped that she did and said the right things to make Po look good. The oceanside villa at which they arrived blew them both away. Exiting the car, Po adjusted the tie that lay beneath his V-neck sweater. His new status would take some getting used to. There were rules to this side of the game that he had yet to learn. They walked to the door and nervous energy pulsed through Liberty. She didn't like the idea of being so close to Samad's associates. Po saw her stiffen, and he leaned into her ear to whisper, "You can trust me. I wouldn't put you in harm's way again, ma. The first time was a mistake. I'd never walk you into the lion's den, Liberty. You're with me so you're good, remember that."

Po rang the bell and was greeted by a white woman dripping in diamonds. Liberty was blinded, the woman was shining so brightly. Her stiff, Botoxed face struggled to stretch into a smile.

"You must be our guests for the evening. Please come in. I'm Claudia," she welcomed. Po and Liberty entered, and Claudia gasped loudly, "You are just exquisite, my dear," she complimented Liberty.

Caught off guard, Liberty stammered a thank you, then followed Claudia into the dining room. The room was set for four and reminded Liberty of a king's celebration. Elaborate place settings laced in gold decorated the table, and a huge diamond chandelier hung above the long, rectangular table.

"My husband will be down shortly," Claudia said. She turned toward the door behind her, and a tall Russian man entered the room. "We guard our home with our life, and we take our privacy very seriously. Please allow Kosov to search you." Her face went from friendly to cold.

Po pulled his gun from his waistline and popped out the clip, handing it to the guard. "Can't do much without bullets," he said as he placed the gun back in its holster. Kosov didn't know that Po always kept one in the chamber. Po was never completely unarmed. Kosov checked the rest of Po's body for wires, and then briefly inspected Liberty before giving Claudia the nod of approval. Claudia's smile returned. "Good," she said. "Please sit. I've had our chef prepare a wonderful meal."

As the threesome sat, a man entered the room. "This is my husband, Sasha," Claudia introduced.

"Po, very good to have you here. You are a refreshing difference from our late friend, Samad," Sasha remarked with a heavy Russian accent. "I hear you have met with Mr. Blue."

Po shook hands with Sasha. "I have. We did good business together."

"I hope you give me the same courtesy as you did him. He bragged quite a bit about the rate you offered. Quite the discount," Sasha said.

"Everything is negotiable. I deal in weight. The heavier your order, the more flexible I can be," Po responded.

Sasha nodded and gave Po a friendly pat on the back. "Quantity won't be an issue with me, Po, but we can talk about that later. Please, introduce me to your lovely companion."

Po turned to Liberty and helped her from her seat. He pulled her next to him as if by his side was where she belonged. "This is Liberty," Po said.

Sasha grabbed Liberty's hand and brought it to his mouth for a kiss.

"My husband is an admirer of beautiful women. I always know if he is stunned by a woman. If you were unattractive you'd have gotten a shake of the hand, but beauty he acknowledges with a kiss. Such the flirt," Claudia said with laughter.

The foursome sat down to a five-course meal, and Liberty was amazed at how commanding Po was. It was obvious that Sasha was more seasoned than Po, but Po's intelligence mixed with his hood savvy easily allowed him to control the tone of the evening. By the end of the evening he had earned Sasha's respect, Claudia's affection, and had established a new business friendship. Po had just flipped another fifty birds and was on a money high as he added up the riches in his head.

Liberty was the perfect accessory. She legitimized him in a way that only a boss could understand. Having a woman as remarkable as her on his arm gave him status. No one knew that she wasn't his, but they played the role perfectly, almost too perfectly for it to be untrue. Liberty charmed Claudia and Sasha all night, speaking only enough to make them feel comfortable. She knew her place and never overstepped her boundaries. Watching her in her element was impressive. It was quite clear that she was meant to be on the arm of a powerful man. She commanded just the right amount of attention to compliment the deal being discussed. Po knew that Liberty had no idea of her own worth. She was a queen that had never been crowned, and Po just happened to have an empty throne next to his.

Good wine, good conversation, and good business flowed between the group. By the end of the night, a firm connection had been established. Po might as well had been the weatherman because he was making it snow all over Southern California. He had bitten off way more than he could chew when he met Liberty. She was his road map to riches far beyond anything he had ever imagined. As he stared at her he found it funny how life had knocked him down, and then put him right back on his feet. He had thought that he was hustling on a large scale back in Detroit, but his grind back home was nonexistent to what L.A. had to offer. By the end of the night, Sasha was completely comfortable with his new supplier, and Po was a quarter million dollars richer. What had once taken him years to amass, he had made in a three-hour time frame this evening. It almost seemed too good to be true.

Liberty and Po stood to leave.

"Thank you so much, Claudia, for your kind hospitality," Liberty graciously said.

"Anytime, doll. Please do not be a stranger. This lifestyle can be quite boring sometimes. I'd love to have you over for brunch sometime soon," Claudia offered.

"Sounds like a date," Liberty smiled.

The men shook hands before Liberty and Po departed. As soon as they were outside Po rejoiced. He picked Liberty up off of her feet and spun her around in excitement. "We getting money, ma! You were brilliant in there! You had them eating out of the palm of your hand," he shouted.

"I didn't do anything. It was all you," she responded. Liberty laughed heartily for the first time in months as he lifted her in the air. She had been so distracted by her failing health, and then by A'shai's passing that she never noticed how long it had been since she had genuinely found something funny. It felt good to laugh, but she felt badly because A'shai was no longer able to hear her happiness. How could she even feel joy without him?

"Shh! Before they hear you! They can't know we were winging it!" she said. Po put her down, and she walked toward the car as the driver held the back door open for her.

Suddenly Po grabbed her hand and said, "Take a walk with me." He turned toward the driver. "I'll call you when we're ready to be picked up."

Po dragged Liberty toward the dark beach. Liberty removed her shoes as her feet touched the sand.

"You know, I've never been to a beach," she said solemnly.

"Like ever?" Po questioned in surprise.

Liberty shook her head and replied, "I don't really like the ocean. The sound of the waves reminds me of the time I spent on the trafficking ship that brought me to the States."

"Ship? Like a *slave* ship?" Po asked.

Liberty nodded, "That's exactly what it was. Getting on that boat was the biggest mistake that we ever made."

"We?" Po grilled.

"A'shai and I. He had been by my side since we were kids. Through everything he was always there," Liberty reminisced. "I never felt alone because even when life separated us, I knew that he was out there somewhere waiting for me."

Po's thoughts drifted to Scarlett. She had been the Bonnie to his Clyde, the Jackie to his Kennedy. Yet he found himself getting jealous whenever Liberty spoke of her lost love. How could he miss Scarlett but be drawn to Liberty simultaneously? His growing connection to Liberty made him feel disloyal. Liberty kicked the sand with her feet as she walked with her head down.

Po stopped and pulled her hand, causing her to face him. His stocky frame loomed over her, and he grabbed the back of her neck with authority, with compassion, as he kissed her lips.

Liberty's body melted into Po as she kissed him back,

tasting the wine on his tongue as her body became ablaze with suppressed pleasure. How was it possible that another man was making her feel the exact same passion that A'shai had? Liberty wanted to stop, but then again, she didn't want to stop. She lingered in his embrace as their bodies pressed against each other. The thin fabric of her dress wasn't enough of a barrier between them to stop her arousal. The firmness of his manhood as it bulged in his slacks made her wet as his hands slid down her back and pulled her ass into him. She moaned against her will; she was caught in his rapture. Never in her life had Liberty wanted to be fucked so badly. She needed to release the tension, the sadness, the chaos that had been building inside of her. But when she closed her eyes, it wasn't Po's face that she saw. She imagined that his hands were A'shai's hands, his tongue A'shai's tongue.

"Ooh, Shai," she whispered. She realized her mistake as soon as the words left her mouth, and she pulled away in embarrassment. She covered her mouth as tears came to her eyes. "I'm sorry. I'm so sorry, Po," she apologized.

Po wiped his mouth with his hand as his nostrils flared from the intensity of his breathing. Liberty had him fiending to feel her body against his, to have her as a replacement in his life. He wasn't mad at her for thinking of the past, because he was guilty of having the same thoughts. They were trying to fill a void in each other's life, but they each had huge shoes to fill.

"It's okay," he replied. "I understand."

"How could you?" she shouted. "No one understands what I lost."

Po sat down in the sand, disregarding his expensive threads, and patted the spot next to him. Liberty sat and leaned her head on his shoulder.

"I have to tell you something, Liberty," Po stated. "My girlfriend was murdered. The day we met at the hospital, I was going to collect some of her things. A nigga I had issues with in the street came into the home that we shared and killed her. They tortured her trying to get answers out of her. Thinking that she wasn't cooperating they murdered her, but they didn't know that she couldn't give them what they wanted. She was deaf. She couldn't hear them," Po revealed.

"Oh my God," Liberty whispered as she grabbed his hand and intertwined her fingers with his. "I'm sorry."

"Her name was Scarlett. She was an organ donor, Liberty," Po stated. "I have no way to be certain, but I think the last-minute heart that they found for you used to beat inside of Scarlett's chest. You remind me so much of her."

Liberty let go of his hand and looked at him in shock as her chest caved in. She lost her breath for a moment as she processed the bomb he had just dropped on her. "What?" She abruptly stood to her feet and dusted off her dress. "So this kiss? You wanting me around? All of this was about your dead girlfriend!" Liberty yelled. "This . . . this . . . connection that I feel to you is because you are trying to have a living memorial to her!"

"No!" Po defended. "It's not like that, Liberty!" Po stood to his feet.

"Oh really? You sure?" Liberty drilled.

Po rubbed the top of his head, frustrated. "I don't know!"

"You don't even know if I have her heart! I'm not her! I won't be her!" Liberty said as she hit her chest with the palm of her hand for emphasis. "I'm not a living shrine!"

"I know that, Liberty!" Po answered.

Liberty didn't know why she was so upset. She shouldn't want him to be attracted to her. *Why do I even care?* she thought.

"It wasn't a good idea that I stayed here, Po. I'm sorry for your loss, but I cannot stay in L.A. I don't belong here with you," she whispered as she walked away from him, unsure of where she was headed.

Po waited up all night for Liberty to come back to the hotel. The hollow pit that had formed in his gut had him sick with worry. It was 4 A.M., and he still hadn't heard from her. He wasn't sure if she was coming back or not. The one thing that gave him hope was the money that she kept in the safe. *She has to come back eventually,* he thought as he leaned over and pinched the bridge of his nose. When he heard the lock on the hotel door open, Po stood and went to the foyer. As soon as she stepped inside their eyes locked. He could tell that she had been crying because her eyes were red and swollen.

"I'm sorry. I have no right to be mad at you. I was emotional. The wine had me tripping," she said. "You can't put Scarlett on me though, Po. I'm not her. There are a million people who donate organs in this world. The odds are impossible that she's my donor. This heart is my heart." Liberty had never thought about who had lost their life in order for her to live, but with Po standing before her she was being forced to accept the cold truth. She felt like a science experiment, like she didn't know whose life she was living. Was she attracted to Po, or was her heart pulling her in a direction of its own?

"I know, Liberty," Po said as he stepped closer to her. He took her face in his hands. The last thing he wanted was for her to disappear. Despite what she said, she was a constant reminder of Scarlett. The fact that Liberty needed what Scarlett so desperately wanted to give someone was connection enough. Yes, Liberty reminded Po of Scarlett, but he could also appreciate the differences he saw.

"I'm sorry. You're more to me than some replacement for what I lost. You remind me of Scarlett because you're a good person. You don't meet too many of those these days. I'm here with you though, Liberty. I see you when I look at you, I hear you when you speak. Scarlett's gone, and you are the only person who gets what I'm going through. Tonight I went too far. I crossed a line, and I get that. I respect you, and I'm sorry I hurt you. Your friendship means a lot to me, ma, but I understand if you want to leave."

Liberty hesitated and looked up at Po. "I've spent a lot of time telling you about my life. About Shai, about Sierra Leone. I haven't done much listening, Po. Tell me about her," she said.

Po kissed the top of her forehead and said, "She was a lot like you. Very dear to me, but she's gone, and you're here. We're here, ma, so let's live."

Liberty gripped his hands tightly while looking up at Po.

"Let's live," she agreed. She kissed his cheek and walked away.

The tension between them was so thick it could be cut with a knife, but inside, they both knew that neither of them could walk away from the other. Something was happening between them, a friendship so organic that it seemed as though it was constructed by lost loves. As Liberty lay in bed staring at the wall she couldn't help but wonder if A'shai and Scarlett were pushing her and Po toward each other, simply so that they wouldn't have to be alone. She touched the scar on her chest and closed her eyes. *Thank you, Scarlett,* she thought, knowing that a girl that she had never met had died so that she could live. "Let's live," she whispered, before falling asleep.

SEVEN

PO AND ROCKO WERE GETTING MORE MONEY than they
could spend. Together, they were the perfect combination.
Po handled the weight, and Rocko ran the streets. As a
pair they quickly dominated the streets of L.A. Po was
able to sell the coke at dirt-cheap prices because it was 100
percent profit to him. With Rocko as his street lieutenant
and enforcer, they were taking over the streets with ease.

Rock had assembled a small squad of hungry young
goons from Compton. They were all live wires and under
the age of eighteen. Each of them was loyal because before
becoming affiliated with Po they were starving. Po fed them
well, and because of this, they all were ready to shoot on Po
or Rocko's command. Rocko provided them with money
and put them onto the game with Samad's cocaine. The
young boys went from catching buses and standing on
blocks to driving new whips and running trap houses. They
looked at Rocko and Po like they were gods.

Po sat in the backroom of Rocko's main trap spot running cash through a money machine. One of his youngins had just sold three bricks to a crew in Crenshaw and things were rolling. Po was flooding the streets with uncut cocaine so rapidly that he was making a name for himself. He had always hustled. He had never been legit a day in his life, but this level of the dope game was a different ballpark for him. Things were going good, but he had to find another coke connect; the bricks he had relieved Samad of were dwindling quickly. Soon he would be out of product. He needed to find a plug immediately.

"Yo, Rocko! Send one of the youngins back here," Po said as he rubber banded the last G-stack. Rocko sat on the front porch along with six youngins; they were all strapped, protecting the territory.

"Yo, run back there and get that from Po," Rocko commanded the youngest of the crew, Mikey, who quickly stood up from the stoop and entered the house. He went to the backroom and saw Po zipping up the duffle bag. A blunt hung out of the left side of Mikey's mouth as he approached Po.

"What's up, big homie?" Mikey asked as he approached Po with an open hand.

"Yo, put that shit out around me," Po said, referring to the blunt Mikey was smoking.

"Oh, my fault," Mikey said as he quickly put the blunt out on the bottom of his shoe. He walked over to Po and grabbed the bag from him.

"Put that in the back of my truck," Po said without making eye contact with Mikey.

Mikey was only seventeen, but he was as ruthless as they came. He didn't care about life, not his own or anyone else's. He was a true live wire, and that's why Rocko had recruited him.

Po usually wouldn't have been posted in the trap spot like he was that day, but he liked to show his face from time to time to make sure that niggas knew who they were eating off of. If he disappeared too long his presence wouldn't be felt. Po ruled with an iron fist, and at no point or under no circumstances would he loosen his grip. If any of his workers got sticky fingers, Po would cut them off, literally. Luckily, his crew had remained loyal so far, and, as always, the money was on point.

Po made a mental note to watch Mikey. He noticed the look in the young boy's eyes when he grabbed the bag full of money. It was the look of greed and envy. Mikey left the room as Po stood to his feet. He was about to pull Rocko's coattail about his suspicions but the ringing of his cell phone interrupted him.

"Hello?" Po answered.

"I need to speak to Po." A voice with a heavy Hispanic accent boomed through his receiver, and he immediately picked up on the larceny in the caller's tone. Whoever it was, this wasn't a friendly call.

"Yo, who is this?" Po asked as he frowned and looked down at his caller ID. He noticed that the number was blocked.

"This is Castro, and I can be your best friend or I could be your worst enemy," the man said boldly.

"Yo, how did you get this number, and who the fuck are you again?" Po said, getting more upset with each passing second. "Matter of fact, come see me. I'm not hard to find. Fuck this phone shit." Po pressed the END button, deading the conversation. He shook his head in disbelief and headed outside to join Rocko and the crew on the porch.

"Yo, I got to get my number changed," Po said as he stood in the doorway and rubbed his hands together. He looked down the street and saw a couple corner boys standing at each corner and smiled. They all worked for him, and they had the whole strip jumping. The strip was like a drive-thru for drugs, and Po had managed to take it over. Everybody on it worked for him or bought from him. He owned the block.

"Yo, what's good?" Rocko asked, noticing that something was bothering his right-hand man.

"I'm good," Po said as he looked onto the street. "Yo, we need to find another plug. What about the cat you were telling me about from Arizona?"

"Yeah, I checked on that, and I got a funny feeling about him. His prices were *too* low. He had them *federal* prices, feel me?" Rocko said referring to the kilo cost.

"Word?" Po asked.

"Word," Rocko confirmed with a head nod.

A stupid nigga would have easily fallen for the okey-doke, but Rocko immediately sniffed out the setup.

"How much was he talking?" Po asked.

"Like six a pop," Rocko said while shaking his head in disbelief.

"Oh yeah, that nigga federal as hell. You can't get them straight off the boat for that price. Leave that nigga alone," Po instructed. He could smell a cop from a mile away. Usually when cops entered the street game undercover they didn't really know the market and tried to sell low to bait the kingpin. On the other hand, when a fed is trying to cop, they usually agree to buy at a price to which no true hustler would ever agree. Feds sell too low and buy too high. Typical Street 101.

They noticed a custom-painted drop top car pull onto the block. The car stopped directly in front of the trap spot, and three Mexican males hopped out. All of them wore wife-beater shirts and had fully tattooed bodies. The young boys stepped off the stairs with their hands on their guns, meeting the Mexican crew on the sidewalk.

"What's good?" Rocko said as he stepped off the porch. He had a menacing scowl on his face as he immediately felt disrespected that these unfamiliar faces would come on their block.

"Yo, slow ya roll, homes. We come in peace. We want to deliver a message," the leader said as he stepped to the forefront. He was a stocky built, bald-headed, full-blooded Mexican. His eyes were heartless, and he showed no sign of fear.

"Message?" Rocko asked as he stepped into the leader's face. They were the same height, so they were looking at each other eye to eye.

"Yeah, from our big homie. He's looking for someone named Po," the leader said with his head held high. Po overheard his name and slowly stepped off the porch and headed toward the crowd.

"I suggest you get the fuck off this block, homeboy," Rocko said as he began to heat up. The young boys pulled their guns out and aimed them at the Mexicans. "See that?" Rocko asked arrogantly as he slightly smiled.

"We came here in peace. We just need to speak with Po on business. Nothing more, nothing less," the leader said as he put his hands up in peace.

"Who sent you?" Po said as he stepped to the forefront.

"Castro. He wants to make a deal with you," the man replied.

"What kind of deal?" Po asked.

"Well, if you didn't know, this is Castro's turf. This whole strip has been his for years. There are certain rules you have to play by when you are in L.A. You can't just move in and set up shop. You have to pay your taxes. And with these taxes, you get security, a pass from the law, and a green light to sell whatever you want."

"Oh yeah?" Po said with fake interest and a sarcastic grin.

"That's right. We just need 30 percent of your take and you'll be good," the leader said as he rubbed his hands together and smiled.

"Thirty percent?" Po said as he stepped closer to the Mexican. Rocko moved to the side and put his hand on the gun in his waist. "I have a different number in mind," Po added.

"What's that?"

"I was thinking more like zero percent. Fuck outta here," Po said just before he clenched his jaws tightly, causing veins to form in his neck.

"You don't know who you're fucking with. You just made a big mistake," the leader said as he shook his head in disappointment.

"Have a nice day, gentlemen," Po said as he stepped back and looked past them as if they weren't even there.

"Have a good day," the dude said as he turned around still shaking his head in disbelief. He gave them a look that said, "You just fucked up" and Po caught on.

At that point, Rocko was heated. He leaned and whispered to Po, "Just give me the word and it's a wrap." Rocko acted like a loyal pit bull waiting to get released off of his chain.

"Go head," Po said giving his approval. He wanted to make a statement to the streets. There was a new sheriff in town, and his name was Po! As soon as the words slid out of Po's mouth, Rocko went into action. He drew his gun and quickly shot twice, hitting two of the Mexicans in the ass. His crew ran over and grabbed the third guy, who was the leader, and stripped him of his gun. While the other two Mexicans were on the ground in agony, they were getting stomped out by Po's crew. In a lot of ways the beating was worse than the bullet as the young wolves stomped the Mexican crew ruthlessly, introducing their skulls to concrete. Po stood back and watched with his arms folded. He didn't have to put in his own work. He simply pressed the buttons.

"Hold him up," Rocko instructed. They held up the leader, and Po walked over to him.

"Yo, tell Castro that I'm not paying shit. I'ma do me, and he can do him. He has nothing to do with my business. He send any more messengers this way and I'm sending 'em back in pine boxes," he said just before he walked to his truck. As he reached the door, he heard two gunshots ring out. Rocko had rocked two of the Mexicans to sleep forever.

The game had just got real. Rocko had let the leader live, so he could run back and tell Castro what time it was. Rocko smiled sinisterly as his goons threw the two bodies in the backseat of their own drop top car. He let the leader drive off, but they knew they would see him again. He sped off and the sound of screeching tires filled the air.

Po sat in his truck and started his car as Rocko entered his passenger seat. He looked at Rocko and said, "We have to move the trap spot. Tell everyone to strap up and keep their eyes open because I know they're coming back."

"Fuck them niggas. We right here! This is *our* strip," Rocko said as he put both of his hands out.

"Then ready your li'l niggas for a war. Them Mexicans are heavy out here. If we staying put, then we blazing on every one that come on our block," Po said.

Rocko nodded his head and slapped hands with Po before he exited the car. Po pulled off knowing that this was the beginning of a war.

Po entered the penthouse and the smell of cooked food filled the air. He smiled as he shut the door with the duffle bag in hand.

"Liberty," he yelled as he entered the main floor and saw

her standing in the kitchen over the stove. "Damn, you got it smelling good in here."

"I got hungry and decided to whip up some steak, potatoes, and broccoli," Liberty said as she snatched off the apron and began preparing her plate.

"You didn't have to cook, ma. You could have ordered room service," Po said.

"I wanted to," she replied with a warm smile. "Of course, I didn't go shopping for the stuff myself. The concierge did a grocery run for me, so it wasn't too much trouble."

"Well, in that case, did you make enough for me?" Po asked as he set the duffle bag on the couch and walked toward the kitchen.

"Of course I did. Is that ready for me to count?"

"Yeah, it's the week's take. You can take care of that in the morning though. Just hook me up one of those plates. I'm starving," Po said. They had a routine. Po would come in every so often and drop off money. Liberty would then count and put it away in the safe for him.

"Okay. One plate coming up!" Liberty said as she began to make both of their plates. Po sat at the bar-styled counter and looked at Liberty. She had such a natural beauty, and for some reason she looked as if she was glowing that day. Her smooth skin and soft hair enhanced her pretty face. Po then looked down at her body and sexual tension began to grow. He admired her plump ass that her comfortable yoga pants couldn't hide. Her small T-shirt displayed her enticing frame, and Po licked his lips in admiration.

"Here you go," she said as she slid the plate in front of

him. She then sat across from him, and they both began to eat.

"Thanks," Po said as he glanced into Liberty's eyes. She quickly looked away out of embarrassment. She still felt funny about the kiss they shared days before. "It seems like there's an elephant in the room," he said.

"What do you mean?" Liberty replied as she cut a piece of steak and put it in her mouth.

"Come on, Liberty. You know exactly what I'm talking about. The kiss," he said.

"Oh, the kiss," she said as she dropped her head and blushed with a smile.

"I can't lie. I kind of enjoyed it," Po admitted.

"I did too," she confessed as she looked into his eyes. It seemed as if Po was looking straight through her. His piercing eyes were sincere and so warm. It made her heart flutter, and that was a feeling she hadn't experienced in quite some time. Not since A'shai had shared special moments with her.

They both locked eyes and seemed to stare into each other's soul. There was nothing being said aloud, but their eyes communicated perfectly. Po wiped his mouth and stood up, and Liberty did the same. It was as if she was having an out-of-body experience. Po slowly walked toward her and put his hands on her hips. Liberty looked up at Po, and that's when Po went for it. He leaned down and gently pressed his lips against hers. Slowly he slipped his tongue inside of her warm inviting mouth and began to kiss her passionately. Liberty wrapped her arms around his neck and felt her panties begin to get wet.

Po scooped her up, palming her plump cheeks as she wrapped her legs around his body. He carried her to the kitchen sink and continued to kiss her. Liberty felt her clitoris begin to throb intensely. She hadn't given herself to a man in a very long time, and honestly, it never crossed her mind because she was mending a broken heart.

Suddenly, Samad's face popped into her mind as she flashed to the brutal rape that she had endured at his hand. She wanted to hesitate. She was unsure if she was ready, but Po was intoxicating, and she found him hard to resist. She didn't want to think before she acted. Liberty threw caution to the wind as her clitoris throbbed, her nipples stiffened up, and she couldn't control her hands.

She quickly pulled off Po's shirt, exposing his tattooed chest. She then reached down to her love-box and began to touch herself. It was neatly shaven and swollen from her wanting. She had no panties on so it was easy access. Her vagina lips were glazed with her juices, and her erect clitoris slightly peeked out of her thick lips. The sight of her nakedness alone made Po's manhood become rock-hard. Liberty looked down and saw the thick imprint of his dick through his boxer briefs and licked her lips in anticipation.

"It's so thick," she admired as Po began to stroke her clitoris with his thumb.

He then dropped to his knees and tongue kissed her box sensually. He took his time as he maneuvered his tongue with precision. His warm tongue sent delicious chills through Liberty's body as she arched her back in pleasure. She threw her head back and gripped the top of Po's head as he gave her oral sex. His tongue expertly moved from side to side and up and down as he slipped two fingers inside of her. He slowly began to finger her while stimulating her love button with his tongue. Liberty hadn't felt that good feeling in so long. She was ready to explode just that quickly.

She pushed his head away, wanting him inside of her, and Po did not hesitate. He slid his boxer briefs off and slid inside of her, drowning in her wetness. He began to slowly stroke her, going as deep as he could. He palmed her ass cheeks tightly as he pulled her close to his body with each thrust.

"Ooh, Po. You on my spot," she crooned as she dug her nails into his back and bit her bottom lip, which was only motivation for Po to go harder.

The sounds of his balls smacking against her anus filled the air, and they were both in bliss as they sexed away. Po slid out of her and quickly sat on the kitchen chair. Liberty straddled him and her wet vagina engulfed her thick ride. She began to slowly move her body like a snake as she rode him like he was a stallion. He gripped and sucked her supple breasts as she worked him. Liberty felt a long overdue orgasm approaching and began to bounce up and down, smacking his pelvis with each landing. She felt an explosion coming, and so did Po. They were both approaching their orgasm at the same time. They gripped each other tightly and moaned in pleasure as Liberty continued to bounce away. The built-up tension made the sex that much better as they both chased their sexual release.

They erupted together, and Po released his fluids inside of Liberty's womb. His body went limp, and he stretched out his legs and curled his toes. Liberty collapsed onto him, and they both remained silent while breathing heavily in unison. They were at the point of no return. They both realized that they had feelings for each other. In a strange way they both were helping each other heal.

Po stared at the ceiling fan as it slowly spun above his head while Liberty rested her head on his chest. They were in the master bedroom, and the room transformed from pitch-black to an amber glow as the sun rose over the beautiful city skyline. They continued round two in the bedroom and stayed up talking into the morning.

"It feels so good to be held, Po," Liberty said as she listened to his heartbeat.

"It feels even better holding you," he responded. She snuggled closer to him and he willingly embraced her. "You got me on some cake shit, ma," he said with a chuckle. Po had never been the type to play lover boy, but Liberty had him open. She laughed, and then rubbed his chest softly.

"What now?" she asked.

"I don't know. You tell me. Are you happy?" Po asked as he ran his fingers through her hair.

"I honestly don't know what happy is. All my life I have had to deal with pain," she answered honestly.

"Tell me . . . tell me what was it like growing up," Po asked, wanting to know the truth about Liberty's life. There was a long silence that filled the air, and Liberty thought long and hard before she answered.

"It's hard to explain. Let me show you," she said as she sat up, looking straight into Po's eyes.

"How can you show me?" he replied in confusion.

"We have to go where it all started . . . in Africa. That's where I'm from, and I always wanted to go back to my old village. I don't have much family left, but my cousin is the last member of my family I saw alive when I was a little girl. I can show you, and also I can get closure," she said as tears began to form. "Can we go? Will you take me there?" she asked.

"Sure. Sure, we can go," he agreed as he hugged her tightly.

He could hear the devastation in her voice, and if she needed to travel across the world to face her past demons, then he would willingly oblige her request. The sound of her light snores quickly filled the room, and he realized that she had fallen asleep. Scarlett's face popped into his mind, but he shook her from his thoughts. He couldn't dwell on his past love when there was a new, healing one developing right in front of him. Liberty was helping him live again, and whatever was happening between them was something that he wanted to explore.

EIGHT

LIBERTY AWOKE WITH HER BACK TO PO'S chest, and the feeling of his arms wrapped around her body warmed her to the core. She turned to face him and noticed that he was already awake. Her body was sore in a good way from the way that Po had worked it out the night before. Every part of her tingled in the aftermath of sexual bliss.

She touched his cheek with the palm of her hand and kissed his lips. With Po, her life had been rebirthed. She didn't feel as though she was living in a fog of grief anymore.

"Is this wrong?" she asked.

Po shook his head. "Nothing about this is wrong, ma. Scarlett and A'shai aren't coming back. We aren't cheating. They're gone. We're here. So why can't we be happy together?"

Po's words made perfect sense to her, and suddenly, any reservations she had about being with him were erased. Po spread her legs with ease and climbed on top of her, but he froze when he heard the faint sound of the electronic lock click open. Liberty felt him stiffen, and she frowned in confusion.

"What's wrong?"

His hand covered her mouth, and his expression went from loving to cold. He put one finger to his lips, and she nodded her head as her eyes widened from the fear of the unknown.

Po grabbed his .45 from off the nightstand and flicked off the safety. He slept with his pistol locked and loaded. All he had to do was tickle the trigger to end a life. Po had instructed the concierge that no one was to enter his room under any circumstances without prior notice, so the fact that someone was coming through the door sent red warning flags waving wildly. He stood and wrapped the hotel sheet around his waist before creeping out into the living room. He let his gun lead the way.

"Agh! Señor!"

Po lowered his gun when he saw the maid standing next to a laundry cart as it propped the door open.

"I apologize. We're good on the sheets," Po said. "Calm down . . . calm down." He breathed a sigh of relief. "Let me get a tip for you. I didn't mean to scare you."

He turned his back to her, and the familiar sound of a gun caused his life to flash before his eyes.

CLICK CLACK

"Fuck," he whispered, scolding himself because he knew that he had just been caught slipping.

He waited for the blast that would end his existence.

"Who sent you?" he heard Rocko say.

Po turned around and saw the maid lower her weapon. An unexpected Rocko had arrived just in time, and now his gun was aimed firmly at the back of her head. Steel against skull . . . he was itching to off the bitch.

Outraged, Po was across the room in ten seconds. "Who sent you, bitch?" he boomed as he grabbed her neck and pushed her into the wall so hard that the drywall cracked.

The woman stubbornly didn't respond so Po tightened his grip, cutting off her air supply. "Who sent you?" he demanded through clenched teeth.

"Castro," the woman choked out. The L.A. crew had just become an eminent threat. Po had underestimated them. Obviously, they had leverage in the streets if they were able to find out where he rested his head.

"Castro who?" Po shouted, so angry that he spat in her face as he said the words.

The girl trembled as she stammered, "The leader of Los Familia. Please don't hurt me . . . this is just my initiation."

Po's temper flared to the point where he lost control. He slapped her so hard with the butt of his gun that he knocked her out cold. He tossed her limp body like a rag doll toward Rocko.

"Make an example out of this bitch and send a message to these Los Familia mu'fuckas. One that they can't help but hear. Call me when it's done," Po ordered, still outraged. Rocko nodded and tossed the chick in the rolling laundry bin. Before Rocko left Po turned toward him. "You're always right on time, fam."

"Always, my nigga," Rocko replied.

Po walked back into the room. "Liberty!" he called. She was nowhere in sight. He went into the bathroom. "Liberty!"

"Po?" she called back.

Po went to the shower and found her huddled in the bottom, his extra gun clasped in both hands raised to her face in fear. He knelt down and took the gun out of her trembling hands.

"Everything's okay, ma. We've got to get out of here though. It's not safe. Pack up all your shit and clear the safe. You said you want to go back to Africa. Well, let's take a trip. I need to get away for a while," he said, knowing that it was best to blow town until things cooled down.

A trip to the motherland couldn't have come at a better time. Po was out of product. Samad's stash didn't last long. With the connections Po had made, he had easily gone through most of the bricks. He needed to re-up, but that meant finding a connect who could provide him with the quality and the high quantity of coke that his customers were used to. It was time to get away and restructure his life. He had hustled low-key in L.A. He didn't know how Los Familia had found out where he rested his head, but now that they knew, it was time to switch it up. He wasn't sticking around to wait for them to come back. Po had always been the predator in the equation. He would never fear another man, but he fought smart, not hard. By the time he came back from Africa he would show Los Familia how he got down. But in the meantime, he and Liberty were on the first flight out of LAX headed to the motherland.

* * *

Rocko stood atop of the famous HOLLYWOOD sign while gripping the "maid" tightly at the elbow. She struggled against him, but it was no use. Her small frame was no match for his 220 pound physique. He manhandled her with no remorse, not taking her gender into consideration. Rocko was well aware that the sign was heavily monitored. The black mask he wore concealed his identity as he forced the girl to the edge of the sign. Normally, he wouldn't even risk doing dirt in a place so conspicuous, but he wanted the world to see what he was about to do. His pistol dug so deep into the girl's ribcage that she cried out in pain as he held her hostage.

"Please. Please don't shoot me," she pleaded, her entire body trembling from fear.

Rocko knelt down and tied the thick brown rope he carried across his shoulder to a metal bolt behind the letter H.

"I'm not gon' shoot you," he replied.

For a brief second she felt relief as she took a deep breath. It was the last breath that she would ever take. Her eyes popped open as she felt the noose slip around her slim neck.

Rocko turned her around and grabbed the sides of her cheeks, squeezing so hard that he dislocated her jaw and her mouth popped open. He stuffed a note inside her mouth, then duct taped it shut. She tried to scream, but no sound came out. With a clenched jaw and malice in his eyes, he leaned in and whispered what he had written on the note in her ear. "Fuck Los Familia." Then he lifted his foot and forcefully kicked her off of the edge of the sign. Her body suspended in the air for a brief moment before gravity jerked it down, snapping her neck instantly and causing her to sway like a pendulum.

As Rocko hightailed it away from the crime scene he nodded his head in satisfaction. The message he had just sent couldn't get much clearer. If niggas wanted to go to war, Po and Rocko were ready, and with them there were no rules of engagement. They played for keeps.

NINE

THE SOUNDS OF PROPELLERS AND PLANES TAKING off on the runway sounded as Po and Liberty stood outside of the airport. Rocko unloaded Liberty's luggage and rolled it to her at the curbside. He slapped hands with Po, and they embraced.

"You sure you don't want to roll?" Po offered to Rocko as they released the hug.

"Naw, I'm good, kid. I got to hold it down here while you're away. I can't leave these knuckleheads here by themselves anyway. They wouldn't know what to do without me," Rocko admitted as he looked around, completely aware of his surroundings.

"Yeah, you right," Po responded thinking about the war that they had just ignited. "Lib, why don't you go grab us a spot in line," Po said as he looked inside of the airport. He wanted some private time with Rocko before he left the country.

"Okay," she said as she grabbed the handle of her luggage. "See you later, Rocko," she smiled and waved goodbye. Rocko nodded his head acknowledging Liberty and stepped closer to Po so they could talk. Po waited until Liberty was out of earshot and began to discuss business.

"That was a wild move you put down. When I said send a message, I didn't mean to the world," Po said through clenched teeth.

"Listen, bro, we have to show these mu'fuckas we not playing out here. We got now, we don't care who got next. This is our turf," Rocko stated, meaning every word that came out of his mouth.

"I understand that, but we have to move smart. The whole city is on fire now," Po said as he looked around.

"I sent a message to them Mexican mu'fuckas and to anybody else that want to step on our toes," Rocko said as he noticeably got heated.

"Okay, just lay low until I get back. After you run through the bricks, stay out of sight. We have to let things cool down, and on top of that we need a plug so keep your ear to the streets. We have to start shopping," Po said. If he didn't find another supplier he would be out of business.

"I got you," Rock said. "You just enjoy your vacay to the motherland."

"Yeah, I'm going to try. Liberty is really excited about going back home, and this will give me a chance to get my mind off the bullshit and relax. But when I get back, it's back to business," Po said as he extended his hand. Rocko shook his man's hand.

"Say no more. Have a good trip, bro," Rocko replied.

"Peace," Po said as he grabbed his luggage and headed into LAX. He was on his way to Sierra Leone and away from the madness with his new love interest, Liberty.

After a twenty-two-hour flight they had arrived at their destination. Their plane had landed in the beautiful country of Sierra Leone, Liberty's home. Po and Liberty looked out the window and admired the beautiful landscape. They landed in the city of Freetown, and it had an urban feel similar to any major metropolis in the States, which surprised Po. When he thought about Africa, he thought of open land and a more rural setting. The high-rise buildings and highways weren't what he had in mind.

"It's beautiful," he whispered to Liberty as they both looked on.

Liberty looked at him with an emotionless expression, and then back out the window. She had mixed feelings about the country. Some of her best memories were of growing up in Africa, but her absolute worst memories were there too. She had witnessed her family get slaughtered and also it was where she had been tricked onto the *Murderville* ship many years ago. It was a bittersweet homecoming for her. However, she felt comfort knowing that Po was by her side.

They exited the plane and headed into the local airport. Liberty held on to Po's arm tightly, feeling secure while in his presence. Po accepted the job as her protector with honor. He couldn't deny that a part of him was falling for her. They made their way to the baggage claim, and then through Customs to find themselves just outside of the airport where the cabbies were waiting.

Po flagged a cabdriver, and he instantly popped his trunk and went for Liberty's bag.

"Where to, mister?" he asked with a heavy accent.

"Dunku Village . . . in Sierra Leone," Liberty said in a shaky voice. Just saying the name of her family's old village sent chills through her body.

"Oh no. I don't think that's a good idea. That is not a tourist area," the cabbie said as he stopped in his tracks. The look of fear was plastered all over his face.

"We know. We still need to go there," Po said as he reached into his pocket and pulled out a hundred-dollar bill.

"No, I don't think you understand. That area is not controlled by the government. If you go there . . . there is no guarantee that you will come back. Let me recommend some great places in downtown Freetown," the cabbie said as he smiled, displaying his gapped teeth.

"Maybe this will change your mind," Po said as he reached into his pocket and pulled out another crispy one hundred-dollar bill.

"You don't understand, sir. I wouldn't go over there if you gave me a million dollars. It's a concrete jungle. Let me show you something," the cabbie said as he looked around.

"Yo, fellas. He wants to go to Dunku!" he yelled. Almost instantly all the cabbies shook their heads no and an abundance of declining offers filled the air. It wasn't that they didn't want to take them . . . but they were afraid. Po looked around and couldn't believe the protest. He looked at Liberty who looked disappointed. She really wanted to go, but the chances were looking slim.

"Make it five hundred and I will take you," a voice came from a distance. A tall, slim man stood up from a crate while smoking a pipe. He had on a small top hat that slightly tilted to the right, and his skin was as black as tar. He walked with a cane and had a slight limp as he approached Po and Liberty. Po smiled and knew that he was the man for the job. He knew he had some spunk to him.

"Deal," Po said as he grabbed his luggage and followed the man as he led them to his Jeep. Po helped Liberty with her bags and then into the back of the Jeep. He hopped in and before they took off the man held out his hand and rubbed the tips of his fingers and his thumb together. Po reached into his pocket and peeled off five hundred-dollar bills.

"There you go, potna," Po said as he laid the bills in his hands.

"Thanks. My name is Serge, and I'm your tour guide for the day," he said as he laughed at his own joke. He started up the car and pulled off. Po and Liberty viewed the city as they rode through the streets of Freetown. Beautiful black people were everywhere. They were all shades and sizes. It was a different experience for Po. About an hour into the ride, Serge broke his silence.

"So, what makes you guys want to go into Dunku?" he asked, curious why someone would want to go to such a dangerous place such as Dunku Village.

"That's where I'm from," Liberty answered first.

"How long has it been since you have been home?" Serge asked.

"A very, very long time," she responded.

"Well, let me be the first to tell you: it's not how it used to be. It's a red zone now," Serge explained.

"What's a red zone?" she asked.

"That is an area where rebels frequent and recruit people to work the diamond mines. Not peacefully either. They force them into modern-day slavery. The government doesn't interfere so it's dog-eat-dog. It's a total war zone with no rules," the cabbie explained.

Po soaked up the information and began to second-guess going to the conflicted area. He looked back at Liberty, and the look in her eyes spoke a million words. She wanted to go back, and there was nothing that was going to stop her. They had come too far. Po smiled at her to give her assurance, and it was like he sent a warm shot to her heart because she instantly smiled back. He didn't know what he was getting himself into, but he was ready for anything. He only wished that he had his strap, which would have put his mind at ease.

After a couple of hours the city surroundings began to drop off and what once were paved roads became dirt roads. Tall buildings became trees and fields. They approached an area that had small houses and narrow roads, and it all began to become more familiar to Liberty. They had just entered the village and Liberty was home. Kids were in the streets playing soccer and momentarily stopped their game as the Jeep cruised through their village. The kids weren't used to seeing cars so they began to chase the Jeep down the road after it passed them. They believed that the passengers were rich just because they had the privilege of riding in the vehicle. It was a beautiful scene as the kids yelled and pounded on the windows as the Jeep crept down the road at a low speed. Liberty smiled while dropping tears, remembering how she and her childhood friend used to do the same thing years ago. Once they got deeper into the village, Liberty knew exactly where they were.

"Turn right here," she said as she pointed to the right. The visions of her father getting killed after the rebels bombarded their community appeared in her mind. She grabbed Po's hand for comfort as she tried to erase the horrid pictures from her thoughts. However, there was no erasing them because they would be forever etched into her soul.

"Stop right here," she yelled out as she looked at the place she was raised. It looked slightly different from what she remembered. What once was a circle of huts were now small raggedy houses. She waited for Serge to stop and quickly got out of the car, her eyes glued to the spot where her family's hut used to be. Po followed suit and got out also.

Serge hurriedly retrieved their bags from the trunk and immediately headed on his way back to Freetown, leaving them on the curb. Liberty's mind was racing, and she tuned everything out as she thought about her dead parents and the memories of growing up in Dunku. She never thought she would ever see the village again, but there she was. She was home. She wanted to find her cousin, Dahlia. Liberty had no idea if she was even still alive. There was no telling what Dahlia had gone through after that fateful day they were torn from each other, but if she was still in Dunku then Liberty was determined to find her.

"What now?" Po asked as he put his hands on his hips and looked around.

"There used to be a small hostel up the road. We should see if it's still there so we can get a room," Liberty said as she pointed up the road and led the way. Po grabbed both of their bags and followed her.

As they made their way up the road Liberty's sadness slowly left and joy filled her heart. She began to point out things to Po that she remembered growing up: all good memories. Po listened closely and noticed her demeanor changing slowly. He saw a spark in her eyes that he had never seen before. He immediately lost any regret for coming to Africa. That spark in Liberty's eyes made the trip well worth it.

About a half mile down the road, the same hostel Liberty remembered was still there. It was more run-down then she remembered. In America, it would have been condemned, but in Dunku, it was a luxury. Po and Liberty got a room and dropped off their luggage. Once they entered the bare room, they noticed how small it was. It was a far cry from the Trump Tower, but Po didn't comment on it, not wanting to be offensive. It had the bare minimum: a bed, nightstand, and a tiny, dirty bathroom.

"Wow, this place looked more glamorous from the outside as a kid. I always wondered what the rooms looked like," Liberty said as she sat on the bed.

"I'm not complaining. I've slept in trap houses much worse than this," Po lied as he set the luggage down.

Liberty watched as Po went to the bathroom and bent over the sink. He splashed water on his face. She admired his swagger. She didn't want to, but she was kind of falling for Po. He was so gangster. He was so different from A'shai but equally as intriguing. Po was more street . . . straight from the bottom and moved like a goon, whereas A'shai moved like a boss. However, Po's roughness was becoming sexy to Liberty. He looked over and caught her staring. "So what's next, ma?" he asked.

"I would like to look for my cousin Dahlia," she replied.

TEN

ON A QUEST TO FIND LIBERTY'S FAMILY, they went about the village asking questions to see if they could find any leads. Nobody knew who she was or where to find her. She went to every surrounding home, but no one seemed to know Dahlia. They inquired about her to anyone they saw, but it was to no avail. Liberty began to get discouraged. She knew it was a long shot, but something deep inside told her that if she came back that Dahlia would be there waiting for her. There were losing sunlight and decided to head back to the hostel to get some shut-eye.

They made their way to the hostel just as the sun set. It had been a long day and they were both exhausted; sleep was the only thing on their mind. Soon after getting back to the room, it did not take long for both of them to pass out in deep slumber. Humidity and heat had a way of draining a person's energy, and they learned that firsthand.

"Get de' fuck up!"

Po heard the order loud as day and opened his eyes to find himself staring down the barrel of an AK-47 assault rifle. He realized that he was being held at gunpoint and quickly sat up, putting his hands in the air.

"Whoa! What's going on?" Po shouted as he looked around the room and noticed five other African goons. One of them had Liberty held by gunpoint. Po's heart dropped as he saw the tears streaming down Liberty's face as she also had her hands up.

A man without a gun began to talk in a language that Po didn't understand as he pointed at him. The medium-framed man stood about six foot with a strong posture. He had strong, deep facial features and a scar that ran along the entire left side of his face. Po frowned and shook his head trying to comprehend what the man was saying. He didn't know a lick of anything other than English. However, Po knew whatever the man was saying, he was irate about it and it showed.

"I don't understand you," Po pleaded.

"Who sent you?" the only man without a gun asked as he stepped forward.

"No one sent me. My friend is from this village. We were looking for Dahlia . . . her cousin," Po explained.

"Stop lying. Why do you go around asking questions in MY village?" the man yelled with malice in his voice.

The men spoke in their native tongue among themselves and not even Liberty could understand them. She herself was raised to speak English when she was in

Sierra Leone. Her father knew that she would have a better chance to prosper if she was raised speaking English, so she was in the dark also. They had been ambushed, and Po's heart beat with regret as he saw his life flash before his eyes.

"Please! He's not lying! My name is Liberty Ibaka. My father's name was Bu Ibaka, and my mother's name was—"

"Jolie Ibaka," the man said, finishing her sentence for her and his frown slowly faded from his face. He yelled something to the guard, and they quickly lowered their guns. He stared deep into Liberty's tearful eyes and slowly walked to her in disbelief. The names that she dropped hadn't been spoken of in over twenty years.

"You are Liberty?" he asked as he walked over to her staring at her intensely.

"Y—yes. Yes, I am," she admitted nervously.

"Oh my God. My mother used to be very good friends with your mother. That was before the rebellion led by Ezekiel came through the village and they slaughtered her and my entire family," he said. His pain was written all over his face. "I've never met you, but I have heard so much about you. On the day that they raided our village, I was away hunting with my older brother. I was the lucky one," the man said as he dropped his head.

"My name is Omega. I am Dahlia's husband," he said as he extended his hand to Liberty.

"Hello," Liberty said just before she took a deep sigh of relief.

"I'm sorry. Let's get you two out of here. Please come to my house. Dahlia will be happy to see you," he said as he unleashed a smile.

"She's here? Oh my God," Liberty said as she covered her mouth and her heart warmed. She looked over at Po who had lowered his hands and observed as everything unfolded.

"Yes, she is. I'm sorry for this," he said. "I didn't know. I have to protect my village and the people in it. The threat of rebels coming through is real," he added. He looked at his goons and threw his head in direction of the door, signaling them to leave immediately. They filed out, leaving only Omega inside with Po and Liberty.

"I'm sorry. I didn't catch your name," he said as he turned to Po and extended his hand. Po looked at Liberty and hesitantly reached for Omega's hand.

"I'm Po. Nice to meet you," he said as he let go of his reservations. He didn't like the fact that he had guns in his face, but at the same time Po respected it.

"Take your time. I will be downstairs waiting for you guys and will take you to Dahlia," Omega said as he nodded to both of them and exited the room, closing the door behind him.

Liberty and Po stared at each other in silence. So much had just happened in the past five minutes, and they both were speechless. Liberty broke the silence with a chuckle, and it made Po smile back. They had accomplished their goal.

"I think we're a good team. What you think?" Liberty

said as her heart fluttered. Their detective work worked for them and served as a small accomplishment on the road to Liberty's happiness. Closure was the name of the game and the ultimate goal.

Po and Liberty rode in the bed of the Jeep and watched as three other Jeeps followed them up the mountains where Omega resided. They soon discovered that Omega was the leader of the village from the respect that he was shown throughout the community and the way the kids cheered him on as he rode by. You would think Barack Obama was riding through town. At all times, he was surrounded by young gunmen that were equipped with assault rifles, ready to lay down their lives to protect him.

The altitude got higher as the Jeeps wrapped around the mountain that sat in the middle of Dunku. Omega's estate sat at the top and what looked like a small house soon proved to be much bigger once they got closer to it. Liberty admired the beautiful trees and fresh air. It was a scent that she had long forgotten until now. The smell of rain always filled the air, even though it hadn't rained in months in Sierra Leone. The cool damp air was refreshing, and the deeper they got, the more exotic and beautiful it became.

"We have been living here about for seven years now. I had it built for my beautiful Dahlia right at the top of the mountain so that she could look down over our beautiful village," Omega explained as he sat in the passenger side of the Jeep.

Po listened closely as Omega pointed out different trees and exotic birds. Africa was, hands-down, the most breathtaking place Po had ever been. Liberty couldn't stop smiling about her reunion with Dahlia. She was the only family she had left.

They had finally reached the top of the mountain where the gigantic brick estate sat. Young militants were scattered everywhere on guard protecting their queen. Omega was very protective of Dahlia, and it was obvious as soon as they pulled up.

The Jeep stopped in front of the home, and they all got out. The tall house resembled a plantation-styled home and shooters paced the upper wraparound porch. Some were even on the roof. Po was definitely impressed.

Africa got some gangsters too, he thought as he hopped out of the bed of the Jeep and held his hand out, helping Liberty down.

They followed Omega toward the house and every time Omega passed a militant, they saluted him by putting their hand to their forehead. You could feel the aura of power coming off of Omega.

Once they entered the magnificent house, the refreshing central air hit their bodies like a ton of bricks. Although their country was somewhat less advanced then the U.S., the inside of Omega and Dahlia's home wasn't. Black life-sized cougar sculptures sat by the doorway, and marble floors set the tone for the extravagant home. The high cathedral ceiling had a diamond chandelier hanging eight feet down to add flair. It was simply amazing. From the outside, one would never think the interior would be so upscale.

"Welcome to our home," Omega said as an older lady approached him. She had on a maid's outfit, skin the color of butterscotch, and a head full of gray hair. She smiled and nodded at Po and Liberty, and then walked over to Omega.

"Please take their bags up to the guest room on the west wing," Omega said as he gently put his hand on her shoulder. The lady nodded and quickly got to work. Po instantly wondered what Omega did to get his money. Whatever it was, he knew that it was lucrative. The hustler in Po made his mind begin to churn. But he knew that he wasn't there for business, just to support Liberty and get away from the madness that was waiting for him back home.

"Dahlia! Honey, I have a surprise for you. Dahlia!" Omega yelled as he looked up the grand staircase. The opulent double stairs were the centerpiece of the room as they met at a balcony at the top. Moments later, all eyes were on the second floor when a dark-skinned beauty queen appeared. Her flawless chocolate skin, thick, full lips, and curvaceous body were breathtaking. Po looked up in awe as he admired her thick body and beauty. She wore black lipstick, which matched her jet-black hair, and was a bombshell. She wore a black silk robe that didn't do much to hide her body. Her legs were thick and toned, as if she was a professional athlete. Her ass was juicy and sat up perfectly as it jiggled with each step she took. Dahlia looked down onto the main floor, and when she laid her eyes on Liberty she immediately recognized her. It wasn't hard to forget someone as fair skinned and lovely as she. Dahlia put her hands over her mouth and stopped dead in her tracks as she and Liberty stared at each other.

"Oh my goodness," Dahlia whispered as she couldn't believe her eyes. She immediately rushed down to Liberty, and Liberty met her at the bottom of the stairs. They embraced each other and both began to cry as they squeezed each other with all their might while rocking back and forth.

"I missed you so much. I looked for you for so long. I always knew that you would come back to me. I always knew! Something deep in my soul told me that you were still alive," Dahlia said as the tears fell and she closed her eyes.

Omega and Po stood back and watched the reunion. The love was genuine and so pure. You could tell that they were close and the love had never wavered, even though many years had passed them by.

"They took me away. I never wanted to leave . . . you," Liberty said while sobbing.

"They took me too," Dahlia said as she dropped her head. Dahlia wiped Liberty's tears away and held both of her hands. "I love you."

"I love you, too," Liberty replied, her heart filled with joy.

"These were the people going around town asking for me?" Dahlia said as she smiled and looked at Omega. He grinned and nodded his head. "And who do we have here?" Dahlia asked as she focused her attention on Po.

"This is Po. He is responsible for bringing me over here," Liberty said.

"How do you do?" Po said as he extended his hand.

"Hello," Dahlia said as she looked down and avoided making eye contact with him.

Dahlia looked at Liberty and hugged her once more. "We have a lot of catching up to do," she said as she grabbed her hand and led her to the den. Po and Omega watched them walk away and a moment of awkward silence filled the air.

"Let's have a drink while the ladies reacquaint themselves," Omega suggested.

"Thought you would never ask," Po said jokingly. They shared a laugh and headed to the liquor cabinet for scotch.

A week had passed as Liberty and Dahlia shared laughs, cries, and heart-to-heart conversations, while Po and Omega were building a mutual respect for each other. The purpose of the trip somewhat changed on the second to last day before they were scheduled to return to the States. Po was in the kitchen on his cell phone talking to Rocko, and Omega accidently overheard business.

"So all of the squares are gone?" Po asked Rocko over the jack. He paced back and forth as he tried to figure out his next move. Every day he was without coke he lost just under one hundred grand in net profit. He knew he had to make a move and do it quickly.

"Okay. Sit tight. I'll be home in a couple of days," Po said just before he pushed the END button harshly. He had been getting calls from Samad's old connects all week but never picked up the phone, not wanting to tell them he was dry. That would kill a business relationship quick, and he understood that. He was anxious to get back to the States and find a plug pronto. He thought about going back to his hometown of Detroit to see what he could scuffle up there. He had a couple of B.M.F. plugs there, but he wasn't sure that they could fill the order he needed. He needed fifty birds at least, and he needed them quick.

"Fuck!" he said harshly under his breath as he leaned against the kitchen counter and crossed his arms.

Unbeknownst to Po, Omega was standing in the doorway with a big smile on his face.

"Here I am thinking you are a rookie . . . and we are in the same line of business," Omega said announcing himself. Po looked up startled as he put his phone in his pocket.

"What are you talking about?" Po said, not fully understanding what Omega was referring to.

"In America, you call cocaine *squares*, right?" Omega inquired, checking to see if his assumption was correct.

"Yeah, sometimes. What's it to you?" Po asked as he stood straight up and cocked his head, trying to figure out Omega's angle.

"Come on. Let's take a ride. I want to introduce you to my friend, Zulu."

The rugged sounds of the four-wheeler engines echoed as Po, Omega, and a crew of Omega's militants weaved through the jungle. Zulu's factory was just ahead, and it was deep in the wilderness, just outside of Dunku.

"We are almost there! It's close," Omega yelled as he looked back at Po who was riding just a couple of yards behind him. Po maneuvered the powerful machine as good as he could as he tried to keep up.

Just as Po was growing tired, an open area appeared where all of the trees were cut. It just looked like an empty field. The only thing for the next one hundred yards or so was piles of hay and lines of plants that stretched the whole hundred yards. Omega and his crew stopped and got off their four-wheelers. Po slowed to a stop and looked around in confusion.

"Why did we stop? You gotta take a leak?" Po asked as he turned off his ignition and stepped off the bike.

"No. We are here," Omega said as he opened his arms and slowly spun around.

"What type of shit is this?" Po asked, suspicious. Something wasn't right.

"Follow me," Omega said as he waved over Po.

Po looked at the militants who all had ice grills and mean mugs as they gripped the assault rifles that hung by their shoulder straps. Po then looked at Omega who was walking away and reluctantly followed him. Po's heart began to pound; he didn't know what type of sick, twisted game Omega was playing with him. Omega stopped at the biggest hay pile and looked at Po with smile.

"Come on," he said as he reached down into the pile and grabbed something. It was a handle. Omega pulled up a hidden door.

A flight of stairs appeared, and Po's eyes grew as big as golf balls as he realized what it was. It was a secret passageway to an underground cellar. He was blown away. Po shook his head in disbelief and cracked a smile as he stepped down and Omega followed close behind. The damp wood stairs led about fifteen feet underground, and then opened to a spacious cellar that was set up like a major sweatshop. Young workers, both male and female, were working diligently factory-style in an assembly line.

"This is where everything is made. The cocoa leaves are crushed here," Omega said as he began to walk through. He pointed at the workers who were using a weed whacker inside the barrels to do so. "And this is where it's mixed with sea salt and gasoline," he said as he walked down the line and pointed at the gigantic mixing pots being stirred.

Po looked on in awe as he tried to take everything in. He had never witnessed the process from the infant stages. He was used to getting his drugs straight off the boat in powder form, but this . . . this was different. This was something that very few people got to see.

"This is the end result right here," Omega said as he pointed at the potato sacks full of pure cocaine.

"Damn," Po whispered looking at the sacks and sacks of cocaine. He had never seen so much white in his life.

"Let's go to the back so I can introduce you to Zulu," Omega said. They walked through the corridor to a steel door at the end. An armed man that was as black as night with shades on stood post.

"I need to see Zulu," Omega said as he approached the man. The guard opened the door and stepped to the side. Omega walked in, and Po followed closely behind. A chiseled man sat in a chair while two of the thickest women Po had ever seen massaged his shoulders. One girl for each side of his body.

The two men began to speak in their native tongue while Po just stood there, unsure of what was being said. They were going back and forth about something, and Po was dying to know what the topic of discussion was. After a couple of minutes Zulu stood up displaying his six foot three frame, then walked over to Po and shook his hand. At that very moment, Po was plugged. Cocaine would never be a problem again.

They left that corridor with an agreement that Po would be their United States distributor of cocaine. The next day, Po left for the States and Liberty stayed in Africa with Dahlia. She wanted more time with her cousin, and since Po expressed that he was returning, she decided to stay for a couple extra weeks. Po was about to set up shop and not only take over Castro's territory, but the entire country.

Po and Omega returned from the Zulu meeting and things were very clear. Omega would go into business with Po.

With Zulu's blessing, the plug had been made and Po would be a part of a long pipeline that would flood the streets back home. Omega had been doing export business with a few people from the States, but no one stayed consistent since his old connect Baron Montgomery. Omega had a good gut feeling about Po. He loved his demeanor and felt a good vibe with him. Zulu was the head honcho, but Omega was the underboss and usually dealt with the day-to-day. Once they reached the house, Omega went into detail with Po.

As they parked the four-wheelers in the back of the house, Omega began to brief Po. They both hopped off the bikes, and Po wiped the sweat from his brow with the back of his hands.

"This is a big opportunity for all parties. We have been looking for a young partner that can make moves in the States. Can you handle what's about to be bestowed upon you?" Omega asked as he slid his hands in his pocket, and they headed toward the house.

"It ain't nothing to me. I can move bricks in my sleep. Not being arrogant, but I'm just telling you the truth. If I can get my hands on that product I just saw, that unstepped on raw, I can make them bitches disappear. Believe that," Po said confidently.

"How much can you handle?" Omega asked as he stopped and crossed his arms, looking Po directly in the eyes.

"I can move fifty a month easy," he replied confidently.

Omega paused and remained quiet as he intensely

studied Po's eyes. Po nodded his head up and down, assuring him that he could do the numbers easy.

"I was thinking more like five hundred."

Po couldn't believe his ears. This was every dope boy's dream. He was actually connected with the source and with the right moves he could become richer than he ever fathomed. Tony Montana rich.

"Let's do it," Po said as he extended his hand. Omega smiled and shook his hand, loving Po's ambition and willingness to go hard.

"Now, getting them to you is very easy. The only thing you would need to do is pick them up from the port of Miami. We will take care of everything else. Our coke is catered," he said while slightly grinning.

"Beautiful," Po smiled as the plan was coming together.

"Our coke is moved on the ship we like to call *Murderville*. We hide the coke in hidden compartments on crates. We use various imported items to move it to the States, such as detergent, corn, and even coffee beans. We have friends at the border, so everything usually goes smoothly. Your point person is Mrs. Beth. A blond-haired, blue-eyed exporter that is a master at what she does. We have been working with her for years. She will let you know what the fee is when you meet her," Omega explained as they headed toward the house.

Po listened closely as he soaked the game in and was very impressed on how organized this African was. He listened carefully as Omega continued.

"You know how a connection that, if used right, can

make you a rich man. Along with this connection, you have
protection. We are all family in this business. So if someone
has a problem with you . . . they have a problem with our
mob," he said in his heavy accent.

"That easy, huh?" Po asked as he soaked it all in.

"That easy. Welcome to the underworld."

ELEVEN

PO MADE THE TRIP BACK TO LOS Angeles with a new coke connect and the strength of the African mafia behind him. It had always been a two-man team with Po and Rocko, but now they had shooters for days. The States hadn't seen a crew as ruthless as the one with which Po was now affiliated. He led the way through the crowded airport with an African goon squad behind him. All arrangements had been made. Two black Maybachs waited curbside for the gentlemen, and as Po stepped inside, his adrenaline raced. He could feel the money in his hands before he even made it. He had sales lined up with all of the major buyers in L.A. His hustle was limitless now, and after he took L.A., he planned to dominate the entire West Coast. He was building an empire that would feed his kids' kids. The amount of money he was about to come into couldn't be spent in one lifetime. He was about to eat like a king, and everybody in his circle was invited to the feast.

He pulled up to Rocko's spot and was taken off guard when Ayo said, "We always get out first."

Po frowned slightly, and Ayo explained, "Dig it: Stateside, you're the boss. You step out last after me and my crew have secured the area. If bullets fly, you should be the last one hit, not the first. You're not on the front line no more. We're your protection; we're the muscle. Use us."

Po nodded and relaxed as Ayo and his men exited the car. Rocko appeared on his porch with his gun sitting on his hip. He threw up his hands.

"Fuck is up? There a problem?" Rocko asked with bravado and limited patience. Ayo smirked, then sniffed as he grabbed at his nose. If all the hustlers in America were as pompous as Rocko they would have some problems. Ayo and his men moved silently. They didn't need to bring the circus to town to put their murder game down. He didn't rock with clowns; he was associated with killers. Men that would slit your throat, and then show up at the funeral to pay proper respects. The African mafia was a business. An organization of great structure. The niggas in the States were in it for the image and the ego. The two things that could get you killed.

"No problems, unless you want them, homeboy," Ayo responded in a thick accent.

"What, nigga?!" Rocko said. The tone of his voice alerted Ayo's goons, and within a split second, seven guns were pointed in Rocko's direction. Rocko reached and kissed Ayo's forehead with the steel of his gun. Ayo's jaws clenched. The men were testing each other. Po immediately emerged from the car.

"Put the guns away. You're on the same team. Save that shit for Los Familia," he ordered. Rocko kept his aim steady until every single gun was lowered off him.

"Rocko," Po said sternly.

Rocko spit between his teeth toward Ayo's feet, and then finally let his gun fall to his side. Po stepped between the two of them and laid down the ground rules.

"Never pull your pistol on my man again, you got me?" he said to Ayo.

"Understood. I didn't know. My apologies, Po," Ayo replied. He held out his hand to Rocko, but Rocko simply stared at it.

"Rocko, play nice. These the mu'fuckas are about to help us get rich. You two might as well get used to each other. You're my right hand, Rock, but now, Ayo is the glove that protects it."

Rocko reluctantly shook Ayo's hand, and the men entered Rocko's spot.

"The plug came with all this?" Rocko asked, referring to the new partnership.

Po nodded and lowered his voice. "This connect came with any and everything we need to not only take L.A. over, but the entire West Coast. So I need you to play nice, fam. They were real hospitable to me over there, so we got to return the favor. This is so much deeper than some street shit, Rock."

Rocko nodded.

"What's that Los Familia situation looking like?" Po asked.

"They lying low, but after what I did to ol' girl, they won't stay that way for long," he replied.

Ayo stepped up and interrupted. "We'll settle that beef before it becomes a problem. It's nothing," he said. "I'm not trying to step on nobody's toes. I'll follow your man's lead when it come to the drugs if he follows my lead when it comes to the war. I come from war. That's what I do. You command in your field of expertise, and I'll take the lead when it's my arena. Anything you need . . ."

Rocko nodded his head. He couldn't help but to respect it. Now that Po had his two lieutenants on the same page it was time for the takeover. He was about to show the streets something they had never seen.

Being at home gave Liberty a peace that she hadn't felt since she was a little girl. Her life had been marred with so many bad memories that she had completely erased the good times that she had experienced in Sierra Leone. The last time she had seen her village it was burning to the ground, but today, it thrived and the community of people that lived there seemed so happy. "I never thought I would be able to come back here," Liberty said as she looked around, smiling, feeling complete, as she took it all in.

"They rebuilt it nicely, and, of course, Omega and I donate money and goods to the economy here. Sierra Leone is transforming, Liberty. This is home," Dahlia said. "I am so glad that you finally found your way back to it."

"Me too," Liberty replied. They held hands as they walked through the village, and it seemed as if their family bond had never been broken. A lot of years had passed, but time and space had not distanced them. Now that they were reunited they were just as close as they had always been. Liberty had forgotten how pure Sierra Leone was. Growing up in the States had taken away her appreciation for nature, for community, for simplicity. She was jaded by labels, wealth, and the hustle, but as she became reacquainted with her roots she realized that none of that mattered.

"I want to stay here forever," she said.

"Then stay, Liberty. You are enslaving yourself by not living your life by your own standards. You're free now, Liberty. Do what *you* want to do," Dahlia said. "Who would your decision displease? Po?"

"He wouldn't move here. He's too . . ."

"He's a city boy," Dahlia interrupted. "He has the city swag, the rugged nature. He can have that here. Besides, I think that he will do whatever it takes to make you happy."

"It's not like that," Liberty rebutted. "Our hearts are linked to people that we can no longer have."

"I see the way that Po looks at you. The only person who doesn't see it is you," Dahlia assured.

"It's complicated," Liberty answered.

Liberty drifted ahead of Dahlia and purchased crafts from the locals and trinkets from the children. She didn't need any of the stuff, but she knew that what she spent on homemade trinkets could help feed a family for a week. The locals were out hustling, but she wondered what her life would have been like had the rebels never invaded her village. Life may have been more peaceful, but she would have never known

A'shai, and fate would have never led her to Po. Having A'shai in her life was worth everything she had been through and finding Po after tragedy was like the cherry on top. Her feelings for Po could not rival what she had once shared with A'shai, but they were strong enough to be the bandage over her wounded heart.

"There is more to Sierra Leone than the simple life, Liberty. You see how Omega keeps me. I do everything on a grand scale. I have the finest jewels, cars, furs . . . but besides the lifestyle, the thing that is valuable most here for a woman is influence," Dahlia schooled. "The circle of women that I introduced you to are the elite few who have the power to start wars, Liberty. Yes, of course, their men are on the front lines. The men are the mouthpiece, the businessmen, the leaders, but the women are behind the scenes, pushing the buttons and pulling the strings."

"Is that what you do with Omega?" Liberty asked.

Dahlia scoffed and shook her head. "No. Omega doesn't grant me that type of power. He likes to keep it all for himself," she admitted with a bit of contempt in her voice. She quickly perked back up and continued. "But Po is different. He will let his queen rule over her court. Po trusts you, and if you play your hand right, you could have it all. Money, power, respect. Po will need you in his life in order to keep his position secure. His business is in L.A., so he won't be here enough to make sure that his will is considered. You are his eyes and ears. Know the connects, make them know you. You hold him down and ensure that his contributions to this game and to the local government are not forgotten. You actually have a man who values what you say, Liberty. When you speak, he listens to you. He acts and reacts according to what you deem acceptable. He cares about you. You're not just a showpiece. You have free will. A lot of women would give anything to have that. Don't squander it because you're holding on to a ghost."

Po watched as large, industrial steel crates were unloaded onto the dock. He stood between Ayo and Rocko as they each waited for the shipment to be unloaded. The operation was flawless. They had a connection with Customs that kept their crates off the log so they could transport as much cocaine as they needed in and out of the port of L.A. Po walked up to one of the crates and frowned when he heard voices coming from inside of it.

He stared up at Ayo. "There are people inside of that crate," he commented.

"Dope isn't the only product coming off of that boat. The *Murderville* ship doesn't discriminate. Women, kids, guns, drugs, counterfeit handbags—it's all about the money."

Po cleared his throat uncomfortably, but his conscience was easily pushed to the side when Ayo pointed to another bin that was being lifted by crane from the ship.

"That's what we're waiting for right there," Ayo said.

The crane operator dropped the large container onto the dock, and the three men approached it.

Po snapped his fingers and Ayo's goons came up from behind them and began to open it. When they popped it open Rocko's mouth watered in greed. "Damn," he muttered, not believing what he was seeing. The weight in front of him made Samad's stash look like something a corner boy hid under his mattress.

Po stepped inside the container and said, "Give me a knife."

Ayo handed him a pocketknife and watched as Po cut into one of the packages and dipped his finger into the snow-white powder. He put the substance in his mouth and within seconds his gums went numb. It was 100 percent raw. He had never had coke that hadn't been stepped on. Even Samad's bricks had a cut on it. Po was about to flip this shit ten times over. He stepped out and slapped hands with Rocko.

"We out. I know everything's good, but being around this much dope out in the open is asking for a federal indictment," Po said. He turned toward his goon squad. "Package that shit up quietly and quickly. Take it to the warehouse. It's time to go to work."

Po, Rocko, and Ayo walked away, each ready for the new era that was about to begin.

TWELVE

PO WAS TOO MUCH OF A HUSTLER to put the product on the streets as is. It was so potent that he could cut it twice and still have the strongest product out. He wasn't compromising his product either. Po refused to hire hood chemists to get the job done. He went to UCLA and found the top ten students in the chemistry department to do the difficult task of stretching one brick into two. With their tuitions paid in full and a handsome pay schedule to match, the young students were more than willing to render their services.

Po's little storage unit was no longer big enough so he bought the entire building, paying off the owner and assuming the property under a fake name. He knocked down the walls between the units and set up shop. Watching the minifactory run successfully was better than anything he had ever felt. Rocko no longer ran the low-level street operation. Po assigned that jurisdiction to Ayo's crew while Rocko and Po handled the big fish.

Once the hood got hold of his dope, his clientele tripled overnight. Within a month, Po became the largest supplier on the West Coast and had ambitions to move to the southern states in the months to come. The way he figured he had three captains. He could maintain the West while Rocko took it back to the Midwest and Ayo took over the South. His manpower wasn't strong enough to expand, but he could easily reach back to Sierra Leone and bring back more thoroughbreds when the time was right. Po was getting it, and money was the most beautiful distraction from the woes that had recently taken over his world.

Castro sat in his car outraged as he looked at the ghost town that had become his block. Nobody was out; no hustlers, no fiends, no police . . . nothing was moving. He had dominated these blocks for the past five years and all of a sudden he was seeing a drop in his profit. No one had ever had enough balls to go against Los Familia. He never had competition because no one wanted to step on his toes. Po's operation had put a permanent halt to Castro's grind, and the lack of income had Castro ready to go to war. The bullshit product that Castro was putting on the streets was no match against Po's. Po was getting his coke straight off the boat. It didn't get better than that.

Castro had been plotting on the out-of-towners ever since Rocko showed up on his block, but after his first attempt on Po's life had failed miserably, he decided to lie low until the opportunity was right. Now Castro feared that he had underplayed his hand. Po's hustle had grown, and the new faces on Po's team gave him the manpower he needed to challenge Los Familia.

Los Familia was one of the most respected gangs in L.A. They put their murder game down over the years and had hidden ties within the LAPD. Reputation had kept them from encountering any adversaries in the past, and they had reigned supreme as the untouchable kings of L.A., but Po didn't care about the hood legends. He was willing to step on any and all toes if he had to. Castro could either accept it or reap the consequences of going against the grain. The choice was up to him, but Castro refused to assimilate. His ego was too large to bow out of the game gracefully. He would rather die on his feet then live on his knees, and if he chose to go to war with Po he just might let his pride take him to an early grave.

Castro walked into the laundromat with a basket full of clothes and looked around, spotting the man he had come to see. The seedy establishment was in the middle of China-town and was half-empty as Castro strolled over to Bower Anders, the police commissioner for the city of Los Ange-les. Under normal circumstances, the two would not run in the same circles, but when Bower married Castro's older sister, Castro acquired a very useful connection inside of the LAPD. Anders kept the police off Castro's ass and out of his territory for the small convenience cash fee of $25,000 per month. Their arrangement had been running smoothly for years . . . until now. Suddenly Castro had come up short, and Anders wanted to know why.

Castro walked over to machine and threw in a light load of clothes, pulling spare change out of his pocket to start it. Any onlookers would never be able to tie the two men to each other. They were simply doing laundry; nothing more, nothing less. Anders sat in the seat directly behind Castro so that their backs were to each other and grabbed the *L.A. Times* that sat nearby. Opening it, he held the newspaper in front of his face.

"What happened to my money this month?" Anders asked.

"I've got a problem on my hands. Some nigger came to town. Opened up shop. Now my blocks ain't making no money. I don't eat, you don't eat. It's that simple," Castro replied in frustration. "I need you to help me get rid of him."

Anders's head spun around as he looked right, then left, making sure that no one was watching or listening. "And how do you suppose I do that?"

"Get him out of my territory. Have your boys raid his spots. I've heard that his product comes in at the port once a month. I'm working with dirty cocaine from Mexico, and this black fucker is getting pure cocaine delivered to him from across the seas. I can't compete with him . . . unless I use you as my leverage," Castro said.

"I don't know about this," Anders replied.

"What do you mean, *vato*? If you want my drug money to keep paying for that pretty house you got my sister and nephews living in then you better help me fix this," Castro stated.

Anders sighed, regretting the day that he ever got involved with the street life. He was once just a dedicated beat cop until he met his wife. When his connection to Castro started he became crooked and began to contribute to the crime that he had once been so determined to stop. The money had blinded him, but now he was so far in that he couldn't pull out. He was living way out of the means of a police commissioner and needed Castro's drug money to maintain his lifestyle. He had to provide for his family. He couldn't go back to the straight and narrow.

"What's his name?" Anders asked.

"Po."

"Po what?" Anders asked.

"Just Po, that's all I know. He runs with a goon named Rocko and some African fuckers. Niggers are black as tar and cold as ice. If you get them out of the picture, then I can get back to business as usual," Castro explained.

"Consider it done. But I want my money immediately. I don't care if you have to pull it out of your personal stash," Anders said.

"I'll have it for you as soon as this nigger's out of my hair," Castro stated. He stood up and before leaving he said, "Kiss my sister for me."

Rocko was like a shift manager at a local factory as he walked back and forth, watching the cook-up team to ensure that no one got sticky fingers. He had no problem being the enforcer. If anybody tested the system he'd put a nigga to sleep. Rocko heard a knock at the door and answered, knowing that it was the local crackhead coming by at her usual time to sell his people chicken dinners.

"What up, Tiny? How many you got for me?" he asked, following his normal routine.

"Ten," she replied as she danced in her own skin, fidgeting, looking around from side to side. She was antsy and excited about the crack that she was about to receive as payment for her meals.

Rocko pulled a knot out of his pocket and handed her a hundred-dollar bill.

"Come on, Rocko," she contested, complaining because she preferred to be paid with drugs instead of money. Rocko always hooked her up and gave her way more than the dinners were worth.

"Man, take that money and go home, Tiny. Put some fucking groceries in your fridge for your fucking kids," he said as he flicked off another fifty and tossed it to her.

She grumbled as she took the money and walked off the porch, cussing him out for being in her business.

Rocko was about to step back inside when he noticed an unmarked police car sitting across the street. The white men inside stuck out like sore thumbs. He hadn't seen a white face on that side of town besides the fiends he served, and the two collared shirts he was staring at were definitely not crackheads.

"Yo' flush that shit! All of it!" Rocko stated.

The workers halted in hesitation and looked at him questioningly.

"Flush it now!" he yelled.

Rocko didn't know how long the police had been sitting on him, but he was sure that if they were that close, then it wouldn't be long before they were kicking down his door.

He worked frantically to get all of the white powder down the toilet, but it was no use. Just as he suspected, the front door came crashing in.

BOOM!

"Put your hands up! Put your fucking hands up now!" the police screamed as they swarmed into the drug house. Rocko pulled his gun off his hip and thought about shooting it out with the cops, but he knew that he was outnumbered. "Fuck," he exclaimed. He pulled the window up and squeezed his body through the tiny frame. He fell clumsily to the ground and heard, "Put your hands up!"

Rocko came up shooting and hit the cop straight in the chest. The bullet didn't pierce the cop's vest but was enough to knock him off his feet. Then he took off, hopping the high fence in the backyard over to the next block. He turned around and shot at the officer who was attempting to hop the fence and give chase. His bullets kept the cop at bay while he ran full speed through the back alleys of the neighborhood. He dashed into a local eatery, half-scaring the customers because he was so frantic. He quickly calmed himself, putting his gun in his waist holster, then hurried to the back of the restaurant where the restrooms were tucked away. He pulled out his cell phone and dialed Po's number.

"Hello?"

Breathing heavily he mumbled into the phone. "My shit just got raided, bro! Come and scoop me ASAP before these fucking cracker-ass cops find my ass," Rocko said.

He gave his location to Po, then locked the bathroom door. He leaned over the sink gasping for air as he caught his breath while thinking how close he had come to spending the rest of his life in prison. "I know I moved smart," he said to himself wondering how the police had gotten the drop on his spot. The raid had come out of nowhere, and he was just grateful that he hadn't been caught.

"What the fuck happened?" Po grilled as Rocko discreetly slid into his front seat.

"I don't know. Nigga, you know how I move. My shit was clean, the trap was discreet, no bullshit, no traffic in and out," Rocko explained.

Po's phone rang, and he put up a finger for Rocko to be quiet as he answered. "What up?" he said.

"We've got a problem," Ayo informed.

Po exhaled deeply. "Nigga, you fucking right. Rocko's shit got raided an hour ago," he informed his lieutenant.

"I wish that was the biggest problem on our plate right now," Ayo replied. "The shipment got flagged by Customs at the port. Shit got intercepted."

"Fuck!" Po shouted outraged. It seemed as though suddenly the house of cards he had built was starting to crash around him.

* * *

Po's business was on a standstill as Omega worked to get him a new shipment as soon as possible. Po's entire warehouse was dry, and since he couldn't supply the streets, Castro stepped right in and picked up where Po had left off. The streets weren't loyal, and Rocko's customers quickly jumped ship. Po's elite clientele were more understanding after Po assured them that he would give them a good deal if they exercised patience.

Castro's hold on the hood was stronger than ever. Now that he was back on, he refused to be knocked off again. His operation was secured, and anybody that was not affiliated with Los Familia wasn't welcome to eat at their table. Castro wasn't playing any games. He used his LAPD connect to ensure his safety, paying Anders double just to make sure that he had police protection when he needed it.

"I don't want no black faces on my block unless they copping. A nigger ride through this mu'fucka you light they shit up," Castro told his workers.

So as Po lost his footing in the drug game in L.A. Castro found his, and this time, he wasn't going to let go. He would go to war with Po and leave the African mafia leaking in the streets before he took another loss.

Po sat in front of his computer screen and waited for Omega to enter their Skype session. The time difference kept them on separate schedules and since he returned to L.A., Omega had not been able to speak with Po directly. Ayo kept him informed on the daily business, but with the emerging street war with Los Familia, Omega felt that it was time to step in.

"Omega, how are things in the motherland?" Po asked.

"Aghh, they are good, Po. You know I'm fostering good relations with our current allies and always establishing new ones. But I don't want to shoot the shit, Po, so I'm going to ask you directly, what is going on with you and the local gangs in L.A.?"

"Things got messy, but it's nothing I can't handle. I've got everything under control," Po replied.

"I don't doubt that, Po. I know that you are more than capable of running your own ship, but I need you to understand how valuable you are to my organization. You are my only American connection. Which means you have the best plug of all the hustlers in the States," Omega said with an arrogant smile. "Why are you even engaging in a street beef? Leave those crumbs to the fucking Mexicans while you eat at the big table."

"That's the difference between me and every other nigga with the product. They forget about the roots. I'm at the top of the tree, and I'm grateful for that, but I still water my roots. There is too much money in the streets for me to just ignore them. I want every dollar," Po stated.

Omega sighed and paused to choose his words carefully. "The loss that we just took, we cannot take again. It draws attention to me, and it's money that can't be recouped. You need to pull out of the street shit. We don't have time to fight a war over your ego. You and Castro are in two different leagues now. You no longer shoot at the same baskets.

You are above selling to fiends. Focus on moving weight. We are all in a good situation and stand to make a lot of money if we play it smart. Dead the beef with the Mexicans, and I will handle the catastrophe that happened at the port. This isn't a request, Po," Omega ordered.

Po had to bite his inner cheek to stop himself from responding with harsh words. He knew that Omega was right, but his ego was in overdrive, and he wanted to destroy Castro. Omega was far removed from the streets, but Po had just come off of them. It would take time and a lot of hard lessons to give Po the refinement and tact that Omega already possessed.

"It's dead," Po said.

"Good. Let him have a few blocks, Po. Meanwhile, you take over the world. Keep the big picture in mind. We'll catch up another time. I'll have your next shipment out in two weeks," Omega stated.

Po ended the Skype session and slammed his laptop shut in frustration. He knew what he had to do, but just the thought of standing down put a bitter taste in his mouth. He had never backed down from anyone in his life, and it would be a huge, yet necessary, pill to swallow.

Two months had passed since the last time Liberty had seen Po. While she was being initiated into the right circles in Sierra Leone he had been establishing a solid hold in the streets. She knew that he was busy and the last thing that she wanted to do was crowd him, but she missed him terribly. Being away from him for so long confirmed that she had it bad for Po, and as she walked into the airport she knew that it was time to return to L.A. What she had assumed was a rebound fling seemed to be growing into much more. It wasn't the romance or sex that she craved; she missed his friendship most. He was the first person who had made her smile after A'shai's death. Po made living without A'shai easier.

Scarlett's death had left Po with half a heart and losing A'shai had left her equally pained. Together, they possessed a whole heart, and although it had been hurt, bruised, and abandoned, it still worked. She couldn't wait to see him. The flight was mind-numbing, and her impatience played a torturous joke on her until she finally touched down. Sitting still for such a long time was the worst type of cruelty to Liberty. Being in Africa had rejuvenated her. She had transformed into a different young woman: one who was ready to face anything ahead of her.

She exited the plane and pulled her Bvlgari sunglasses down over her eyes as she headed toward baggage claim. Butterflies filled her stomach. *Did he miss me like I missed him? Will he be happy to see me?* she pondered as she went down the escalator. Through the crowd, she saw a man holding a sign that read her name. She waved her hand slightly and got his attention. She immediately knew that it was one of Omega's men. He was dark as night, and Liberty noticed that his neck was on a constant swivel as he surveyed his surroundings.

He nodded his head at her, and she approached him.

"Po couldn't make it, but I was instructed to retrieve

you and your things, and then bring you directly to him."

Liberty nodded and pointed to the conveyer belt. "My luggage is over there."

He tipped a skycap to carry her things, and then led her to the Maybach that had now become Po's preference when it came to transportation. Liberty climbed inside and the goon got up front with the driver before they pulled away.

Liberty didn't know what to expect when she saw Po. If life had taught her anything it was that nothing was guaranteed. She closed her eyes and saw A'shai's face behind her lids. That was the only place where he still lived, in her memory, and she tried as best as she could to keep him alive without becoming stuck in despair. But every day she lived and with every breath that she took, she was forced to accept his death more and more. She was coming to terms with her new life. A'shai was her past, and he would always be a part of her, but she was ready to bury yesterday's strife and focus on tomorrow's survival. *Don't feel guilty for living. That's what he wanted you to do,* she thought. She was in her emotions, and the ringing of her cell phone brought her back to reality.

Liberty smiled when she recognized Po's number.

"How was your flight?" he asked.

"Long," she replied.

Po looked around the Beverly Hills estate that he had purchased. He knew that if it weren't for Liberty he would have never planted roots in L.A., but he wanted to create stability for her. This house was his way of showing her that he wanted to build a future with her. He couldn't wait until she saw it. "Well, I have a big surprise for you. Hurry to me, ma. Where are you now?" Po asked, eager to see her face.

"We're passing Sepulvada and 96th," she said as she noticed the street sign out of her window.

RAT TAT TAT TAT TAT TAT TAT

Out of nowhere bullets flew through the car. "Aghh!" Liberty screamed as she hit the floor, dropping her phone and covering her ears. Glass rained down on her as gunfire erupted all around her. Liberty didn't know what to do. She had no time to react. All she could do was cower in fear and plug her ears as the madness around her ensued. Her pulse raced as terror gripped her body. "Please, God, please, please," she whispered as she balled her body into a tight knot, praying not to get hit.

Finally the firing ceased, and she heard the sound of screeching tires as the shooters sped away.

Liberty's body trembled, and she crawled to open the door. Delirious, she could barely regain her composure to crawl from the car. Blood covered her face and hands from the minor cuts she had received from the windows being blown out.

She heard the sound of coughing coming from the front seat and turned to see that Omega's worker was struggling to breathe.

"Oh my God . . . oh, God . . . hold on, just hold on," she said, not realizing that she was screaming in panic at the top of her lungs. She touched the blood-filled hole in his chest, trying to stop the bleeding, but her fingers just drowned in redness.

She glanced over at the driver, who was slumped onto the steering wheel, the weight of his head causing the horn to blare. The man's breathing was erratic as he began to choke on his own blood.

"T-tell Po . . . It was Castro," he managed to say before his body shuddered and his time on this earth came to a tragic end. In the distance, Liberty heard sirens and climbed from the car. A small group of gawkers had gathered around her. It felt as though a thousand sets of eyes were on her, but no one offered to help. Her legs were like Jell-O, and they barely kept her standing as she put both hands on the side of her head in distress.

The police finally arrived and approached her cautiously. "Ma'am, are you hurt?" one of the officers asked.

All Liberty could do was shake her head in response. She was too traumatized to do anything else, and she wasn't answering any questions until Po was by her side.

THIRTEEN

PO WAS SO LIVID THAT HE COULDN'T contain himself. He stood at the long, rectangular table with both hands planted firmly against the Brazilian wood. His head hung low in contemplation as Rocko, Ayo, and the rest of his goons sat around the table, waiting for him to speak. No one dared interrupt the deafening silence that took over the room. The tension was thick as everyone stared at Po.

"Find this mu'fucka and bring him to me. I want his blocks shut down. I want everybody in his crew tied up. I want him burying his bitch and his kids by the end of the week. Anything that has to do with Castro and Los Familia is to be destroyed," Po ordered. He spoke calmly, but the bulging vein in the center of his forehead revealed his anger. Rocko had known his man long enough to know not to take Po's calm demeanor as a weakness. Po was past the point of loud charades. It was the still before the storm, and he was about to make the city bleed.

"You know we've got eyes on us right now. We go any-where near Castro's territory, and the LAPD becomes a problem. The mu'fucka is protected by them or something," Rocko said.

"If they on his payroll we'll give 'em a mysterious raise," Po answered. "Then they'll be on *my* payroll."

"I don't know how he got the police on his team, but I don't think they choosing sides. Word on the street is he in like Flynn with them mu'fuckas. He won't be easy to get to," Rocko said matter-of-factly while shaking his head.

"Find a way. I don't care how you get to him. He's become a thorn in my side. Niggas think I'm playing out here. Get rid of him, this time for good," Po demanded.

Po left the room, leaving the men to their thoughts as he climbed the stairs to his home. He was so angry that his head pounded with fury and his nostrils flared as he thought of how badly things could have turned out. He had lost one woman whom he cared for due to the streets. He wasn't prepared to lose another. Just the thought of it threatened to send him over the edge. He stopped outside of his bedroom and took a deep breath before opening the door. The recessed lighting was low, and he could see Liberty's silhouette as she lay in the bed. Not wanting to disturb her sleep he began to close the door until her voice stopped him.

"Don't leave," she said.

Po entered and walked over to her. She stared at the wall as tears fell from her eyes and onto the satin pillow. "I don't want that life, Po. I've been around death and violence all my life. I don't want that to be all I know. I want to live carefree. I want to be happy," she said. She sat up and leaned against the headboard as she looked him in the eyes.

"What happened today shouldn't have happened. I give you my word, ma, on my life, that you will never be put in danger again," Po assured.

"I won't let it happen again, Po. If I ever feel unsafe with you, then I will leave. Someone gave their life for me to be able to live mine. I can't squander it trying to play wifey to a drug dealer," Liberty said.

Her words flew at him like daggers, causing him to become defensive. "A'shai was a drug dealer," Po shot back. "All of a sudden that's not good enough for you?" His voice was low, and she could hear that she had slighted him.

"You can be so much more than a hustler, Po. I just wonder if you know it. I don't want this to be my life forever," she whispered. "I don't want to be afraid to turn over the ignition in my car every morning. I don't want to fear for my future children, thinking they'll get snatched and tied up somewhere behind some beef that you have!" she defended.

"Do you trust me?" he asked.

"I do," Liberty replied.

"You're safe with me. I would never let that happen.

I want you in my life, ma, but if the day ever comes when you feel like you need to walk away from me I will understand, and I will make sure that you're taken care of when you leave. You won't ever want for anything, ma . . . with or without me, but I hope you'll give me a chance to make this up to you," Po said sincerely. "You don't have to make your choice now. It's been a long day for you. Just rest."

Po kissed her forehead, and then walked out of the room, his chest hollow with the feeling that she may leave. If she walked away from him, his next best chance at happiness would disappear before his eyes.

The next morning Po sat in his dining room reading the morning paper when Liberty entered the room. She smiled sheepishly at him while standing in the doorway.

"I'm not leaving," she said.

"I know," he replied. Outwardly he appeared confident, but inside, he was grateful for her presence. Now all he had to do was make good on his promise and send Castro to meet his Maker. She stood awkwardly and looked around the large minimansion, taking in the new home for the first time.

"I like the house," she said.

"Good, because it's your job to fill it up with furniture, with love, with memories," Po said, causing her to smile. He nodded to the chair at his left. "Take a seat."

She joined him at the table, and he reached over to squeeze her hand gently. He slid a black velvet box across the table to her before returning to his reading.

Liberty stopped breathing when she saw the box. Her eyes shot up and met his. He could see the terror set into her bones.

"Relax, it's not a ring," he said with a smirk.

Liberty breathed a sigh of relief. "Thank God," she whispered as she placed a hand over her heart.

Po couldn't help but chuckle. "It would have been that bad?" he asked with a charming smile.

She gave him a friendly scowl and replied, "Of course not. You just took me by surprise. We're not . . . I mean . . . I don't want to get married . . . we barely . . ."

"Just open the box," Po said, easing her nervousness.

Liberty opened the box, and then froze. Her face dropped, and she placed the box back on the table, then slid it over to him. It wasn't exactly the reaction that Po was expecting. "It's beautiful, but I can't accept these. Please never buy me diamonds, Po. Those are blood diamonds."

Po had forgotten that Liberty wasn't the average hood chick. She had a complicated past that left her sensitive to a lot of issues, and he kicked himself for not being more considerate. Diamonds were a sign of affluence and luxury where he was from. They were a sign of affection. But to Liberty, they symbolized murder, mutilation, tyranny. The fact that Po had given them to her was a blunt reminder that they came from different worlds.

"I'm sorry," Po stated.

"It's okay. You didn't know," Liberty said. She reached over and touched the diamond bracelet he wore. "But now you do," she said.

He slipped the bracelet off of his wrist and held it in his hand, then reached over and kissed the back of her wrist. In a lot of ways she was just like Scarlett, but he was slowly learning that in many others she was very unique, and he loved every part of her. He just wanted to have her as his own.

Rocko and Ayo sat in an old Chevy Caprice while watching Castro's every move. Since the shooting, Castro had definitely locked things down. Los Familia was now harder to touch than ever before.

"I say we just dead this wetback mu'fucka right now," Rocko said as he looked on.

"You see that?" Ayo asked, as he pointed to the unmarked police car that sat across the street from where Castro was parked. "This is a ho stroll. There are tricks and johns all down this block, but they not making no arrests," Ayo said. "They're here to watch Castro's back. Whoever he in with down at the police department, it's a deep connection. We can't just open fire in broad daylight."

"So what? We sit out here while he paying for pussy?" Rocko asked.

"Nah, stateside. We sit back and watch *who* he paying for pussy," Ayo replied.

They watched as Castro approached one of the women on the block. Within seconds he was leading her to his car. Once the sexual transaction was complete, the woman got out and Castro drove away.

"Ain't you gon' follow him?" Rocko asked.

"He can go. We know where to find him. That girl is the only person outside of his crew that has been able to get close to him. That's who we need to talk to."

Ayo and Rocko sat on the prostitute all day observing her, how she moved, who she spoke to, and who she reported to at the end of the night. To their surprise she hadn't chosen a pimp: it appeared that the other chicks on the strip had chosen her. At the conclusion of the evening she collected her money from the other ladies, then jumped into a cab.

"Bitch about her paper," Rocko stated with a laugh as they tailed her.

She got out of the cab, and they followed her as she walked up the stairs to her apartment building. She was clueless to their presence until Rocko stuck a pistol in her side.

"Open the door and don't scream," he demanded.

"Fuck my life!" the woman grumbled and turned her key in the door. Rocko pushed her inside immediately, and she turned around with her hands held high. "Look, you fucking assholes, I don't got no money!"

"Sit down," Ayo said.

"I done told you muthafuckas that I'm not worth robbing. You don't look like the type to have to pay for pussy. What the fuck you want?"

"We want Castro, and you're going to help us get him," Rocko revealed.

The woman gave an exasperated look and flopped down on a tattered couch. She reached onto the coffee table and retrieved a cigarette to still her nerves. "Damn, that's all you want? All you had to do was ask. I don't give a fuck about that booty-loving muthafucka," she bitched as she lit her square and inhaled deeply.

Rocko chuckled and looked at Ayo who remained stern. "What's your name?" Ayo asked.

"Ms. Trixie, baby!" the woman responded singing slightly. She then used her natural tone of voice and said, "Or Mr., if you prefer. I can be whatever you like."

Rocko and Ayo were shocked as they both realized that Trixie was a transsexual.

"We've got a proposition for you, Trixie," Ayo said.

"You better be talking good money 'cuz I don't got time for games," she responded.

"My man got a personal beef with Los Familia, and we need to touch him," Ayo explained.

Trixie took a long drag from her cigarette and replied, "Do you know who you're fucking with? Los Familia isn't your average gang. They run all of this shit." Trixie waved her hand from side to side as she spoke, lowering her voice a bit as if she didn't want to be heard. "If Castro even finds out I'm having this conversation, then that's my ass."

Ayo put both hands in front of his body, folding them near his belt as he squared his shoulders. "Let's just say there is a new sheriff in town. Castro's reign is over and we're moving in whether you help us or not. So you can be on the winning team or you can choose to sink with Castro's ship. Now we're bringing war to Castro. You can help us do it quietly, or we can spray your entire block with bullets since it is in Castro's territory. That type of bloodshed will have your operation dried up for months. Your tricks will be too afraid to drive down your strip by the time we're done."

Trixie was silent as she thought about how long it had taken her to establish her track and knew that rebuilding elsewhere would take too much effort.

"We want you to help us set Castro up," Rocko pushed.

"That shouldn't be too hard," she said, giving in. "All of Los Familia come through here and trick with me and my girls. I can deliver 'em to you on a silver platter, no problem. The question is . . . what's in it for Trix?"

"My man got five racks on every member of Los Familia you give us," Rocko stated.

Trixie let the offer linger in the air as she mulled it over in her mind. That was good money. It would take her an entire month, maybe two, to make five grand. There was no way she was missing out on this lick.

"All I've got to do is throw a pussy party," Trixie said, thinking aloud.

"A pussy what?" Ayo asked. "Be clear, paint the picture for us."

"I throw pussy parties. Niggas come trick with a group of my girls for the night and do the freaky shit that they can't get from their proper girlfriends and wives. Every time I throw one, Los Familia comes through, spending big money. I can guarantee that Castro will be there, along with a few of the others, and they will be unarmed. No guns are allowed," she said confidently.

"Let's make it happen. The party needs to go down sooner than later, you understand?" Rocko asked.

Trixie nodded and said, "Done."

Jay-Z's classic lyrics from *Can I Live* pumped through the dimly lit room, providing the soundtrack for the evening. Trixie had escaped from the clutches of pimps and drug dealers long ago. Now she was the one collecting the money and running an entire strip of working girls on her own. Trixie wasn't new to the game. The notion of exchanging sex for money was as natural as breathing for her. She had no love for the men she serviced; she was only infatuated with one: Ben Franklin. She was a true professional and although Los Familia had been showing her block love for years she had no loyalty to them. She was married to the money, and the offer to set up Castro was too lucrative to turn down. She made sure she put everything together perfectly and went all out to ensure that the setup went off without a hitch. She spent the last of her hard-earned money to rent out a hotel suite and pay the front desk clerk to make sure the hotel security cameras weren't functioning that night. The last thing she needed was her face to be connected to whatever Rocko and Ayo had planned. She was spending her last dollar to make her next dollar, and she prayed that it was worth it.

She sat back sipping a glass of cheap cognac as she watched a few members of Los Familia trickle in. The usual suspects were present, but Castro had yet to darken her door. She tapped her long, blood red fingernails against her glass impatiently. The girls were mingling and getting their paper. Nothing was off limits. Trixie's dolls were down for whatever: sucking, fucking, anal, fetishes, bondage, three-somes. They fulfilled the wildest of fantasies with expertise, and on a normal night Trixie would be right in on the action, but tonight was different. Tonight she was the ringmaster to the circus that was sure to ensue. She already had her escape mapped out. As soon as shit popped off, she would disappear, then meet with Rocko and Ayo to collect her money.

Trixie was beginning to think that Castro would not show, but then he finally walked into the room. She walked up to him and greeted him personally.

"Hey, daddy, Ms. Trixie got something special for you tonight," she whispered seductively in his ear, wetting it slightly with her tongue. She put her hand down the front of his Dickie pants and felt his manhood stiffen instantly. *It's a shame I'm about to put that big dick to sleep,* she thought as she removed her hand and strutted away.

"Can I have your attention, divas and gentlemen!" she shouted.

"Tonight, I have something especially freaky and tantalizing for our guests. If I can have all my working girls up front, and all of our guests seated in the chairs," she instructed.

Everyone did as they were told, and Castro took a seat front and center, eager to see what sexual escapades Trixie had come up with this time. She was known for putting on a show at her parties, and they always left her guests fully satisfied. "I have some new girls I'd like to introduce to you, and they're here just for Los Familia," she said. "Ladies!"

Seven women stepped up from the back to the front, wearing silky short robes and stiletto heels. Castro's crew loved Trixie because she had the best trannies in town. They tricked with the he-women often, and they all were paying close attention as they anticipated the freak fest to come. In the blink of an eye the women opened their robes, but the surprise that they had was deadly.

PSST! PSST! PSST!

PSST! PSST! PSST!

The women were actually men, Po's men, and they opened fire on Castro and his crew. The silenced shots whistled through the air, and Trixie's girls scattered like roaches trying to make sure that they weren't caught in the crossfire. Trixie got lost in the crowd as she headed for the nearest exit. Without weapons, the Mexican gang members were like sitting ducks, and the African mafia gunned them down one by one, leaving a river of blood flowing through the room. Trixie hightailed it out of there. While all of the other ladies hit the stairs, Trixie sauntered over to the elevator and tore down the OUT OF SERVICE sign that she had posted earlier. She pressed the call button and the doors opened immediately. She stepped inside and smiled in satisfaction as the doors closed behind her.

When Rocko got the call he looked at Po and nodded his head in confirmation.

"How many came?" he asked into the phone.

"Castro and fifteen others," Trixie replied.

Rocko made arrangements to have the money delivered to her, and then hung up the call. "We owe her 80 racks," Rocko said with a chuckle in disbelief that she had actually pulled it off.

"Pay her and make sure you express our appreciation for her cooperation and discretion," Po stated. "Somebody like that is a good ally to have on the team."

That night Po entered the bedroom he shared with Liberty. It was 3 A.M., and she was already asleep. He didn't wake her. Po pulled out the pearl necklace that he had gotten in exchange for the diamonds she had refused. He put it around her sleeping neck and then leaned down to kiss her forehead. "You're safe now, ma. Good night."

Omega slammed down the phone, outraged that Po had disregarded his orders. He understood that Po was retaliating and had reacted in haste, but Omega realized what was at stake. They were running an international drug ring, and Omega was testing Po to see if he was ready to get to the real money. Cocaine was a black man's game. Eventually, if Po proved worthy, Omega planned to introduce him to the diamond trade. Diamonds didn't discriminate, and Po would be initiated into a different world, but first he had to prove that he could control his temper and check his hustler's mentality at the door. To lose a load of bricks to Customs was nothing, but to have a shipment of pure diamonds with zero imperfections stopped would be the death of Po. Minor adversaries like Castro would always pop up. Omega needed Po to learn the art of diplomacy and manipulation before he moved him to the major leagues of international trade. Omega had learned to put his emotions to the side and rely less on his guerilla tactics long ago. His mind was greater than any automatic weapon. When Po learned to outwit the competition he wouldn't have to exhaust his muscle to keep control.

"Is everything okay, Omega?" Dahlia asked as she entered the room. She wore a long see-through robe and stiletto heels as she stood in his doorway, ready to attend to his every need.

"I'm beginning to wonder if I misjudged Po. Maybe he's not ready for this," Omega said more to himself than to her.

"I think that Po just needs a checks and balances system. You don't have time to oversee his every move, and Ayo works for Po, not beside him," Dahlia said. "He can't stop Po from making a mistake beforehand. You need better eyes in the States."

Dahlia was itching to get to America alone. She loved the independence that Liberty had. Yes, she had gone through hell to get it, but to be with a man like Po who allowed her to move freely and to think freely was worth the years of enslavement . . . or so Dahlia thought. When Po called for Liberty to come back to L.A., Dahlia couldn't help but wish that she was going too. She and Omega had been many times. In fact, he took her all over the world. But Omega was cut from a different cultural cloth than Po.

Being his woman was like being his child. There were strict rules that needed to be followed and high expectations that Dahlia must meet. Even her opinion wasn't highly respected. In order to get her way, Dahlia had to plant a seed inside of Omega, and then nurture it until it bloomed into an idea that Omega thought was his own manifestation. It took a lot of work to be in her shoes, whereas Liberty's spot was carefree. Her only requirements were love, looks, and loyalty. As long as she held those three down, then Po was satisfied. The dance that Dahlia did with Omega was much more difficult. The submission he demanded was suffocating. To outsiders, her life appeared so grand. She walked around with her head held high and flaunting her status to mask her true feelings. In actuality, she was like a caged bird, dying for her owner to mistakenly leave the door open one day so that she could fly free.

"You're tense, baby. Let me make you feel better," she whispered. Dahlia dropped to her knees and unbuckled his expensive slacks, then slid his zipper down slowly. Just the thought of Dahlia's head game had Omega's manhood standing at attention, and he squirmed in his seat in anticipation. She handled his throbbing dick gently as she removed his thickness and massaged it softly, jacking it in her grip. A small moan escaped Omega's lips. He didn't have to coach Dahlia. She knew exactly what to do. First, kissing the tip, she slid her warm lips onto his dick, taking it into her mouth inch by inch until she was full of his strength. She sucked on his dick until his toes curled, and he couldn't contain the euphoria that was building inside of him.

"Shit," he moaned as he pushed her head down into his

lap and grinded his hips in ecstasy. He released, and she swallowed every drop of his nectar, causing his body to tense up until she released him.

"All better?" she asked as she looked up at him with a smile.

His head fell back in amazement. "All better, baby," he replied with a hearty laugh.

Dahlia stood and headed out, her seductive legs moving with a model's precision. "If you need more than that, you know where to find me," she said. Just as she was about to disappear from sight he called after her.

"Dahlia!"

She peeked back into the room.

"Yes, baby?" she asked.

"I'm sending diamonds to Po in his next shipment. This isn't cocaine, and I'm not sure if he can handle this game. I need someone in L.A. to watch Po and keep an eye on my money. Pack your bags. I'm putting you on a plane tomorrow evening," he said. Under normal circumstances he would have never given Dahlia the freedom or authority to do such a task, but he needed eyes on Po 24/7. Since Dahlia was Liberty's cousin, she was the only person who would be able to get inside of Po's home with an open invitation. When dealing in diamonds, Omega couldn't take the same risks as he did with cocaine. Dahlia would be a live-in checks and balances system for Omega.

Dahlia nodded and replied, "Whatever you need from me."

She hid her smile until she was out of sight. Just like

clockwork, she had manipulated him into having her way. She couldn't wait to get to California. She had never been so far away without Omega by her side. She was ready to test the waters on her own and see how she could make this temporary freedom last forever.

FOURTEEN

WHEN DAHLIA STEPPED FOOT OFF THE PLANE she fell in love with L.A. at first sight. The warm weather, the hustle and bustle of the city, and the palm trees made her feel like a socialite. She made her way through the airport, her beauty mesmerizing the other patrons. Dahlia's aura exuded sexuality and beauty like no other. She was used to getting attention for her dark, exotic, sensual looks, and she welcomed it. She was about to make America her runway as she put on a show. She made her way down the escalator and the first face she saw was Liberty's. She smiled brightly, genuinely happy to be reunited with her cousin. After decades apart, it felt so good to have her bloodline around her.

"Dahlia!" Liberty squealed as they embraced and swayed from side to side. "I'm so glad that you're here!"

"I couldn't wait to come, Lib. I was so sad when you left Sierra Leone. Now we're back together, and you get to show me around your city! La La Land, isn't that what they call it?" Dahlia asked.

"The land of dreamers," Liberty said with a head nod. "Po asked me to bring you directly to him. I know that you two have a lot of business to handle. But after he's done with you I can't wait to spend some time with my cousin."

"What hotel am I staying in?" Dahlia asked.

Liberty smiled and replied, "I would never put you in a hotel. You're staying with me and Po. We have more than enough space."

Liberty took Dahlia to their home and showed her to her room. Dahlia admired the elegantly decorated mansion, and although it was slightly smaller than Omega's place she could tell that Po was getting money. The way that Liberty beamed with happiness told a story of new love, and Dahlia knew that Liberty was a kept woman.

Po knocked on Dahlia's bedroom door and stood with his hands in his pant pockets as he greeted her. Po's brown skin, stocky stature, and handsome face were hard for any woman to ignore. Dahlia was always taken aback when in his presence. Po had an energy that screamed "rich nigga," and women loved it.

"Is this room big enough for you, ma?" he asked.

Dahlia looked around the thousand square foot space that was expensively furnished and nodded with a smile. "It's fine. Thanks, Po."

"I know that you will want to rest after that long flight. Whatever you need Liberty can get for you. I know y'all got some bonding or some girl shit to do, so I'm gonna leave you to it. I'm expecting a new shipment in today," Po said.

Po had no idea that the shipment would be different than any other he had received before. Omega was hitting him with the diamonds unexpectedly, to see if he could handle a new hustle. If not, Dahlia knew what to do and would coach Po until he was ready.

The port was busy with imports coming into the city as Po, Rocko, and Ayo headed toward their crate.

"That's us right there," Ayo pointed out as a crane operator lifted a heavy steel crate from the ship and placed it onto the port's dock. The white man looked down at Po and nodded his head, knowing that a $20,000 payment would be waiting at his doorstep later that night. The operation was so flawless that it was almost impossible to be caught. Anyone who could have made it hard for Po was on his payroll. As long as everybody ate, nobody complained and money was good.

Rocko cracked open the package, and the three men stepped inside. Po frowned when he saw that it was full of fish tanks. He walked over to one of the fragile cases and picked up the clear rocks that lay inside.

"Fuck is this? You sure this the right bin, fam?" he asked Ayo as he let the rocks filter from his hand back into the fish tank as if he were playing in sand. "This shit look like it belong to an aquarium or something. This can't be for me."

Ayo chuckled, and then replied, "Oh, it's for you." He walked over to one of the tanks, lifted the lid, and picked up one of the rocks.

"Looks like a bunch of bullshit to me," Rocko stated.

"They're diamonds," Ayo said. "You've just graduated to another level. This is an entirely different game, Po. Omega must think you're ready."

Po's heart galloped inside of his chest as he thought of the money to be made.

"What about the niggas we got waiting for bricks? I've got a nigga in Denver waiting on fifty. That's a lot of money to miss," Rocko said.

"That's li'l nigga shit compared to what we on now. Trust me," Po said as he held up a diamond. "These are on the market for everybody. Crack is a black drug, coke is for the hood niggas, but everyone buys diamonds. White, black, shit, purple . . . this hustle don't discriminate."

"The biggest market will be the Arabs," Ayo said.

"If that's the case, then we got a problem, cuz they ain't gon' cop from us. Those Arabs hate black mu'fuckas," Rocko stated seriously.

"They hate black *men*," Po rebutted as he traced his five o'clock shadow with his hand. "But they *love* black women, and I happen to have two in mind that no man can resist."

"Who's that? Because unless you sending Liberty in there—"

"That's exactly who I'm talking about," Po interrupted.

"Who's the second chick?" Ayo asked.

Po rubbed his hands together and replied, "Dahlia."

Ayo looked at Po in surprise because it was rare that Omega sent his woman anywhere alone. But with a shipment so valuable no measure was too extreme.

Rocko stepped up and said, "I've got a third bitch in mind if we need her."

"Call her and set up a meeting tonight. Let's get these diamonds packaged and get the fuck out of here," Po replied. "It's money time, fam."

Po knew that he would never be able to establish a relationship with the Arab jewelers, but once he sent Liberty and Dahlia their way it would be a wrap. It was the perfect plan because diamonds weren't a violent game. He could send the women in without the threat of danger. It was time for Liberty to come off the bench for the team. He needed her, and she was one of the few people that he trusted with something so valuable.

FIFTEEN

LIBERTY AND DAHLIA WERE LIKE MOVIE STARS as they destroyed Rodeo Drive, so exquisite that even bitches turned their heads with a mixture of jealousy and admiration as they strutted past. Stunning in Italian designer fashions, the two looked as if they had stepped off the front cover of *Vogue*. The ladies were VIP in all the stores. Champagne and caviar awaited them before they even stepped foot inside the doors.

Dahlia was in heaven. She couldn't believe that Po allowed Liberty to roam around the city on her own. Omega always made Dahlia feel as though she were on a very short leash. If he couldn't escort her, then he sent a guard with her, and it was more for control then for protection. Omega had to know everything about everyone all the time, and he was especially invasive when it came to Dahlia.

"So you and Po seem comfy," Dahlia said in a girlish, giggly tone as they walked arm in arm like they used to as kids.

Liberty blushed and nudged Dahlia with her hip. "We are. He's so good to me," she admitted, finally feeling no guilt for the way she felt about him.

"I'm happy for you, Liberty," Dahlia said. She noticed the glimmer in Liberty's eyes when Po's name came up. She looked like a girl in love. Liberty absolutely glowed from happiness, and Dahlia was jealous. Her man was more powerful than Po, but when it came to catering to his woman, Omega didn't know the first thing about pleasing her. Yes, he was friendly with his money and showered her with every material possession she could ever want, but Dahlia craved intimacy. She wanted to be his queen. The one who sat beside him on the throne, not the one who kneeled at his feet to earn her scraps. Dahlia wanted what Liberty had, plain and simple . . . an American boy.

The two made their way home, riding with the top down in Liberty's silver Aston Martin Virage and enjoying the feel of the ocean-misted air whipping through their hair. Dahlia couldn't help but think, *This is the life*. L.A. was where she needed to be. Liberty was crazy, because if Po was Dahlia's man, she would be running things, and the entire city would be her kingdom while the people in it . . . her peasants. *She don't know what to do with a man like Po. With all this freedom she has, I'd be the queen,* Dahlia thought. Liberty was weak; she played in the background because she was so tormented by her past. Dahlia understood, but she knew that the past was the past. It couldn't be changed. *Fuck it, the shit happened,* Dahlia thought. She refused to let it dictate her future. She had come up hard, so as a result, she became hardened to the point where she was only out for self.

Dahlia was in such deep thought that it felt as though they arrived back home in the blink of an eye. The two women walked into the house, laughing and conversing about the day's events. They entered the great room and paused when they saw Po, Rocko, and Ayo standing in a circle looking as though they were in the middle of an important conversation.

"Oh, sorry, Po. We didn't realize you were busy," Liberty said as she turned to head out of the room. Dahlia stayed put, eyeing the men curiously before following Liberty.

"Liberty, Dahlia, I need to talk to you," Po said.

"Is something wrong? Did something happen?" Liberty asked.

"Everything's fine. I want to show you something. Sit down, ma," he instructed as he motioned toward the leather sofa. He nodded to Dahlia and said, "You too."

He pulled a silk pouch out of his pocket and emptied a small diamond into his hand. He held it up in between his forefinger and thumb for them to see. The stone caught the light in the room, and an array of colors danced in the diamond, resembling a disco ball.

"Where did you get that?" Liberty asked, her heart pounding from the sight of the imperfect stone. She was from Sierra Leone . . . spotting a diamond so pure was instinctive to her. Back home, children died, people were dismembered, and men became devils for stones just like the one Po held in his hand. She shuddered from the memory alone.

"Omega," Dahlia answered for him.

"Why are they in my house?" she asked, lips trembling.

Po could see that Liberty was becoming upset, and he said, "Let me have a minute with Liberty."

Rocko, Ayo, and Dahlia left the room.

"What the fuck are you doing?" Liberty asked angrily. Her question took Po off guard.

"Let me explain, ma," Po said.

"I told you about the diamonds," she whispered. "The men who deal in diamonds have blood on their hands, Po."

"Liberty! Listen to me," Po said, grabbing her shoulders and making her face him. Liberty's jaws locked as she looked at him with watery eyes. "Omega sent these diamonds here. I had no idea he even wanted to bring me into this side of the game, but I'm in now. What you want me to do? Back out? Cuz I don't think it's that easy to get out, ma. You just don't walk away from some shit like this," Po whispered harshly. "Now these diamonds can make me . . . make us very rich, Liberty. I can give you anything you want, ma. We can—"

"We can't do anything, Po," Liberty said. "You don't get it. I would rather be broke and on the streets than get rich off those diamonds. I don't know why I thought you would ever understand."

Liberty was about to storm out when Rocko stepped back into the room.

"Yo, give us a minute, fam," Po said in frustration.

"I don't mean to interrupt, bro, but ol' girl is here," he said.

"Don't let me stop you," Liberty said as she stormed out of the room. But she stopped dead in her tracks when she entered the foyer.

"Trixie?" she called out as she saw her old friend standing ten feet away from her. Her hands flew up to her mouth in disbelief. It had been years since they had last seen each other, but it was a face that she would never forget. Trixie was half the reason Liberty had survived her days on the ho strip. They had been good friends once upon a time.

"Liberty?" Trixie replied.

Po, Ayo, Rocko, and Dahlia all looked on in confusion as Liberty rushed to hug Trixie.

"Oh my God! Trix! What are you doing here?" Liberty asked.

Po stepped up and answered, "She's in on the diamonds."

Liberty looked at Po in disappointment, and she turned to Ayo, to Dahlia for support. They stayed out of it. No one wanted to take sides. The only thing that mattered to them was the money. They could give a damn about the blood diamond crisis. Liberty reached out and grabbed Trixie's hands, squeezing both of them gently.

"I'm going to let you all handle your business, but please don't leave before I get a chance to talk to you," Liberty said. She looked back at Po with hurt in her eyes, then walked up the stairs.

Po wanted to go after her, but he knew that now was not the time. "Follow me into the study," he said.

Po got right down to business breaking down the money plot to the girls. "Dahlia meet Trixie. Trixie, Dahlia. I need you ladies to get to know each other. You'll be working closely together," Po said.

"Doing what exactly?" Trixie asked.

"Moving diamonds," Po replied. "You'll be selling them to jewelers, rappers, open market, black market . . . whoever can afford them."

"Why do you need us? You have plenty of men on your payroll," Dahlia asked.

"Exactly. Men. The Middle Eastern jewelers hate black men. They won't deal with any of my people, but they love black women. That's where you two come in," Po said. "I'll give you 10 percent for every deal you broker."

"I'm in," Trixie said. "Now where did Ms. Liberty disappear to?" she asked flamboyantly while looking around.

Po pointed to the second floor and said, "Take the stairs to the second level. She's in the last room on your right. Rocko and Ayo will be in touch."

Trixie made her exit and as soon as she was out of earshot Dahlia spoke. "She may be content with 10 percent, but *my price* is 20 percent."

Dahlia smirked as Po licked his lips and rubbed his goatee as they stared at each other.

"What's it gonna be, Po? You know I'm worth it," Dahlia said seductively.

Ayo and Rocko shot each other a look with raised eyebrows.

"A'ight, 20 percent," Po agreed.

Dahlia smiled. "Good night, gentlemen," she said as she left the room.

"You better be careful with that one," Rocko cracked under his breath, admiring Dahlia's long legs and fat ass as she walked away. "She'll be the bitch to break up a happy home."

"I might have already done that myself," Po admitted; he had a lot of making up to do to his lady.

Liberty sat at her vanity removing her makeup and jewelry. She was so livid that she didn't even want to see Po's face. She was sure that she would scream at him as soon as he entered their bedroom. She put her face in her hands and leaned onto the glass top, feeling overwhelmed. Her stomach turned from the thought of Po dealing blood diamonds. He was representing everything that she hated. *How could he?* she thought.

Her mouth began to taste like metal, and she felt disgusted as she bent over and hurled up the contents of her stomach. She grabbed the trash can near her feet and hugged it as she threw up.

A knock at the door got her attention, and she looked up, wiping her mouth with the side of her hand. Trixie stood at the door and just seeing her face caused a weak smile to spread across Liberty's face.

"Hey, Trix," Liberty greeted her. She stood and placed the trash can back on the ground.

"Liberty, I know the last time you saw me I did you dirty, but—"

Liberty put up her hand. "It's old news, Trixie. We were all just trying to survive out there. Now if you don't come give me a hug . . ."

The two women embraced.

"You look good, girl! Look at you! You landed on your feet, Liberty. Big fancy house, cars, clothes, that fine man down there," Trixie complimented. "You were always too good for the life. This is exactly how you always deserved to live."

Liberty smiled. "What about you, Trix? You still on the strip? Still stuck? I can get you out. I can help you get away from it all."

Trixie waved her hand in dismissal. "Honey, I haven't been pimped since the day we both made a run for it. Yeah, I'm still on the strip, but that's what Ms. Trixie do, boo. Now all the little chickens on the block are reporting to me. I'm good. Don't need no saving. I'm making money doing what I do best. For some of us, this is all there is," Trixie said.

Liberty nodded in understanding. She knew that she couldn't want more for Trixie than she wanted for herself.

"I'm glad you're well, Trix," Liberty said. "Thank you for looking out for me all those years ago. They would have eaten me alive out there if it weren't for you. You were my guardian angel."

"And you were mine, baby girl. A soul like yours kept me pure when everybody else out there was trying to corrupt me. I love you, Liberty, girl," Trixie stated.

"I love you too, Trix," Liberty replied.

Trixie turned to leave, happy that she was able to apologize for doing Liberty dirty once upon a time. It was the one thing that had haunted her over the years, but now she had been given atonement. Liberty's forgiveness would help her sleep at night, especially now that she knew Liberty was okay.

Liberty awoke to an empty bed and knew that Po had slept in one of the guest rooms to give her some space. She stood and immediately the room began to spin. She ran to the attached master bathroom and barely made it to the toilet before she was throwing up again. Liberty struggled to her feet and heaved in air. *I have to get out of here. I can't be with someone like him,* she thought.

She quickly dressed, and then began to throw her things inside of a suitcase. She had too much stuff to take, so she grabbed a few pieces and cleared her money from the safe that Po had built for them. Liberty wanted to cry and felt as though she should be sad that this was coming to an end, but in her heart she knew that it would never last. Po was not her soul mate. He was simply a replica, a cheap knockoff of A'shai Montgomery, and although he would make the perfect mate for someone, it wasn't her. Liberty was built for someone else.

She grabbed her two vintage Louis Vuitton suitcases and left the room. She bumped into Dahlia who was coming her way with a cup of coffee in her hands. The coffee spilled all over her short kimono robe.

"Oh. I'm so sorry, Dahlia . . ."

"You're leaving?" Dahlia asked, ignoring the spill and eyeing Liberty, and then her luggage.

Dahlia was slightly disappointed that Liberty was

ASHLEY & JAQUAVIS

squandering such a good opportunity to be Po's queen. Liberty was too sensitive, too moral. *Who gives a fuck about the diamond crisis in Sierra Leone? Whether Po has his hand in the pot or not won't make or break the struggle. She better let her man get his money. If she can't hold him down, I have no problem doing it for her,* Dahlia thought.

"I'm sorry, cousin. I just can't stay here," Liberty said.

"Then I'm coming with you," Dahlia said, faking loyalty. Her love for Liberty was true, but her love for herself was greater. She wanted to be the woman on Po's arm, but she had to get Liberty out of the picture first.

"No, you stay here with him. I know you two have business with each other. He needs you here," Liberty said.

Liberty was naïve and made the number-one mistake of trusting another woman around her man. She trusted Dahlia too much. So much so that she didn't question the short robe that Dahlia wore, exposing her long, luscious legs with her cleavage peeking from the top. A seasoned woman would have told Dahlia to respect her house and put some clothes on, but Liberty was blind to Dahlia's manipulation.

"Where are you going?" Dahlia asked.

"A hotel or something until I can figure out something long term," Liberty replied. "I'll be fine. I love you."

"I love you too," Dahlia said.

The sound of her footsteps coming down the marble staircase got Po's attention. He walked into the foyer and when he saw Liberty descending the stairs with her bags packed his heart sank. He had told her if she wanted to leave

that he would let her go. That was their deal, so although he
wanted to stop her from leaving he held his tongue.

Liberty walked right past him and didn't stop until he
called her name.

"Liberty."

She paused, but didn't turn to face him.

"I'ma have Rocko deliver a package to you tonight.
Please text me the address to wherever you are going," he
said. He didn't turn to look at her as he spoke because he
knew that it would break his heart to see her walk away.
Liberty was the bandage that had stopped him from bleeding out after Scarlett had passed away. Now that she was
leaving, he was mourning the loss of two great women.

Liberty didn't respond but continued to walk away. She
kept telling herself that if she didn't stand for something
that she would fall for anything.

SIXTEEN

DAHLIA AND TRIXIE WALKED INTO THE AIRPORT together, but as soon as they were inside one veered right while the other strayed left. They didn't speak and to the average eye it would appear as if they didn't even know each other. Between the two of them they carried a million dollars' worth of diamonds. There was too much at stake for them to engage in pleasantries. They were there on business, booked on two different airline carriers, headed for the East Coast.

Dahlia stood in line with her carry-on luggage. Her demeanor was calm as she waited patiently behind the other passengers on her flight. Check-in went smoothly just as she suspected it would, but the challenge would be getting through security without any alarm. The high-tech x-ray machines picked up on everything, and Dahlia would not be able to explain her way out of this situation if the diamonds were discovered. TSA was the last organization that could be bribed. With the terror threat so high, she knew that they would arrest her first and ask questions later if anything went wrong.

Dahlia's poker face was award-winning as she placed her small suitcase on the conveyer belt and watched it disappear under the machine. She removed her red bottom heels and belt and placed them in a bin, sending them down the conveyer belt behind her bag.

"Step through here, ma'am," the TSA agent directed.

Dahlia stepped inside.

"Put your arms above your head and stand still."

Dahlia did as she was told and waited a few seconds until they gave her the all clear. She stepped out, and when she saw her luggage rolling out, she smiled inwardly.

She grabbed her things, putting her shoes and belt back on quickly before grabbing her rolling luggage and hightailing it down the terminal. She hurriedly went into the bathroom and opened up her luggage. She removed the vitamin bottle in which she had concealed the diamonds. She emptied one capsule out into her hand and then twisted it apart. One beautiful stone fell into her hand. They were the perfect size to fit inside the large capsule. No one would ever suspect that she was moving product through the airport because her hiding place was flawless. She put the diamond back inside, then secured the lid before placing it back in her luggage. The hard part was over. Now all she had to do was make the sales. Her charm and gift of gab would have her buyers eating out of the palm of her hand. Liberty bumped into Trixie on her way out of the bathroom.

The two met eyes but didn't speak as they continued on their separate ways. At least Dahlia knew that Trixie had made it through security. She didn't know how Trixie got her load through, but she was glad that it had worked. Dahlia pulled out her phone and sent a text to Po.

WE GOT THROUGH.

Dahlia boarded her plane and took off into the friendly skies, knowing that this was simply the beginning of a very lucrative hustle.

Trixie rushed into the stall and breathed a sigh of relief as she came out of her blazer. *Damn, a bitch was sweating bullets,* she thought. Trixie pulled off a few sheets of toilet paper and dried underneath her arms. She had been so nervous that she was sure she would give herself away, but was fortunate to have pulled it off. She unwrapped her extra large bun that sat on top of her head and gently shook out the diamonds, making sure to account for every single stone that had been carefully taped into her weave. When she was done, she put the diamonds in a clear ziplock bag, then taped them underneath her fake DD breasts and walked out of the restroom, heading for her flight.

The sounds of the city streets blared around her as Dahlia stepped foot out of the NYC cab.

She looked around cautiously before reaching for the crocodile briefcase she carried. Her stilettos clicked against the dirty concrete as she walked into the jewelry store that sat in the middle of the Diamond District.

"How can I help you?" one of the store's workers asked. The women in the store worked off of commission and as soon as they spotted Dahlia they pegged her as a big spender. Everything from her shoes, her clothes, even her demeanor screamed money.

"I'm here for Ahmad," she announced. "My name is Dahlia. He's expecting me."

The lady nodded her head and disappeared in the back. Dahlia walked around, running one hand on top of the glass displays as she admired the sparkling jewels that were protected below. The pieces were pretty, but compared to what Dahlia was holding they looked like cheap costume jewels. Dahlia was working with quality and knew that her stones were a rare and hot commodity. They would practically sell themselves.

An attractive man with olive skin and shoulder-length jet-black hair emerged from the back and smiled warmly at Dahlia.

"I'm Ahmad," he introduced as he extended his hand to her.

"Dahlia," she replied. She could tell by the way that he stared at her that he was smitten instantly.

"This way please," he said as he led her to his office and closed the door. He took a seat behind his oak desk and motioned for her to sit in front of him. "Let's see what you have for me, beautiful."

Dahlia sat and placed the briefcase in her lap. Popping

it open, she bypassed the small caliber pistol that she carried inside and pulled out the velvet bag that contained the diamonds. She removed one and placed it on a small cloth for him to see.

Ahmad pulled out a looking glass and leaned over to examine the stone. It was so clear that it appeared as though he were looking at glass. He was a man of experience so he knew that Dahlia had brought him stones that were quite valuable.

"They're flawless," Ahmad exclaimed, breathless.

"They're for sale," Dahlia replied.

Ahmad looked up at her and placed the looking glass down. "I'll give you a quarter million for them, right now, in cash," he offered.

Dahlia sat back and crossed her legs while shaking her head. "Now I have a number in my head that I find appropriate. I can tell you that you're not even close to it. Why don't you try again," she said sweetly. Ahmad loved the challenge of a black woman. They were strong, outspoken, and seductive. Haggling with Dahlia made his loins tingle as he stared at her full lips and beautiful cantaloupe-shaped breasts.

"$300,000," Ahmad countered.

Dahlia stood. "You're wasting my time," she stated as she turned to leave.

Ahmad stood and said, "Wait!"

He rounded the desk and pushed the door completely closed so that she was stuck between him and the exit. Her round behind pushed into his crotch, making his dick harden. She turned to face him.

"Make a fair offer or let me leave," she demanded. They stood so close to each other that her lips touched his as she spoke. Her breath smelled sweet, and her perfume danced up his nostrils.

"I bet your pussy tastes sweet like dark cherries," Ahmad whispered.

Her breath caught in her throat when she felt his hands part her thighs as they made their way up her dress.

His handsome face was dark, mysterious, and sexy as he seduced her. "You're not wearing panties," he commented.

She gasped as he inserted two fingers inside of her.

"They just get in the way," she whispered.

Ahmad lowered himself until he was face-first with her pussy, then dove right in while humming in satisfaction.

"Hmm. It tastes just the way I thought it would," he moaned as he sucked on her pussy as if it were a fresh peach. Dahlia's knees weakened as he sucked and licked her with passion. She had never had her womanhood treated so good. Ahmad knew exactly what he was doing as he focused on her clit and made love to her middle with his long, wet tongue.

"Black pussy is the best pussy," he whispered as he took his fingers and spread her southern lips so that he left no part of her undiscovered.

"Oh shit," Dahlia moaned.

Ahmad sucked her until she squirted her juices all over his tongue. He stood to his feet and wiped his face.

"I hope you enjoyed it," he said, pulling a handkerchief out of his lapel and cleaning up.

Dahlia adjusted her dress and cleared her throat.

"$500,000," Ahmad said.

"$600,000," Dahlia replied. "Half a million for my stones and another hundred thousand for giving you a taste of the best pussy you'll ever have."

"Is that the going rate if I wanted to taste it again?" he asked.

"It is," she replied with a sexy smirk as she pulled out a laptop and opened it on top of his desk. "Wire the $500k into this Swiss account and the stones are yours. I'll take my money in cash."

Trixie had never been to Detroit. As she rode in the backseat of the Lincoln Town Car that had been arranged for her, she couldn't help but notice that the cold, industrial city was a far cry from sunny, friendly L.A. that she was used to. She felt as if she were in the middle of a concrete jungle as she was driven to her destination. The Palace of Auburn Hills was the stadium of Michigan's professional basketball team, and she had a meeting with the owner of the organization. She was sure that the stones would move quickly, and as they pulled up she hoped that she could pull off such an important transaction. Since Rocko and Ayo had put her down with the Castro hit, Trixie's income had quadrupled overnight. She was getting money with Po's crew and desperately wanted to keep her spot.

"We're here," the driver announced as he opened his door and came around to let Trixie out. "I'll be right here when you're ready to leave. Just call me five minutes before."

Trixie nodded, and then looked up at the circular building feeling intimidated. A month ago she was turning tricks with down-low brothers on the streets, and now she was about to sit across the table from a multimillionaire. Oh, how life had changed for her.

She entered the building and approached the guest services desk. She made sure to dress conservatively. She didn't want to draw attention to herself by being over the top, but even in the two-piece pencil skirt suit, she still exuded sexuality. Trixie may have been born a man, but she had the woman act down. No one would ever know her sex unless they lay down in bed with her—that's how beautifully she passed as a woman. Trixie was a bad bitch.

"I have a meeting with Mr. Hunter," she said as she pulled at the skirt, fidgeting nervously.

"Your name?" the receptionist asked.

"Trixie."

"Last name?" the receptionist pushed.

"Diamonds," Trixie answered, laughing slightly to herself.

The receptionist eyed her curiously but picked up the phone to announce her arrival.

"His assistant will be down to get you shortly," the woman said after hanging up the phone.

Trixie nodded, then stepped back as she drifted around the lobby, looking at the various trophies and team photos that were on display.

"Trixie, right this way, please," a woman called.

Trixie turned and followed the woman up to the VIP

office. "Mr. Hunter, your 3 o'clock appointment has arrived," she announced as Trixie followed her through the door.

Mr. Hunter extended a seat to her and waited until his assistant left the room before he spoke.

"Welcome, Trixie. I hope your travels were safe," he said.

Trixie nodded. "It was fine."

"So let's see them."

Trixie pulled the diamonds out and laid them across his desk.

Mr. Hunter picked up one of the stones and held it up to the light. Immediately it sparkled.

"Exquisite," he remarked. He put it back on the desk and looked at Trixie. "As are you, Trixie."

Trixie smiled and replied, "Thank you, Mr. Hunter, but trust me, honey, you can't handle what Ms. Trixie has to offer."

Mr. Hunter chuckled. "I beg to differ." He stood and walked over to his floor-to-ceiling window and looked out over the parking lot while thinking. "I want these stones. I'm willing to offer you $450,000."

"You add fifty grand to that number and you've got yourself a deal," Trixie said. "I have very strict instructions. I can't go any lower then that number."

Mr. Hunter turned toward Trixie and said, "I suppose I can do that *if* you agree to accompany me to dinner this evening before you leave town."

Trixie laughed and then replied, "Listen, Mr. Hunter, I like you. You seem like a good man, and I don't want to see your name on the front page of any tabloid. So let me be frank with you," Trixie stated. She cleared her throat, and then spoke freely in her masculine tone. "You don't want what I have to offer. Taking me to dinner will ruin your career."

Mr. Hunter's eyes bulged in surprise. "L . . . let's just conclude the deal," he stammered.

Trixie pulled out a laptop and set up the wire transfer account. "All you have to do is enter your bank information and press SUBMIT," she stated.

Mr. Hunter moved with haste, wanting to get the transaction over as soon as possible. He was clearly uncomfortable. Trixie couldn't help but chuckle to herself.

"All done," Mr. Hunter said.

Trixie collected her laptop and left the diamonds where they lay.

"Nice doing business with you," Trixie said sweetly, waving good-bye as she left.

The knock at the door startled Liberty as she lay in bed staring at her phone and the missed calls from Po. As much as she wanted to reach out to him, she couldn't. Loyalty to her past was stopping her from falling for her future. She arose from the bed and hesitantly went to the door. She grabbed the small .22 mm handgun that she had taken from Po. No one knew where she was. *There shouldn't be anybody knocking at my door,* she thought as she held her breath while walking toward it.

"It's me, Liberty. I know you in there. Open up."

She sighed in relief when she recognized Rocko's voice. Her relief turned to annoyance as she pulled open the door.

"What are you doing here?" she asked, walking away, leaving the door hanging open and Rocko standing at the threshold. "How did you even know where to find me?"

"I followed you the morning you left. Po wanted me to make sure you were okay," Rocko said. He stepped inside and closed the door behind him. In his hands he carried a Gucci duffle. He took the strap off his shoulder and held it out for her. "That's the money he promised you."

Liberty folded her arms and shook her head. "I don't want that money. It's dirty."

Rocko chuckled and rubbed his hands together. He respected her morals, but she was living in a fantasyland. "There's no such thing as clean money, ma. Everybody crosses somebody to get it."

"Well, I don't want it," she said again, this time more sternly.

"Well, I can't take it back. I don't give a fuck what you do with it. Give it to the homeless nigga in front of the building for all I care. Po sent me here to give it to you. I've done my part," Rocko said as he turned toward the door, strolling out with a nonchalant swag. She eyed the bag of money. She respected Po for keeping his word, but hated him at the same time for being too greedy to turn away from the game. Rocko paused and turned to see her battling silently with herself.

"For the record, Po's a good nigga. You should go home. I've only seen him treat one other person the way that he treats you," Rocko said. He thought of Scarlett in that moment, as did Liberty. "The only difference is, she would have never walked away from him the way you did."

He walked out and closed the door behind him, leaving her standing there feeling guilty as if she were in the wrong.

SEVENTEEN

DAHLIA ENTERED THE HOUSE AND WENT INTO Po's office, knocking on the door frame as she watched him pacing the floor as he spoke into the phone.

"Liberty, it's me. Give me a call. I miss you, ma," he said.

Dahlia wanted to gag. She rolled her eyes as he ended the call.

"You still haven't spoken to her?" she asked, when he finally turned toward her.

Po took a seat and loosened his necktie as he leaned back in the plush leather chair. "She won't return my calls."

"The last time I called her she said that she wanted to move on. I don't know a woman who can stay away from the man she loves. It's been two weeks, Po. I don't think she *wants* to come back," Dahlia said sympathetically. In truth, she had not spoken to Liberty since the day that she had moved out, but she was willing to say anything to put a wedge between the couple.

"I saw the transfers into the account. I take it everything went as planned?" Po asked.

Dahlia walked into the room and sat in the chair in front of his desk. "Everything went perfectly," she said.

"Shit is crazy. I just made a $1,000,000 in a week," Po said. "Is this how Omega eats?"

"This is how kings eat, Po," Dahlia replied. "You are a king."

She stood and walked around to him. "We should celebrate," she said as she grabbed his hands and pulled him out of his chair. "It would have taken you a month to make that much money from drugs. This calls for dinner . . . for drinks!"

"Nah, ma, I'm good," Po rejected.

Dahlia pouted and put her hands on her hips. "Come on, Po. You have to get out of this funk you're in. I've watched you walk around here in a bad mood since Liberty left. I just want you to come out and toast to the money you're about to make," she said, her eyes pleading sexily. "Please, Po. I've been in L.A. and have barely seen the city."

Po lightened up and nodded his head. "A'ight, ma. Go get gorgeous and meet me downstairs in an hour."

Po waited in the foyer and checked his Piguet wristwatch as he paced impatiently. Just as he was about to go get Dahlia, he looked up to find her standing at the top of the staircase.

Stunning was the only word to describe her. She looked like Miss America in a short, ivory, peplum cocktail dress that she accented with gold and diamonds. Her gold Jimmy

Choo six-inch peep toes accented her chocolate legs beautifully.

He was mesmerized for a moment and had to shake his head to come out of the trance she had put on him.

"You like?" Dahlia asked, holding her clutch under one arm.

Po nodded once and replied, "I like." He held out his arm, and she descended the steps. She held onto him as he escorted her out of the house.

Po took her to Spago in Beverly Hills where they ate and drank like royalty. The ambiance in the restaurant was perfect for their celebration, and as they ate side by side, they looked more like a couple then friends. Po couldn't help but think that Dahlia was the perfect woman.

"Let me ask you something, Dahlia. What do you think about me selling diamonds?" Po asked.

"I think that you are a businessman, Po, a very good one. I also think that a woman should support her man. You're a provider; you should be appreciated. If you don't sell them, then somebody else will. There will always be a market for diamonds, whether you choose to play or not. So why miss out on the money? It's business not personal," Dahlia replied. "I am from Sierra Leone, but I'm not a savior."

She understood the game in which he played in and respected his position. He couldn't always play the good guy. Sometimes he was the bad guy . . . the villain. He didn't like it, but Dahlia understood that it was completely necessary.

"Omega is a lucky man," Po said. The expensive cognac encouraged him to speak freely. Words were flowing from his mouth that he would have normally kept to himself. "There aren't a lot of women who are strong enough to put up with men in our position."

"I can appreciate a man in your position, Po," she said as she leaned into him. "I'm not happy with Omega. He doesn't realize how good of a woman I am."

"That's his first mistake," Po said. "Cuz you're a different breed, ma." He gently touched her chin and brought her face near his own.

"Here is the dessert menu," the waiter said, interrupting them and causing Po to back up uncomfortably. Dahlia shot daggers at the waiter with her eyes. She could kill him for stopping the kiss that Po was about to give her.

Po stood and threw money on the table. "I think we're done," he said. "Keep the change, my man."

Po was slightly tipsy and knew that it was time to conclude the evening. His loneliness mixed with his intoxication was causing his judgment to be off. He began to walk out of the restaurant and Dahlia was livid as she walked behind him, mad that her evening was suddenly cut short.

When they arrived home Po closed himself in his office and Dahlia changed into something more comfortable. A black lace camisole and black kimono robe barely covered her bottom as she walked through the house. She went down to the wine cellar feeling the need to take the edge off with a bottle of vintage Brunello.

The cellar was dark, only lit by the dim recessed lighting

that Po had installed. Dahlia grabbed a bottle and turned to leave. She jumped when she saw Po standing behind her.

"Oh my God. I didn't even hear you," Dahlia screeched as she put a hand over her racing heart.

"Looks like we both were thinking the same thing," Po said, pointing to the bottle she gripped in her hand. "The finest bottle in the cellar. You are a kingpin's wife, ain't you?" he chuckled.

"Share a bottle with me?" she asked. She grabbed his hand, and they went back to the kitchen.

He reached for the glasses and Dahlia came up behind him, pressing her body against his back. "You go sit down. I'll serve you," she said. He could feel her hardened nipples through the fabric of his shirt, and he stepped to the side as he sat at the island, watching her fix his drink.

As she reached up the fabric of her kimono rose slightly higher then her behind and showed the bottom half of her ass cheeks. Po looked away.

"We never toasted," she said as she handed him a glass. "To new beginnings. I think the million dollars we made today proves that we are very good together. To us."

Po tapped his glass against hers, and they sipped the wine. It wasn't long before they went through half the bottle.

"Wine is my vice," she said as she slipped out of the kimono, showing the lace camisole lingerie she wore underneath. "It always makes my temperature rise."

Po cleared his throat and turned his head, trying to be respectful.

"You can look," Dahlia said. She stood and stepped in

between his legs. He stood, and she stepped closer as she reached up to kiss his lips.

Her lips were so soft that Po devoured her, lifting her so that her ass rested in his hands and her legs were wrapped around his waist. She grinded her pussy into his crotch as his thick nine inches hardened. Po's hands were gentler than Omega's. Po explored her body with the intensity of a roughneck, but the smoothness of a Casanova, electrifying every part he touched. He reached to slide her panties to the side and realized that there was no fabric to move. She was soaking wet and rained on his fingers as he massaged her clit. Po knew that what he was doing was wrong, but he was mad at Liberty for walking out on him. She just ran away from him when he needed her to stand by him and support him. When shit got thick, Liberty deserted him. He needed someone who understood his lifestyle; one who would trust his decisions no matter how bad they seemed.

Po turned Dahlia around and bent her over the island, then slid himself inside of her. His girth took her breath away as he slid in and out of her. She felt his pain as he fucked her hard. His sweat fell onto her back as he held her hips and dug deeper inside of her womanhood, causing her to run. He pulled her back, filling her until her legs shook. He grunted. She moaned. He moaned. She growled. Their bodies flowed to the same rhythm.

He turned her around, lifting her onto the granite island, then slid into her again. His hands ripped her lingerie to shreds as he freed her breasts and took the chocolate mounds into his mouth, suckling on her nipples. The shit was so good that Dahlia called his name repeatedly, "Ooh, Po. Daddy, fuck me! Baby, it's so good. I knew this dick was good." Dahlia was losing her mind. Po was putting in work. She felt her orgasm building. "I'm cumming, Po . . . ooh, baby, I'm cumming," she whispered, as ecstasy took her there. Po made sure that every drop of her love came down before he followed her, pulling out of her cookie jar just in time. He held his head down as he moved away from her and leaned against the adjacent countertop. Dahlia came up behind him and rubbed his head from behind.

"It's okay, Po," Dahlia said. "If it ever came down to it, Po, I'd choose you. Over Omega, over Liberty, over everything . . . I'd choose you. So when the time comes for you to decide, remember that, Po. I can be your queen. You deserve loyalty, Po, and so do I."

Dahlia didn't want to crowd him. She had just given him the best shot of his life and had put her cards on the table letting him know that she was his, if he wanted her to be. A man of his status needed a chick like her. Liberty couldn't handle Po. It would only be a matter of time before her good girl act began to bore him.

Speechless, Liberty stared at the small white stick. The pink plus sign confirmed her suspicions. She was pregnant. Mixed emotions filled her as her hands instinctively went to her flat belly. She turned to the side and lifted her shirt. She miraculously felt pregnant. All of a sudden her nipples hurt. She felt bloated, and the nausea she had been feeling lately took a turn for the worse. Confirming it seemed to bring on all the symptoms at once.

Liberty rushed to the bed and grabbed one of the decorative square pillows off the hotel bed, then ran back to the bathroom mirror. She stuffed the pillow under her shirt and tried to imagine how she would look when her belly started to grow. Tears came to her eyes. She was happy, sad, mad, glad, all at the same time. She had always imagined being a mother, but not under these circumstances. In her dreams she saw A'shai's little nappy-headed boy and beautiful girl. In reality, she was pregnant by Po, and although she loved him, theirs was an imperfect love . . . an unlikely love . . . an incompatible love.

I don't have to tell him, Liberty thought. It had been three weeks since she had left him, and he had yet to come for her. Liberty had enough money to walk away and raise her child without him. *I could just run away and be a good mother to my baby. I could find my happiness,* she thought. The feeling of having life inside of her gave Liberty a newfound view on her existence. *I'm gonna be somebody's mother. You sure you know what you're doing with that one, God?* She chuckled at the thought; she would be clueless when the time came. She would have so many questions and no one to go to for answers, but she was confident that she would make it through. Now, someone else depended on her. She had no choice but to get things right.

She instantly began to feel selfish as she thought of Po. It was his baby too. Didn't he deserve to know that they had created life together? She was so confused that she didn't know what to do. Picking up her cell she texted Dahlia:

CAN YOU MEET ME FOR LUNCH IN THE LOBBY OF MY HOTEL?

Dahlia received the text as she lay in Po's bed, basking in the afterglow of their sex session. Po had put her body through things that she had never experienced before, giving her pleasure through the night as he sexed away his frustration. They both knew that they had crossed a line, but he liked the ease of being with Dahlia. She wasn't hard to please. Dahlia got up from bed and quietly crept out of the room, not wanting to wake a sleeping Po. She replied to Liberty, letting her know that she was on her way. Dahlia showered quickly and dressed before racing out to meet Liberty.

Dahlia entered the restaurant with large Chanel shades covering her eyes. Liberty sat at a table in the corner of the room, sipping a cup of hot tea as Dahlia approached from behind. *She's so green. She's affiliated with Po. Her back should never be to the door,* Dahlia thought as she shook her head. It was clear that Liberty wasn't the type of girl for Po. Someone like Liberty made Po accessible. She made him touchable. Dahlia was trying to make him untouchable. She plastered a smile on her face and sat across from Liberty.

"Hi, Liberty," Dahlia said. "I miss you. Is everything okay?" She sounded so concerned that she almost convinced herself that she was sincere. It wasn't that she didn't care for Liberty, because she did. Liberty just happened to be standing in the way of something that Dahlia wanted.

"I'm pregnant," Liberty blurted out, unable to keep the news to herself any longer. She had to share it with someone. She needed help deciding what she should do next.

"You're *what*?" Dahlia snapped.

Taken aback by her cousin's sharp tone, Liberty frowned. "I'm pregnant," she said again, this time more firmly.

"I'm sorry, Liberty. You just shocked me is all," Dahlia replied. "What are you going to do?" she asked. This was the worst news that Dahlia could be hit with. She knew that as soon as Po found out about this baby that he would go running back to Liberty.

"I don't know," Liberty admitted. "A part of me wants to take this baby and just disappear."

"You're going to have it?" Dahlia asked. "Do you think that's smart? You have options, Liberty. What kind of father do you think Po will be? He's a drug dealer, and he's dealing illegal diamonds internationally. How long do you think he'll even be free? Men like him aren't family men, Liberty."

Liberty's brow dipped in concern because the reality that Dahlia was feeding her was the brutal truth. Her life was not a fairy tale.

"I can't have this baby," Liberty concluded.

Dahlia sighed in silent relief. "I'm so sorry you are going through this, Liberty."

"I'm just glad that I have you. Thanks for listening," Liberty said.

Liberty sat still as Dahlia rose.

"You're leaving?" Liberty asked.

"I'm sorry, Liberty, but I can't stay. I'm going out of town to meet another jewelry buyer for Po. I'll check up on you when I get back," Dahlia promised. "Don't beat yourself up about it, Liberty. We both know firsthand how cruel the world can be. We've been beaten, raped, kidnapped, left for dead . . . Do you really want to birth a baby into such a cold place? Who is going to protect that baby, Liberty? We couldn't even protect ourselves."

Dahlia knew that she had hit a nerve. Liberty was too sensitive not to consider her past when deciding about her future. She reached down and gave Liberty a supportive squeeze on the shoulder, then walked out of the restaurant. As she retrieved her car from the valet, she looked back at Liberty through the large glass windows. Worry covered her face, and she could see her cousin wiping away tears. *Oh dear cousin,* she thought without remorse, *just abort that fucking baby. You're the only thing standing in my way. Remove yourself—before I do it for you.* Dahlia hid her cruel intentions behind her sunglasses as she grabbed her keys from the valet worker, then hopped into her car, speeding away.

EIGHTEEN

AYO RANG PO'S DOORBELL THE NEXT MORNING and was caught off guard when Dahlia answered, half-naked, with a wineglass in her hand. He frowned slightly, then stepped around her before she even invited him inside.

"Good morning to you too," she mumbled as she closed the door.

Ayo looked her up and down. "Don't you want to put some fucking clothes on? Omega know you walking around this bitch looking like a street whore?" he asked, disgusted at Dahlia's behavior. Ayo had grown up in Sierra Leone and had strict ideas of how a woman should behave. This was not the Dahlia that he had watched on Omega's arm. He was an expert at weeding out snakes, and now he was staring one in the eyes. *Snake-ass bitch,* he thought, while shaking his head.

"Don't you want to mind your own business?" she snapped back. "What are you, Omega's *bitch* or something?"

Ayo was about to respond, but Po entered the room, disrupting their hostile exchange. Ayo turned his attention to Po, and Dahlia retreated to her room, both putting their differences aside for now. Ayo made it a point to make sure he put in a call to Omega. Dahlia thought that she was free to do as she pleased in Los Angeles, but Omega always covered his bases. The moment she touched down, Ayo had been keeping tabs on her. He just didn't want to play her too closely. He would give her just enough rope to hang herself. He hoped that Po didn't fall for the bait that she was blatantly throwing out because if so, Omega would mark him a dead man.

"What up, fam?" Po greeted.

"I've got three more buyers, and one of them is out of Korea," Ayo explained.

Po's eyebrows arose in surprise. "Korea?" he questioned.

"Korea," Ayo confirmed. "And he has connections to every major city this way: L.A., Chicago, New York. He's royalty over there . . . an emperor's nephew."

Po saw green as he thought of how much money he could make if this connection went through. He would be the largest diamond supplier in the States if he linked up with the Asian market. Everyone knew that niggas never connected with the Asians. They kept their hustles exclusive. For Po to make that deal would be major. Not even Omega had been able to secure an alliance in the Orient.

"There's only one catch," Ayo said.

"What's that?" Po asked.

"He's on the U.S. Most Wanted list. He's considered a

threat to your country. If you're caught doing business with him, it will be considered treason," Ayo warned.

"If I don't get caught it's a gold mine," Po replied, weighing the other option.

"More money than you can count," Ayo answered.

Po knew that the buyer was federal as hell and that no one in their right mind would take that kind of risk, but he couldn't pass up an opportunity this large.

"I'm in," Po said.

"Be sure about this," Ayo warned.

"Make the arrangements. Put Dahlia on a plane. Send Rocko with her," Po instructed.

Po entered Dahlia's room and saw that she was staring out the window deep in thought.

"Everything a'ight?" he asked, startling her.

She turned toward him. "I'm fine," she assured. "Just thinking. I've never put myself on the line for Omega the way that I'm doing for you."

Po remained silent, unsure of where she was headed with the conversation.

"I would do anything to hold you down, Po. I'm ready to choose you, if you're ready to let me," Dahlia said.

Po saw the sincerity in her eyes and knew that she meant what she said. A part of him felt badly because she was Omega's woman. He was breaking the code by sleeping with her in the first place, but resisting her was proving to be a challenge. Dahlia was ready to invest her time into him, but Po wasn't ready. She had been good company and had taken his mind off of Liberty's absence. He appreciated her for that, but he didn't feel for her the way that he had Liberty, and she couldn't hold a candle to Scarlett.

Dahlia was a beautiful woman who didn't give him a hard time. She was a convenient distraction, but he would never wife her. She had shown that she wasn't loyal. The way that she had easily cheated with Po meant that she would easily cheat on him. *Bitches ain't shit,* he thought to himself. He knew that she was a woman who traded up. She chose the winning team, but what would happen when he started to lose? She would be a free agent again, and choosing season would begin. Po didn't want to distract her from the large task ahead of her. If he denied her now it could fuck up his deal. He had to play her smart.

"You sure you ready for that?" he asked.

"I've been ready," she answered sexily as she reached up to kiss him. The doorbell rang, and Po dodged her kiss, moving his head to the right.

"We'll talk about it when you get back. Rocko's here," he said.

Rocko and Dahlia stood in the Customs line, wedding rings on their left fingers as they pretended to be a doting couple. The two were set to fly into South Korea and then cross the border into North Korea by car. Flying directly into a country that had hostile relations with the U.S. would immediately throw up red flags to homeland security. They had to play their hands more than smart in order to pull off this task. Rocko was more nervous than ever. He was used to holding it down in the streets and felt that he was in over his head. *This nigga Po on some straight boss shit,* he thought. He couldn't believe how far up the ladder his man had climbed. They were a long way from Detroit, Michigan.

Liberty threw the covers off her body in a cold sweat as she rushed to the bathroom. The morning sickness was taking a toll on her, and as she hugged the porcelain toilet she closed her eyes in distress. She knew that an abortion would have been the most logical thing to do, but her heart wouldn't let her get rid of her child. Life was growing inside of her. Every time she thought of it she teared up. How could she destroy a miracle so precious?

Liberty missed Po terribly and needed someone to celebrate with in her excitement, but fear stopped her. Dahlia's voice echoed in the back of her mind, reminding her that Po was not fit to raise her child. He wasn't about that life. A drug dealer and kingpin couldn't convert to a family man. *Or could he?* she thought. Liberty desperately wanted to give her child a safe and ordinary life, but with Po that wasn't guaranteed.

As Liberty thought of her current circumstance she realized that nothing was ever promised. If so, she would still be with A'shai. *He deserves to know,* she thought. Liberty mulled over her decision as she dressed, but in the end she knew that it was not her place to keep Po out of his child's life. She grabbed her car keys off the hotel dresser, then hurriedly pulled the duffel bag full of money he had given her out of the closet before rushing out to find him.

When Liberty arrived in Po's driveway she lost her nerve. She sat in her car, staring up at his house with butterflies in her stomach. *Just tell him,* she urged herself as she finally built the courage to walk to the door. She rang the bell and waited impatiently. She wanted to turn and run away with every second that passed, but her feet felt as if they were cemented to the stoop. When Po opened the door, her heart stopped and she became tongue-tied. There she stood, speechless and afraid. She trembled slightly from the magnitude of his presence. It wasn't until that moment that she realized how much she had missed him. His handsome face, intoxicating scent, intimidating stare . . . She missed it all and although she just stubbornly stood there, she really just wanted to jump into his arms.

He didn't speak or even remove the stern look from his face, but the sight of her was like a breath of fresh air. He loved her as she stood before him, unwilling to admit his affection to her aloud. He stepped to the side allowing her to enter. They stood in the foyer, staring at each other. There was so much animosity between them, but in the grand scheme of things Liberty knew that it was petty. The secret that she was keeping was bigger than everything that was stopping them from being together.

Liberty removed the duffel bag from her shoulder and held it out to him. "I don't want it," she said. "You take it. You take it, Po, and make sure that you take care of us. We need you. We are depending on you. I don't want to do this by myself."

Liberty was rambling, and Po frowned in confusion as

she went on. "We weren't even going to come here today. We weren't going to tell you . . ."

Frustrated, Po reached out and pulled her near him, cupping her face in his hands. "Slow down, ma. What are you saying? Who the fuck is 'we'?" he asked in confusion.

Liberty looked at the floor, and then up at him with emotion in her eyes. She was on the verge of tears as her lip began to tremble. "We is . . . me and . . ."

She could barely get the words out she was so full of nervous energy. She was crying because she was happy, scared, sad, overjoyed . . . She was all of these things, and it made it hard for her to speak.

Po softened at the sight of her so distraught. "What's wrong, ma? I haven't seen you in damn near a month. I've been calling you, and I can't get a call back, but now all of a sudden you show up here like this. Talk to me. Are you okay?" he asked.

Liberty looked up at him and knew that he would take care of her. She didn't know how they would work things out or if he would ever be exactly who she wanted him to be, but of one thing she was certain: he would do right by her. In the short time that she had known him, he had proved himself to be a good man.

"I'm pregnant, Po," she whispered.

Po took a step back, and his eyes instinctively shifted to her stomach.

"You're what?" he asked.

"Pregnant," she repeated.

He turned away from her and put his hands on his head

as he closed his eyes. His heart beat in a rhythm that he had never heard before.. It was in that time and space that Liberty became the love of his life.

"I was going to get rid of it, but . . ."

Po turned around with a brief moment of anger in his eyes. It was quickly replaced with love as he spoke. "Why would you do that, ma? This baby . . . our baby, is all I've got. Don't take that away from me."

Liberty nodded as he kissed her lips. She had only been away for a month, but it felt as if she hadn't seen him in years.

"I love you, ma," he whispered as he picked her up off of her feet.

She paused for a minute, wondering for a second if A'shai would be upset with her. But as she looked in Po's eyes she realized that Po was the one here with her. He was the one who had put his seed inside of her. A'shai would always live in her heart, but to the world he was extinct and it was time to move on.

"I love you too," she replied finally.

Po kissed Liberty all the way to his bedroom and stopped as he was about to lay her on the bed. He realized that he had sexed Dahlia in the exact same place, and he didn't want to disrespect Liberty by placing her in the spot where another woman had slept. He made a mental note to get the bed replaced and turned out of the room.

"Where are we going?" Liberty asked as he carried her back into the hall. Po turned into one of his many guest-rooms.

"Make love to me, Po," she whispered as she unfastened his pants.

Po leaned over her, lowering her down onto the bed and as he ravished her body they both felt different this time. With a baby between them they connected on a different level. After taking the biggest loss that anyone could suffer, they now had the biggest gain. They had found love, and as their bodies became one, so did their hearts. They loved each other without remorse as they sexed until their bodies gave out and sleep took over.

NINETEEN

DAHLIA AND ROCKO ESTABLISHED A CONNECTION THAT was invaluable to Po. The Asian diamond market was a billion dollar per year business, and Po had just carved out his piece of that pie. The trip alone had been worth $10,000,000. He had definitely graduated from his days on the block, and he finally understood the bigger picture about which Omega had been schooling him. He was getting stupid bread, and as a result of his success, Rocko, Dahlia, and Ayo were coming up with him. Even after Omega took his cut off the top Po still walked away nice. He was becoming untouchable.

Dahlia couldn't wait to return home. She was sure that after the deal that she had just put in place for Po that he would be eating out of the palm of her hand. She was what he needed in his life; she just had to get him to see that. As Rocko pulled into Po's estate he said, "Tell bro I'll get with him in the A.M. I'm tired as shit. You can fill him in on everything, right?"

Dahlia nodded, and then exited the car, glad that Rocko had decided to call it a night. She entered the house and noticed that it was pitch-black inside. She dropped her luggage at the door and made her way up the stairs, headed to Po's room. She was about to wake him up to the best head he had ever received in his life. Dahlia crept down the hallway and into Po's room, but she frowned when she saw the empty bed. She turned around confused as she stepped back into the hallway.

She knew that he was home because his car was parked in the circular driveway. She headed toward his office, but paused when she saw that one of the guest bedroom doors was closed. Dahlia quietly turned the knob and peeked inside.

Her stomach turned in rage when she saw Liberty lying peacefully in Po's arms. A fire blazed in her eyes as she cursed Liberty in her head. *What the fuck is she doing here? Does he know about the baby? Did she get rid of it?* Her mind raced, and she could feel herself losing control. She had done everything right; she had everything planned perfectly. She was supposed to be Po's queen by now. Being with him would have meant freedom, but also power to reign with him over his budding empire. Liberty was family, but family loyalty went out the window the day that they were snatched away from each other back in Sierra Leone. Now they were distant, and although Liberty thought it was all love between them, Dahlia felt more envy then anything. Jealousy could create hostility where there was once love, and Dahlia was the perfect example of that.

She stormed off and went into her room. She was deter-mined to claim the spot where Liberty rested her head. It didn't matter what it took. Dahlia was not going back to Omega. Her place was not in Sierra Leone.

Po and Liberty held a special brunch at their home to announce the big news to all of their loved ones. As they sat with Rocko, Dahlia, Ayo, and numerous members of the African mafia, they feasted on a catered buffet. Everyone was happy to see Liberty back on Po's arm. Even Rocko had warmed up to her. He respected her character. She was different than a lot of chickens who could have come after Scarlett, and she made his friend happy. If Po liked it, he loved it and would show his support.

"I'd like everyone's attention, please," Po announced as he stood to his feet. "I want to thank everyone here for the role that you have played in my organization. Every player here has an instrumental role on my team. That power move we just made is gon' take us to the top, fam, and as long as I'm eating, everybody at this table is eating with me. Believe that. On another note, I want to introduce the lady in my life to you. A lot of you already know her, but for those who do not, this is Liberty. In eight months, she will be the mother of my child. You protect her life like it is your life. You do for her as you would do for me. If she puts in a call, then you follow her order. Any nigga that she don't like gets cut from the team," Po said with a smile, but only half-jokingly. "So your best bet is to make a good impression on wifey."

Everyone showed Liberty love and congratulated her on the bun she had cooking. Overwhelmed with the amount of loyalty Po had, she knew that she had made the right choice. It wasn't a conventional family, but she and her child had love . . . love from Po's people and love in the streets. It was everything that she didn't want, but now that she had it, it didn't seem so bad.

Dahlia sat back watching from the corner of the room as she sipped her mimosa. She didn't even recognize the sour look on her face until Ayo pointed it out.

"You better fix your face or you'll expose your hand," Ayo said, letting her know he was hip to her game.

Dahlia gave him a cold look and replied, "You better watch your mouth before you find yourself in my crosshairs."

She walked away and put a fake smile on her face as she barely stomached the rest of the brunch. When she saw Po disappear to his upstairs office she followed him discreetly. Sliding into his office and closing the door behind her she took him by surprise.

"Dahlia," he said with a loud exhale, knowing that he owed her an explanation.

"You're back with Liberty," Dahlia commented.

"I am," he said.

Dahlia crossed the room and came close to his face. "But what about us, baby? What about the way I make you feel?" she asked seductively as she rubbed his broad, strong chest. Po brushed her hands off of him. She grabbed at his belt. "She can't suck your dick like me, Po. She can't fuck you like me," she said as she licked her lips slowly.

"Stop," he said as he slapped her hands away once more. Dahlia was persistent and unzipped his fly, grabbing his dick. "Stop!" he said, this time more firmly, grabbing her wrists tightly, causing her to wince in pain.

"What about *us*, Po? You can't tell me we aren't good together," Dahlia argued, angered to the point of tears. She had never been turned down before and having him brush her off now was a bruise to her huge ego.

"Us?" Po chuckled. "There is no us, Dahlia. Liberty's back. She's pregnant with my child. We fucked a couple times. It was good, but it's over now."

Dahlia laughed and folded her arms. "It's far from over, Po," she said in a threatening tone.

Po grabbed her neck swiftly with fire in his eyes. "Don't threaten me, Dahlia. I don't give a fuck who you're affiliated with. I'll send you back to Africa in a pine box," he said through clenched teeth. He realized his grip was too tight when she began to claw at his hand while gasping for air. He loosened his grip slightly, allowing her to breathe but still held her firmly.

"Liberty is your cousin. I don't want to hurt her, and I didn't mean to hurt you. Maybe if she wasn't in the picture things could have been different, but she came back, and I'm not letting anything get in the way of us being together. Liberty can't ever find out about what happened between us, under any circumstance. Let's just keep it professional from now on," he said sternly, then he let her go.

She felt as if he had punched her in the gut. "Professional?" she shot back.

"You're not a bird brain, Dahlia, so let's save the dramatics. You're not built like that. Have some pride about yourself. You want me, but I want her. It is what it is. Now leave my office before I lose my patience."

Dahlia stormed out of the office feeling rejected. She bumped into Liberty on her way down the hall.

"Are you okay?" Liberty asked, but Dahlia just brushed past her without replying.

When Liberty turned around Po was standing in front of her. "What was that about?" she asked.

"Just business. I gave Ayo some of her clients, and she's upset about it. Nothing for you to worry about, ma. Let's go back downstairs and enjoy brunch."

Dahlia sat back, silently seething all day. As everyone catered to Liberty, she slowly rotted with resentment toward her. *She's weak. She has so much power and doesn't even know what to do with it. She can't handle a man like Po, and if it weren't for that damn baby she wouldn't even be competition,* Dahlia thought. She didn't care that a man had come between her and her only living family. She wanted what she wanted, and that was to be seated at Po's left.

Ayo was too perceptive to not notice the tension in the room. Dahlia's lips were fixed in a smile, but it was her conniving eyes that gave her away. The storm that brewed behind her cold stare was category five, and if it didn't veer left it would destroy everything that Po had built.

Ayo was making money with Po, more than he had ever earned with Omega who was a selfish dictator. All of the work that Ayo put in under Omega's command only fattened

Omega's bank account. He fed Ayo and the rest of his men peanuts compared to the full plate that Po shared. Po ruled with love, and Ayo had grown to respect him greatly, but he wasn't blind. He had to speak with Po before the shit got too far out of hand. If Omega found out about Dahlia and Po, then everybody would be cut off. Omega's wrath was blind to guilt. He blamed everybody, and the good thing that they all had going would crash and burn. Women had been the cause of the fall of many empires. He refused to let pussy lead them down the path of destruction.

Ayo approached Po and leaned into his ear. "Can I speak to you for a minute, fam?" he said.

Po nodded, and then excused himself as he followed Ayo outside.

"I know that look," Po said. "That look is not good." He descended his entryway steps, and the two men began to walk around his massive property.

"I'm about to say something to you, and I mean no disrespect. You're my man, and I have come to love you like a brother . . ."

Po stopped walking, looked behind him, and then back at Ayo. He put his hand on Ayo's chest and said, "Ayo, don't beat around the bush or mince words with me, fam. You got something on your chest, speak it."

"You need to put Dahlia back on a flight to Sierra Leone," he said.

"What?" Po said.

"I know you've been fucking her, and if I can tell, how long you think it'll take for Liberty to notice? A jealous woman is a liability. If I'm out of place right now, please let me know, but keeping a bitch like that around is bound to blow up in your face. When your ship sinks, a lot of men will drown with you," Ayo said.

Po threw one arm around Ayo's shoulder and gave him a friendly pat. "Let's enjoy the party, fam," he replied, not admitting guilt but never claiming innocence either, but Po heard Ayo loud and clear. When they reentered his home he approached Rocko and pulled him aside. He leaned in and whispered in his ear. "Get Dahlia out of L.A. ASAP, bro. Ship her ass back to Omega."

He walked away without any explanation and found his place back at Liberty's side. She kissed his cheek and smiled up at him, absolutely glowing. When he looked up he saw Dahlia burning a hole through him with her eyes. Ayo was right. Her time in L.A. had expired, and he had to get rid of her . . . fast.

Dahlia sat in the VIP of Hollywood's trendiest hot spot with her head thrown back over the velvet booth as she received the best head of her life. The young boy between her legs couldn't have been a day older than twenty-one, but his tongue was seasoned, and he pleased her eagerly as the colorful strobe light flickered throughout the darkened room. Dahlia was drunk out of her mind, sulking in her temporary loss to Liberty as she attempted to kill her second bottle of Ace of Spades.

She moved her hips to the slow R&B song as he flicked her clit to the beat. Dahlia's thighs tensed as she felt her orgasm flowing. Her pussy pulsed as she squirted her love all over his lips. The boy sat up and wiped his mouth with the back of his hand.

"My turn," he said.

Dahlia smacked her lips and replied, "Nigga, please." She didn't give head, especially to a nameless little nigga with no bread and no reputation. She reached into her Birkin bag and pulled out a rubber banded knot of money. Arrogantly, she threw it at him, handing him $5,000 like it was chump change. "Get lost," she said as she stood up, drunkenly stumbling her way toward the bathroom. She locked the door behind her, then walked over to the sink and leaned over it. Her legs were so wobbly that they barely held her up. She bent down and wet her face, then took two deep breaths.

Dahlia had never gotten drunk before. She had never frolicked around one of the world's greatest cities, club hopping. She had never had her pussy eaten in a public place. Dahlia never had the freedom to live like a boss, and now that she had tasted it she wouldn't give it up. She would be damned if she went back to the obsolete existence of being Omega's woman. She wanted Po, and she was willing to do anything to get him.

TWENTY

DAHLIA MOANED AS SHE FELT WARM HANDS caress her legs as slept. She smiled, but she was too hungover to open her eyes.

"Hmm, that feels good," she whispered as she turned over onto her back. The sight of Omega sitting at the foot of her bed startled her as she let out a slight scream.

"Oh my goodness! Omega!" she exclaimed as she sat up in shock. She looked around in confusion. "W . . . what are you doing here?"

"Get your things packed. It's time to come home," he said in a stern voice. He looked at the skimpy gold dress that was strewn across the floor. Dahlia's eyes shot to the six-inch heels that lay beside it and knew that he was waiting for an explanation.

"I had to meet with a buyer for Po last night," she said. She came up on her knees and crawled toward him. "I missed you, baby."

243

Omega grabbed Dahlia's face, tightly holding her at the chin and causing her to grimace. His face was set in anger as he looked at her in disgust.

"Omega, you're hurting me," she whispered.

He was livid as he stared at the makeup that she still wore from the night before. After receiving a call from Rocko that Dahlia was getting out of control, he took the first flight out to L.A. He wanted to retrieve her himself, to pop up on her when she least expected it so that he could judge the situation accordingly. Just from the sight of her he knew that Dahlia was having a little too much fun. Her black mascara was smeared under her eyes, making her look as horrible as she felt.

"You smell like a fucking whore," he said, as he frowned at the stale residue of expensive perfume and liquor. "I asked you to come here to watch my money, to help Po, but I see you have been doing a lot more. Your time here is done. Pack your things and meet me downstairs." He stood to his feet, and she cut her eyes at him as he walked to the door. He stopped before he exited her room. "You weren't expecting me, so whose hands did you think were touching your body?"

He left before she could answer, leaving her feeling like a cornered animal with nowhere to run. Her lip trembled as she hopped out of bed. *What the fuck am I going to do?* she thought as she paced back and forth, beating the sides of her head in frustration. The average woman would have appreciated what she had with Omega. He was a provider. He was handsome, powerful, sexy, but Dahlia despised the control. She was too busy looking at Liberty's lawn to water her own, and Liberty's grass was looking real green at the moment.

Bitterly, she threw her things into her bags, and then left them sitting on the bed for Omega's men to retrieve. She took a deep, calming breath to keep her emotions in check, and then put on the face of a demure, submissive mate as she went to find Omega. He stood at the bottom of the staircase, speaking with Po and Liberty. When they saw Dahlia appear they stopped their conversation, and Liberty looked at Dahlia with sad eyes as she watched her cousin descend the stairs.

Stop looking at me like a sick puppy. I'll be back sooner than you think, Dahlia thought.

"I'm ready," Dahlia said as she stood next to Omega. "Can you have one of the men get my bags?"

Omega nodded for one of his bodyguards that stood guard at Po's front door to go retrieve her belongings.

"I'll show you where her room is," Liberty said as she walked ahead of the guard.

Dahlia stared at Po, and he could see that she was outraged. He avoided her as he spoke directly to Omega. "Business is good, Omega. Let's do everything we can to make sure it stays that way. Thank you for extending Dahlia's assistance, but she is no longer needed here. I have all the hands on deck that I need, and I have everything under control. She's the queen in your empire. I have mine now," he said as Liberty came back into sight. All eyes seemed to go to her as the two men silently acknowledged her beauty.

Dahlia's nostrils flared in annoyance. How dare Po just dismiss her! She had helped him secure his place in the diamond trade, and now he was just shooing her away. She felt slighted, but she knew that his change in attitude was due to the delicate situation growing in Liberty's stomach.

"Yes, you do," Omega concurred, nodding his head in approval of Liberty. Beauty had been both a blessing and a curse since her childhood. She had been raped, sold, and manipulated just to exploit it, but she had also attracted love from two great men as well. Her exquisiteness was a double-edged sword.

"Can we go?" Dahlia said, tired of witnessing the gawking session.

"I'll be in touch before the next shipment comes in," Omega said. "You moved from drugs to diamonds. Next, we'll see if you can handle something bigger."

"What's bigger than this?" Po said.

"Women," Omega replied in a hushed whisper. "But that's for a later discussion."

Po nodded and looked back at Liberty. He knew her past would directly conflict with his ambition, but he would cross that bridge when he got to it. *She don't need to know everything,* he thought.

Liberty hugged Dahlia and grabbed both of her hands. "Travel safe, cousin," she said with a warm smile. Dahlia couldn't even muster up one in return. She simply let go of Liberty's hand, and then walked out, livid that she was being forced to leave.

TWENTY-ONE

DAHLIA AND OMEGA SAT ACROSS FROM EACH other at the candlelit table, but neither of them spoke. He gave her the silent treatment during the entire flight, and now as she ate her dinner she didn't know what to say. *How much does he know?* she thought. Her heart pounded inside of her chest, and her hands shook slightly. She couldn't control her nervous jitters, and she cursed herself silently. If she didn't keep her composure she would give her own guilt away before he ever asked any questions.

Omega ran a tight ship and there would be a serious consequence for her disloyalty. He had never mistreated Dahlia, but she had seen his wrath before. The last place she wanted to be was on his bad side, especially now that she was back in his clutches. Being bold was easy when there was an entire ocean that separated them, but here in his presence, she was reminded of how powerful he was. If only he was less controlling, more welcome to sharing his reign with her, then she wouldn't have to plot to replace him.

She had been enslaved in some form for her entire life, always dreaming of being free to move without restrictions. She had gotten a taste of that life in L.A., and now her mind couldn't go back to the strict rules that Omega demanded she follow. It could no longer be his way or the highway. She no longer wanted to ask to go shopping or ask for his money to purchase something. She wanted to be a boss in her own right. Fuck the king and his rules; she wanted to make her own.

"Tell me what happened in L.A." Omega's deep voice boomed with authority, causing her to look up at him.

"What do you mean?" she asked. "Nothing happened."

"You're not a good liar, Dahlia. Don't insult me. I'm giving you a chance to tell me from your own mouth, in your own words. If I hear it from someone else, it will not be good for you."

Dahlia stood and walked around the table, her nails touching the top of the table with her long red fingernails as she approached him. She opened his legs, turning his body toward her. She could see the skepticism in his eyes. He didn't trust her, and she would have to spin this web very carefully in order to trap him. She straddled him, sitting on his lap, with her warm pussy radiating through the fabric of his slacks. She could hear his desire for her in the way that he grunted slightly. His manhood stiffened, and she knew that once he was turned on, her words would sound more believable. Her sex could cloud any man's judgment.

"You're right, Omega. Something did happen in L.A., but before I tell you, I want you to promise me that you won't do anything stupid," she said.

Omega gripped her chin and looked her in the eyes. "Talk," he commanded.

"I wanted to tell you before, but you were making so much money with Po and things were going so well that I didn't want to be the reason everything fell apart," she said, her eyes watering with burden as she shook her head from side to side. *And the Academy Award goes to . . . ,* she thought.

"Tell it to me straight, Dahlia. What happened?" Omega asked. His jaws clenched as he grinded his teeth furiously.

"Po came onto me. He and Liberty were going through problems, and he kissed me. He was drunk, and I told him to stop," Dahlia said, shedding tears.

"Did you fuck him?" Omega asked.

Dahlia looked at him as if his words insulted her. "Of course not, Omega. Is that all you think of me? I love *you,* Omega. I was over there because you asked me to be. I would never . . ." she paused for dramatic effect as she stood from his lap. "I can't believe you would ask me something like that."

Omega stood and pulled her close, then said, "Stop crying, Dahlia. You should have told me sooner!" He was outraged at the disrespect. He had done nothing but show Po love by putting him on, and *this* was how he was repaid. "I'll handle it. I tried to show him how to get money. I tried to put him on the winning team. Now he's cut off. No more diamonds, no more coke. Nobody eats! I'ma starve the li'l nigga to death!"

Dahlia watched him storm out of the room, and then crept to his office door as he put in the phone call to cut Po out of the diamond trade. Omega was connected worldwide. He had people everywhere, and when he put in the order to excommunicate someone, it was strictly followed. Po wouldn't be able to hustle knockoff bags if he wanted to. Omega seized all that without remorse. It was that part of Omega that made Dahlia wet and reminded her of their earlier years when she had fallen head over heels for him. Little did Omega know, once he placed that call he was collateral damage. He was playing right into her hand.

The moonlight illuminated Dahlia's bedroom casting a blue glow over her sleeping husband as she lay folded up beneath him. The red numbers on the digital clock were her focal point. She didn't even blink, she was so focused. She had been lying in the exact same position, contemplating her next move. The scent of Omega sickened her. He was not who she wanted to be underneath right now and what was meant to be a loving embrace as she slept felt like unbreakable chains.

3:54 A.M.

3:55 A.M.

3:56 A.M.

The minutes ticked by mind-numbingly slow, torturing Dahlia to the point of insanity. She was losing control, and she desperately needed to put things back on track. She didn't foresee her jealousy causing Po to send her away. She had underestimated his affection for Liberty. She wouldn't make that same mistake twice. *I can't do anything with Omega's watchful eye on me at all times,* she thought. She eased her body from underneath Omega and paused when he shifted in his sleep. Her heart almost stopped from the fear of him awaking. Dahlia looked at him. He had been good to her. He had rescued her from the streets of Sierra Leone and showed her a life that she would have never known without him. His one mistake was keeping her too close, protecting her too much, secluding her from everything. Dahlia was suffocating from too much love from Omega. A man in his position came with too many chains, too many rules, and she was about to break free.

Dahlia slipped her hand under her pillow and pulled out the hunting knife that she had hid there the night before. She touched the blade softly. It was so sharp that it cut her finger slightly. A small dot of blood appeared on her fingertip, and she licked it away. She was like a shark, and the taste of blood made her thirsty for more. She took the blade and slid it across Omega's neck. His eyes shot open, and his hand instantly went up to his neck as he bled out. He stared at her, pleading with his eyes as he gurgled, struggling to breathe.

Dahlia stood as he reached for her, moving out of the way just before he touched her, and watched with a stone face as Omega's life slowly faded away. It looked like a painful death, but Dahlia never blinked. She was cold, and in his last moments on this earth, Omega finally saw her true colors. She was the devil in human form.

Omega's funeral was like a huge parade as his coffin was carried on the shoulders of his henchmen as they proceeded through the town of Sierra Leone. The mourning viewers that crowded the streets cried for the generous man they had come to know. Dahlia and the African mafia clapped loudly, slowly, in honor of the old burial ritual. It was to ensure that Omega was really dead and not just in a trance. They clapped to wake him, but everyone was well aware that it was for tradition only. Omega had been murdered. His neck slit from ear to ear. There was no coming back from that.

Dahlia's face was covered by a black veil. The black peplum style dress she wore matched the black lace gloves that covered her hands. She had dressed to a model's standard for the occasion and had made sure that Omega was just as sharp. There was no way that she would send him home half-assed. When he was alive, he did everything in style, so in death she gave him the ceremony worthy of an African king. *That's the least I can do considering,* she thought in amusement. Dahlia marched at the head of the procession with her head lowered until they finally reached the cemetery. She played the grieving widow well.

Po walked up toward the grave but was stopped before he could pay his respects. Dahlia watched as Omega's men turned him away. The anger on Po's face could be seen a mile away. The last thing that Dahlia wanted was a scene at

Omega's funeral. As the clergyman read a passage from the Bible, Dahlia excused herself, quietly slipping away from the group to walk over to the altercation.

"Dahlia, what the fuck is this? I'm not welcome here?" he asked, his brows dipped in irritation.

"It was Omega's wishes, Po. He had you cut off," Dahlia whispered.

Po looked perplexed as Omega's men stood between him and Dahlia, who looked sympathetic. "Meet me at my place in an hour," she said. "Now please go and let me lay him to rest."

She watched Po retreat, and she had to check the smile that spread on her face. Omega's death had brought Po back to Africa without Liberty, and it was the perfect opportunity for Dahlia to level the playing field. Before Omega's untimely demise he had ensured that Po be locked out of the game. Dahlia was equally connected and knew all of Omega's contacts extremely well. She knew that they would allow her to fill Omega's shoes. Dahlia wasn't naïve, however. She knew that a woman with that much power could not rule without having a strong man as the face to protect the empire. Niggas would try her. They would test her left and right, assuming that she was too weak to defend her throne, and she would be without Po. Omega's will was strong even in death, and no one would go against his wishes to railroad Po, except Dahlia. She could easily unlock the doors for Po and welcome him back into the fold of things. She could be his new connect . . . if he saw things her way.

* * *

"Why the fuck was I cut off?" Po asked as soon as Dahlia opened the door. Her red eyes and solemn face immediately made him regret the question.

"Hi to you too, Po," Dahlia replied as she stepped to the side and allowed him to enter into her home.

"I'm sorry. I just don't understand. How did all of this happen? Did you see who killed him?" Po asked.

She shook his head. "I didn't. It was dark, and I couldn't see much. I heard the struggle. By the time I turned on the lights Omega's neck had been slit. I only saw the back of the killer as he ran out. I called for help, but by the time help came, Omega died in my arms. It all happened so fast, I didn't know what to do," she whispered as a single tear slid down her cheek. She quickly wiped it off of her face. She shook her head and looked up at Po. "You want some coffee, some food or something? I know you had a long flight," she offered.

"I want answers, ma. Since when have I been cut off? Omega and I were doing good business . . . profitable business," Po argued.

"He thought you were skimming money from him. He wouldn't tell me everything. You know how private Omega was, but I overheard him on the phone saying that you had been stealing money. Telling him that you were selling the diamonds for a higher price than what you told him and keeping the difference. I tried to tell him that it wasn't like that, but he wouldn't listen," Dahlia said.

"Who the fuck planted that seed, Dahlia? You're not telling me everything. There's nobody close enough to me to know how much I'm selling shit for. Who would tell him that, especially knowing that it wasn't true?" Po yelled in frustration.

Dahlia knew that if she threw a name out directly that Po would not listen, but if he came up with a suspect on his own he would hear it loud and clear.

"I don't know, Po! I told you a long time ago that I would do anything to be there for you! Don't you think if I knew I would tell you?" Dahlia defended, crying. "The only people who even knew about the diamonds were me, Ayo, Rocko, and Trixie . . ."

"But Rocko and Trixie didn't even have access to Omega . . ." Po's words drifted off as his mind pointed him to Ayo. *He the only nigga that even knew how to get to Omega,* Po thought.

Dahlia saw Po putting the pieces together in his mind and knew that he was accusing exactly whom she had implicated. Ayo was a problem and a thorn in Dahlia's side. Ayo would stand in her way because he saw right through her, but if she had her way, Po would knock Ayo for her.

"I can't think about this right now," Dahlia said, feeling overwhelmed as she took a seat. "That isn't even important right now. What am I going to do without Omega? Somebody came into our home and murdered him. Am I next?" she asked.

Po sat beside her and put one arm around her shoulder. "No, you're not next, ma. You know the risks that Omega took. There's no telling what went bad or what enemies he had. Everything will be okay," Po comforted her.

Dahlia rested her head on his chest. Po knew that without Omega's blessing that he would never be able to do business out of Africa again. There were no diamonds as clear as the ones coming out of the mines of Sierra Leone. He needed a new connect. Po thought about stepping away from the game. He didn't need to be dealt back in. In the short time that he had done business with Omega he had accumulated more wealth than one man could spend, but the power fed his ego. He was addicted to the money and wasn't ready to let go of the hold he had over his empire.

"I need this connect," he mumbled.

Dahlia raised her head and touched his cheek with her hand. "I can get you the diamonds, Po. I told you that I was ready to ride for you before you had me exiled from L.A.," she said with a small smile, only half-jokingly.

"You were out of pocket, ma. You were wearing your heart on your sleeve. You know my situation," he replied.

"I know the connect, Po. He won't do business with you, but he *will* do business with me," Dahlia whispered. "We can be a team, Po. We've always played so well together." Her voice was low and seductive as her lips touched his ear as she spoke. His loins tingled from her touch. Dahlia's sex was the best he had ever had, and she had a way of working her tongue that made his knees buckle. Dahlia was like that poisonous apple in the Garden of Eden. He just had to pick her. His hands fell down her back until they rested on her round behind, and he pulled her into his crotch.

"What about your precious Liberty?" Dahlia asked, breathing heavy in lust.

Po ripped her shirt open and feasted on her breasts. "Don't talk about her," he said as he ravished her body, pushing her against a wall.

"Fuck me, Po," Dahlia said as she stuck her sweet tongue in his mouth.

Her body always tasted so good. It was as if she used the syrup from the earth to lotion her skin, and Po indulged in her, sopping her up as she removed his shirt. Every place she touched caused goose bumps to appear on his skin. Dahlia made her way south, her warm tongue licking a trail to the V cuts that outlined his lower abdomen. She gripped his stiff penis firmly and licked around his chocolate rod, then engulfed it. She sucked on his dick gently while her hands jerked him off, twisting and turning as he fucked her face. The pleasure she was giving him was irresistible, and Po was backed up. With Liberty pregnant, he felt that she was too delicate to be intimate with so it had been awhile. His head fell back as Dahlia slurped sloppily on him, making sure to keep her mouth nice and wet. Po's body tensed as he let go. He tried to pull away from her, but Dahlia grabbed his ass and kept him close as she swallowed every drop of his nectar.

"Hmm," she moaned. "I missed you."

He adjusted himself, and she stood to her feet. "There's a lot more where that came from, Po. We're good together, baby. You'll see soon enough."

Dahlia pulled her hair up into a ponytail and eyed him

sexily as he watched her retreat to her room, hoping that he would follow.

Po shook his head and let his body fall down on the couch. For some reason he couldn't resist Dahlia. Telling her no was damn near impossible. He had hoped that sending her back to Africa would be the answer to his problems, but now that Omega had died things had changed. She was going to be around, and if she could get the diamonds he would be working hand in hand with her. He would have to tread lightly to keep the two women in his life in balance. Of course, Liberty came first, but Dahlia was hard to turn away, especially when she knew how to make him feel so good.

TWENTY-TWO

THE KNOCK ON HER DOOR WAS INEVITABLE, and her heart beat quickly as she slowly stood. The La Perla silk robe she wore was feminine, sexy. It hugged her body in all the right places and left everything to the imagination. Dahlia was a master seductress and knew that it was more appealing for a man to wonder what lay underneath than for her to lay it out on the table. That's where other women fucked up. They were too sexual. There was no chase. Dahlia was like a rabbit at a dog race. You had to chase her around the world before you got the prize for catching her.

Dahlia strutted in six-inch heels until she reached her front door. She smiled seductively as she pulled it open. She knew exactly who had come knocking. She was expecting him. In fact, she had boldly invited him.

"Hello, Zulu," she greeted, staring Omega's old connect in the eyes with deep sincerity. "Thank you for coming."

"No problem, Dahlia. One of my best men has fallen. You were his wife. There is no way I would not have come to your aid when you called upon me. What do you need? Money?" he asked.

Dahlia shook her head, declining the money offer. "I need diamonds," she whispered in his ear as she gripped the collar of his white button-down shirt. "And I'll do anything to get them."

Zulu's eyes opened to the size of small saucers as the tip of her tongue wet his ear. He wasn't used to this aggressive nature in a woman. Most women in Africa were too afraid to be so pushy with a man; even their husbands didn't get to experience the inner freak that dwelled inside of them. Zulu turned to the two suited men that stood behind him. They stood stone faced and obedient. Zulu never went anywhere without protection. He cleared his throat, slightly embarrassed by Dahlia's flirting. He had a wife and children at home. He kept his playthings hidden from all eyes, so the fact that Dahlia had come onto him in front of his guards didn't please him.

"Check the house, and then wait for me in the car," Zulu ordered.

The men pushed past Dahlia, and she stepped back, crossing her arms as the two men quickly went through her entire home, securing the area.

"There's no one here. It's all clear," one of the men announced.

"Then leave me," Zulu replied.

The men exited, and Dahlia stepped toward Zulu and

stood directly in front of him. Zulu turned around as if he were about to leave, and then out of nowhere, he spun back, slapping the taste out of Dahlia's mouth.

The salty taste of blood filled her mouth as a slight cut formed in the corner of her lips. She wiped it away with the back of her hand, and then pressed her lips against Zulu's.

Zulu roughly pushed her back against a wall. He shoved with such force that her head put a crack in the drywall. She winced in pain, but then her mouth fell open in pleasure as he held her hands above her head with one hand while molesting her neck with his tongue. Zulu's large, chiseled body easily overpowered Dahlia as he tore open her robe with his free hand.

"You want to throw the pussy at me? Now I'm going to take it," Zulu said. His voice was so deep that his words sounded animalistic, as if he were growling in her ear.

"You don't have to take it, Zulu. I'm giving it to you," Dahlia whispered in pants of ecstasy as he slid two fingers inside of her. He removed his fingers and dipped them into his mouth, closing his eyes as he savored her sweet nectar. Dahlia pulled out a condom from her bra and opened it with her teeth. "Put it on," she said.

"Mmm," he moaned. Hurriedly he unzipped his pants and let them fall around his ankles. His dick was mandigo hard and was the largest, thickest, juiciest piece of male flesh that Dahlia had ever experienced. He slid the condom on anxiously, then lifted her and pulled her ass cheeks apart as he sat her on his crotch, inserting himself inside of her.

"Oooh!"

The moan escaped her lips against her will as he fucked her against the wall. Her pussy ached in a good way as he roughly pounded her out. Dahlia could tell that he wasn't being fucked at home. At home, he was being forced to make love, but here inside of Dahlia's lair, he was in true form. At the essence of his being he was an animal.

Man.

Lion.

Conqueror.

He was all these things with only one mission on his mind—to bust his nut. He commanded Dahlia's body, sucking her huge black nipples as he hit the back of her womanhood. She had to admit he was working her over. This was the best sex she ever had in her life. Zulu was twenty years her senior and was seasoned in the art of pleasing a woman. He removed his erect penis from her and got on his knees to taste her. He spread her pussy lips outward and ran his hot tongue up her walls, causing her knees to buckle. He pulled her waist down, causing her to sit on his face as he devoured her.

Dahlia's legs shook uncontrollably. Zulu had no limits. He stuck his tongue in her rear and warmed her there as well, sending Dahlia into convulsions. He knew every button to push, as if he had designed her body himself. Dahlia looked down and noticed that he was stroking his manhood, his black, firm hand moving up and down on his rod. The visual alone took Dahlia to the point of no return and her orgasm came down. She melted into his mouth.

Dahlia climbed off of him and grabbed his hand, leading him to the couch.

"Turn around," she whispered. He did as he was told and Dahlia put her knee between his legs to spread them and bend him over the couch. Then she got on her knees and licked the crack of his ass. She reached around and grabbed his dick, slowly masturbating him as she let her tongue please his backside.

When she felt his rod begin to pulsate, she knew that the rumors of homosexuality were true. She had overheard Omega saying that Zulu liked to have sexual relations with some of his soldiers, and there was no doubt in her mind that this was a fact. She reached under a couch cushion and grabbed the strap-on dildo. Quickly, she placed it in the rim of his rectum.

"What the fuck are you doing?" Zulu asked as he turned around and grabbed Dahlia by the neck.

"Relax, baby. It's just you and me here. I want to make you feel *real* good," Dahlia whispered. She put the dildo in her mouth and licked it seductively. Then she put her hands on his shoulders and turned him back around, bending him over once again. "Relax," she coached.

Dahlia stuck the dildo up Zulu's ass, and he yelped in pleasure as he threw it back for her. Dahlia wanted to burst into laughter. *This big gay-ass nigga,* she thought as she rammed him anally. He masturbated as she played with his anus until he couldn't take it any longer.

"Ah! Ah!" he moaned as he shot his load off, his semen so backed up that it flew out of the tip of his dick.

Dahlia stepped back, and then picked up her robe. She slowly redressed, waiting for him to turn around and face her.

Zulu looked at Dahlia, and she stared him in the eyes. The look of lust she wore earlier was replaced by a look of determination. She had let him have his fun, now it was her turn to get what she wanted.

"Now let's talk," Dahlia said. "I need diamonds, and I need them at a better price than what you were giving to Omega."

Zulu laughed as he stepped into his pants.

"And why would I do that? You know that diamonds are not a woman's game, and the price is the price. I was giving Omega a good deal," Zulu said.

"You were raping Omega. He was stupid enough to pay top dollar, but I want the discount. You see, you will do business with me, and you will give me the deal of a lifetime," Dahlia said with a sneaky smile.

"Oh really? Now, tell me why would I do that? That tight little pussy isn't *that* good," Zulu said arrogantly.

"Let me show you something," Dahlia said as she walked over to the entertainment system and grabbed a remote control. She pressed a button, and instantly, Zulu's image came up on her seventy-inch television screen. His loud moans echoed through the house as the sexual escapade they just had played before him.

"You bitch! You recorded me!" Zulu said as he stormed toward her.

"Uh-uh!" Dahlia warned. "This system is hooked up to the Internet. I press one button, and it goes viral. The fact that you like to get butt fucked will have 1,000,000 views on YouTube by next week. Imagine the look on your wife's face when she sees this. What about your soldiers? Your business partners? Who will respect you after this?" Dahlia was like Picasso when it came to the art of blackmail. She had mastered that craft.

Zulu wanted to snap her neck, and he breathed like a bull as he contemplated her words.

"If you supply me with the diamonds you never have to worry about this seeing the light of day," she said. "But my deal is only good for a few more seconds. In fact, I upload this video in 5, 4, 3, 2—"

"Okay!" Zulu yelled. "You have yourself a connect!"

Zulu stormed out of her house, and Dahlia smiled to herself. Po wouldn't be able to resist having her by his side when he found out the deal that she had just brokered.

"How did you get Zulu to lower the price?" Po asked excitedly as Dahlia stood in front of him. She knew that she was playing a dangerous game with such a powerful man. As long as she was in Africa, Zulu's reach would be far, so to ensure her safety, she hopped on the first flight back to L.A. to deliver the news to Po in person.

"If I told you, I'd have to slit your throat in your sleep," she said coyly. Her mind flashed to Omega's murder briefly, and she smiled because Po didn't know the truth behind her words.

"You're the shit, ma!" Po said as he hugged her, lifting her from her feet and spinning her around.

Liberty walked into the room and frowned in confusion. "What's going on now?" she asked.

Po put Dahlia down and couldn't contain the smile on his face. "Dahlia's a fucking genius."

"I thought you were staying in Africa," Liberty said.

"Nah, ma," Po answered for her. "I need her here now. She's in L.A. permanently. Help her get comfortable."

Liberty was slightly taken aback by Dahlia's presence. She was looking forward to the idea of living alone with Po, and she felt as if Dahlia was intruding into their lives. *Stop being selfish. She just lost Omega,* Liberty scolded herself.

"Of course," Liberty said. "I'm so sorry about Omega. I can't even imagine how you must be feeling."

"Thank you, cousin. How are you?" Dahlia asked.

Liberty rubbed her stomach and said, "I can't see the baby bump yet, but I definitely feel it. I'm sick all the time. They should call morning sickness, all-day sickness."

"Aww, poor baby. Well, now that I'm back, I'll have to take care of you. I know Po is busy with business so you must be lonely all the time," Dahlia said, sneakily pointing out one of Po's flaws.

Liberty shook her head and went to Po's side. "Actually, he hasn't left my side since he found out."

Po leaned down to kiss her, and Dahlia saw red. Vomit and bile rose up in her mouth, but she was able to swallow it down and keep the fake smile plastered on her face. Seeing Po so affectionate to Liberty made Dahlia sick to her stomach. She knew that she would have to break their bond. It seemed as though Liberty's pregnancy had brought them closer together, and Dahlia wasn't about to let some bastard child stand in the way of what she wanted. The baby had to go.

Rocko sat in the leather chair across from Po's desk silently thinking about the repercussions to his actions. His head hung low and his fingers were intertwined as Po's order rang in his ear. Rocko had never questioned Po's actions before, but this time it didn't feel right. What Po wanted Rocko to do felt wrong.

"You know I've never second-guessed you, my nigga, but I have to ask you . . . are you *sure* about this?" Rocko asked.

Po nodded his head. "The nigga got to go. Rock his ass to sleep and make sure he feels it," Po instructed.

Rocko stood and locked hands with Po, but doubt filled his mind. He had never had a conscience before, but his gut was telling him to protest against Po's rule. But being the loyal goon that he was, he kept his mouth shut and headed out of the house. He went to his car and hopped in the driver's side.

"Everything good?" Ayo asked.

Rocko nodded. "Yeah, fam. Everything's one hunnid. He

just added a job for me. I got to meet this nigga under the Santa Monica pier."

"Let's do it," Ayo replied.

Rocko nodded his head to the beat of Drake's latest hit as he guided his car through the city traffic. "Yo, roll up for me, bro. Let's blaze one," Rocko said.

Ayo pulled a blunt out of the glove box and replied, "You left me waiting so long at Po spot I rolled one while I was passing time." Ayo lit the blunt and took a deep pull before passing it to Rocko.

Rocko hit the cush-filled cigarillo as smoke filled the car.

"You got family back in Africa, Ayo? A bitch and some kids?" Rocko asked, feeling the effects of the blunt.

"You stateside mu'fuckas real loose with your lips," Ayo said with a laugh. "I don't refer to my woman as a bitch. I have someone back home, and we have one son together. I'm applying for citizenship here, and then plan to bring them here when shit is established. This street game ain't forever for me, Rocko. As soon as my ducks are in order, I'm making my exit and living right."

"I feel you," Rocko replied. "I'm in it until the casket drop. That's why I don't keep no steady hoes."

Ayo cleared his throat, and Rocko laughed as he hit the blunt. "My bad, fam. I mean, I don't keep no steady woman, and I don't have any kids. If something happened to me it wouldn't be fair to them. But I see my niggas like you and Po with families. If anything ever happened to where you couldn't take care of them, I'd step in. They would be straight. That's what a real nigga do."

"Indeed," Ayo answered as he took the blunt. "Appreciate that."

Ayo noticed that they had arrived, and he nodded. "This is it? Where we supposed to be meeting your man? Who is it again?"

Rocko shrugged. "Some nigga Po know. He meeting us under the pier on the beach. Let's go."

Ayo slid out of the car, and Rocko followed. The carnival-like atmosphere on top of the pier was crowded and noisy, but the beach below was deserted. It was so dark that they could barely see underneath the pier.

They stepped out onto the sand, and Rocko looked around to ensure that it was deserted. When they were at the edge of the water Ayo stepped underneath the pier. The waves crashed into the wooden columns that held up the pier, providing a peaceful soundtrack to the night.

"Where is he?" Ayo asked.

His question was answered when he felt the cold steel of Rocko's gun on the back of his head.

"I meant what I said about your lady and your son. Rest in peace, my nigga," Rocko said. He pulled the trigger just as the roller coaster above them zoomed across the track. The ride was so noisy that no one heard the gunshot that ended Ayo's life. His body hit the sand with a thud, and Rocko pushed him into the water, allowing the waves to carry him out to sea.

Po had told Rocko to kill Ayo slow for his betrayal, but Rocko couldn't torture the nigga that he had spent every day with for the past few months. Rocko felt in his bones that Po was calling out the wrong play, but as his lieutenant, it wasn't his place to ask questions. Rocko snuffed Ayo's lights out because that's what the order had been, but out of respect, he made it quick, and he hoped that the weed helped to make it painless. Dahlia had planted a seed of deceit in Po's head that had caused him to have Ayo hit. Rocko had no idea how true his intuition was. He had just killed an innocent man.

TWENTY-THREE

LIBERTY HUGGED THE TOILET AS SHE VOMITED her soul into the bowl. Her body was so weak. She had no idea that carrying a child would be so hard and the further into her pregnancy that she got, the more symptoms arose. Po held her hair and rubbed her back as he tried his best to comfort her. He felt horribly because it was his seed that was causing her so much pain. Liberty had demanded that he take her to three different doctors because they all told her that she was just fine, but she didn't feel fine. In fact, it felt as if she were dying in order to birth this little person.

"I can't keep anything down," she moaned miserably in between heaves.

"Everything is going to be okay, ma. Just be strong for our little one. You can do this," Po said supportively.

"And what the hell are *you* going to do?" Liberty asked whining, because she felt that she was going through all the hard stuff while Po just watched. "You got to do the fun part. I have to put up with this."

Po couldn't help but laugh as Liberty pulled herself up from the floor.

"It's not funny!" she cried as she hit Po on the chest.

"Why don't you take a warm bath? Relax, and I'll go get you some crackers, cheese, and sparkling cider," Po suggested.

She nodded and reached up for a kiss, but Po dodged her lips. "No offense, ma, but you smell like throw-up," he said with a charming smile.

Liberty shook her head pathetically and said, "I can't believe I have seven more months of this torture!!"

Po kissed her on the forehead and walked out of the room. He went to the kitchen to make Liberty a light meal and saw Dahlia standing over the blender. Fresh fruit littered the counter.

"Oh, hey!" she said in surprise when she noticed him standing in the doorway. She quickly grabbed the small, crushed up pills in front of her and threw them into the blender. Then she pressed the button and made the blades spin, dissolving the pills into the smoothie she was preparing. "Lib is having a hard time, huh?"

Po nodded and said, "Yeah, that baby's fucking her up."

"Well, I think a fresh fruit smoothie will make her feel better. It's not solid so she shouldn't have a hard time keeping it down, and it's healthy for the baby," Dahlia said.

She poured the concoction into a glass and placed a straw inside. "There you go."

"Thanks, Dahlia," he replied as he took the glass and headed out. He stopped and turned around abruptly. "Thanks for understanding. She's pregnant, and she needs us both. I don't want it to be uncomfortable between us . . ."

Dahlia waved her hand dismissively. "Don't worry about it, Po. I know my place. We're partners now. I'll never blow up your spot, and I'll keep it professional, unless you ask me to do otherwise," she said, openly flirting with him. "Anytime you want me to . . ."

"We can't, Dahlia. Not anymore," Po replied. "It's good, ma. Very good," he said as he eyed her voluptuous body, "but she's the mother of my child."

Dahlia nodded and watched him walk away to cater to Liberty. She smirked and mumbled, "She won't be the mother of your child for long." She pulled out the bottle of Plan-B pills that she had purchased from a street dealer and gripped it tightly in her hands. She read the warning:

Do not take if already pregnant. Can cause miscarriage.

She would stuff those smoothies down Liberty's throat every day if she had to. There was no way that Dahlia was letting that baby be born into the world. It was the only thing standing between her and Po. At this point, Dahlia wasn't even sure if it was her attraction to Po that made her want him. Dahlia just didn't like to be told she couldn't have him. It only made her crave him more, and anyone who knew her well knew that she refused to lose.

* * *

Po fed Dahlia's smoothies to Liberty every day, and Liberty never questioned what she was ingesting. She trusted Po too much to ask what was being put in it, and because she barely left her room she had no clue that it was Dahlia that was actually making them. Dahlia was slowly sabotaging Liberty's pregnancy and felt no remorse about it. It was one of the sacrifices in the war she had waged against Liberty. The only problem was Liberty didn't even know she was fighting one. She couldn't defend herself when she had the enemy sleeping in her home, right beneath her nose.

Po and Liberty descended the stairs as Dahlia went into the kitchen to prepare another batch of her magic potion. She knew that they were headed to a doctor's appointment, and she hoped that they came back with bad news. Dahlia was getting impatient. *When are these pills going to work?* she thought.

"We'll be back a little later. We're going to the doctor's, and then I'm going to see if some shopping will make Liberty feel better," Po said as he wrapped one arm around her shoulder and kissed her cheek.

"Nothing is going to make me feel better. I'll feel better once this baby is out of me," she said.

That will make two of us, Dahlia thought. "Have fun you guys," she said aloud.

Po nodded and replied, "Lock the door behind us."

She waited until she saw Po's car disappear from sight before she rushed into the kitchen. She was finally home alone so she could experiment with her smoothies and try to make them as potent as possible without altering the taste. She had been spoon-feeding Liberty the Plan-B pills, only putting a little bit in at one time because she didn't want Liberty to detect it, but her patience was running thin. Watching Po's love for Liberty grow by the day was disgusting. Liberty only had one advantage, and as soon as that was out of the equation the playing field would be equal. She couldn't snatch Po as long as he was playing the role of doting father.

She pulled all of the fruit out of the refrigerator, and then pulled the Plan-B pill bottle out of her handbag. She put it on the center island, and then grabbed the blender from out of the cabinet.

"This fucking baby is messing up everything! Po would have been mine if it wasn't for Liberty's stupid ass getting pregnant!" Dahlia mumbled harshly as she took a silver spoon and crushed the pills into a fine dust. "This bitch is in my fucking way . . . stupid bitch!" Dahlia's frustration was on ten. She had all of her ducks in a row, and Liberty was the only loose end.

"What the fuck is wrong with you, bitch?"

The voice behind her caused Dahlia to freeze. She immediately put down the spoon as she turned to find Trixie standing behind her. Trixie held a white bag in her hand and she held it up slowly. "I know Lib's been sick so I brought her some soup . . ." Trixie peered around Dahlia at the countertop behind her.

"Mind your own business," Dahlia said.

"What are you doing?" Trixie asked. She pushed past

Dahlia and saw the white pills crushed up on the counter. She noticed the fruit that was thrown into the blender.

"These are the smoothies that Liberty's been drinking?" Trixie asked. She turned and picked up the pill bottle. "Plan B!" She knew exactly what the pills were for. She fed them to her own hoes on the strip to ensure that they didn't come home pregnant. Trixie had also seen the devastating effects that those pills could have on an expectant mother. She had made the mistake of giving one to a ho that was two months in and within a week she had miscarried. Trixie put two and two together, then opened her mouth in disbelief. All the femininity left her body as her voice deepened to its natural octave.

"What the fuck are you doing to her?" Trixie turned toward, Dahlia to confront her, but stopped dead in her tracks when she saw Dahlia standing behind her with a .22 in her hand.

"Bitch, you done lost your fucking mind," Trixie said. She pulled off her wig and removed her earrings, placing them on the table. "What, you gon' shoot me, ho? How you going to lift my big 200 pound ass up outta here to hide the body? Huh, bitch? You're poisoning your cousin! Do you know what that will do to their baby?"

Dahlia chambered a bullet into the head of the gun and screamed, "I don't have to hide your fucking body, you fucking faggot. You shouldn't have come here today, Trixie, but now I can't let you leave. Get your ass in the basement!" Dahlia said as she put the gun to Trixie's head and forced her to move.

"Ooohh, you sneaky, dirty bitch," Trixie said. The situation was too serious for Trixie to put on any character. She was all-man as she walked down the basement steps. "What did Liberty ever do to you?"

"Stop talking," Dahlia said coldly. "See, this wasn't in my plan, but it's brilliant actually. You came here today to rob Po's safe. I had to stop you, so I shot you," Dahlia explained.

"Liberty will never believe you. She knows me!" Trixie said.

"Liberty doesn't have to believe it. Po will," Dahlia replied. "Now turn around." Trixie slowly turned, and without even thinking twice, Dahlia put a bullet between her eyes.

Trixie dropped to the floor instantly, and a foul stench filled the room as her bowels released in death. Dahlia quickly went up to her room and removed one of her guns from the top of her closet. She had an arsenal of dirty guns that she had purchased off the streets of L.A. She may have been a female, but she was never unarmed. Dahlia stayed strapped so that no one would try to test her. In this circumstance she needed to make it look as if shooting Trixie was self-defense. She ran back to the basement, grabbed Trixie's hand, and wrapped it around the gun.

Next, Dahlia removed her cell phone and dialed Po's number. When he answered the performance began. She burst into tears instantly.

"Po . . . Po, please, you have to come home. Please turn around. Trixie . . . I shot her! Please hurry!" Dahlia cried. She hung up without saying anything further, then stepped over Trixie's body with a smirk on her face. "Let the games begin."

Po immediately called Rocko who met him at his home. They rushed into the house with Liberty on their tails, and as soon as Liberty saw Trixie's body she rushed to Trixie's side and fell to her knees. "No! No! No! What happened?" Liberty yelled as she looked up at Dahlia.

"I don't know," Dahlia said shakily as she put her hand to her forehead in distress, forming tears of her own. Her hands shook. Po touched Dahlia's shoulders and made her face him. "It all happened so fast," she cried as she looked into his eyes.

"I need you to calm down and explain it to me, Dahlia," he said grimly.

Rocko went to Liberty and picked her up from the floor. She shook her head from side to side, distraught that after everything Trixie had been through, she had died like this.

"How could you do this to her?" Liberty shouted.

Po shot Rocko a look that told him to remove Liberty from the basement.

"Yo, Lib, let's get you upstairs. You don't need to see this," Rocko said.

"No! Trixie was my friend," Liberty protested angrily.

"I was upstairs when I heard the front door open. I was stupid. I left the front door unlocked after you guys left. I thought you had come back for something, but it was Trixie. When she saw me she pointed a gun at me and forced me into the basement. She tried to make me open the safe. She came here to steal the diamonds. She was going to kill me! I didn't have a choice! I had to shoot her before she shot me!"

"That's a lie!" Liberty shouted.

"Liberty!" Po barked, louder than he intended to. "Let her speak," he said, this time in a calmer voice.

"I'm sorry, Po. I didn't know what to do. It just happened. I pulled the trigger before I could think. I thought I was going to die," Dahlia cried. Her eyes were so sincere that Po felt sorry for her. He pulled her close for a hug and felt that she was shivering in fear.

"It's okay. I'm home now. Me and Rocko gon' take care of it. You did good, ma," Po said.

"What?! Po! Trixie wouldn't do this! She wouldn't steal," Liberty argued.

"Didn't you say she stole from you back in the day, Liberty? Open your eyes! The bitch was dirty. Dahlia gave her what she deserved," Po said harshly.

Rocko shook his head and spoke up. "I got this. I'll clean this mess up, fam."

Po placed a hand on Rocko's shoulder, then escorted Dahlia to her room, consoling her as he went.

Liberty paced her room for hours waiting for Po to emerge from Dahlia's bedroom. She was livid and her mind was racing. Liberty saw a thousand holes in Dahlia's flimsy story, and it was at that point that she began to look at Dahlia through a suspicious lens. *I know Trixie. There is no way she came here to rob that safe.* Finally, Po came into the room.

"She's resting now," Po said. "She was traumatized."

"She's lying, Po," Liberty blurted out. "Why would Trixie come here to rob you? She could have easily just waited until the next job to flee with your diamonds. You've sent her across country, and she came back with your money on point every time! Think about it, Po!"

"I'm done talking about it, Liberty. Just stay in your place, ma. Don't worry about my business. I hate that you had to see that. Just let me handle it," Po replied.

"Po!"

"Liberty! I said drop it! A murder just happened where I rest my head. Let me think," Po shouted.

Liberty stormed out of the room. She saw Dahlia heading toward her. Liberty had a gut feeling that there was so much more to the story than Dahlia was exposing. The two women faced off silently as Dahlia walked past her. They locked eyes, and Liberty noticed a slight smile of arrogance cross Dahlia's face.

There is something very wrong about this. I don't trust her as far as I can throw her. She's lying about something, and I'm going to find out.

TWENTY-FOUR

LIBERTY SAT AT HER VANITY, LEANING OVER with her elbows resting on the glass top as she inhaled to stop herself from throwing up. Po knocked and entered to see her. Despite the fact that she felt horrible, she was the vision of beauty. The peach one-shoulder, Grecian-style sundress she wore complemented her skin tone well. Her small baby bump was barely visible as she stood up.

"How do I look?" she asked.

"Beautiful, ma," Po replied.

"I don't know if I can make it through this. I can barely keep anything down," Liberty said. "I might throw up on my guests."

They shared a laugh, and the unlikely couple stared at each other, foreheads pressed together in joy. This child would be the glue that held them together.

"Come down when you're ready. Take your time," Po said. "I know that what we have isn't perfect, ma, but it's ours, and I love you."

Liberty smiled and replied, "I love you too."

Liberty took her time and waited until all of her guests had arrived before she made her appearance. Dahlia stood beside Po with a glass of champagne in her hand. "She looks beautiful," Dahlia complimented honestly. Even she was taken aback by the brightness of Liberty's glow. She cut her eyes as she took her seat, while Liberty worked the room.

Rocko approached Liberty and hugged her gently. "Congratulations, sis," he said.

"Thank you, Rocko," she replied, overjoyed at all the love people were showering her with. She didn't know many of the guests. Most of them were there on behalf of Po, but they were more than generous.

Liberty's baby shower was a success, and expensive presents overflowed on the gift table. Dahlia sat back as Po's workers and their girlfriends and wives approached Liberty. She rolled her eyes in disgust. Liberty was so overwhelmed that she didn't even wear her crown right. *Bitch don't even know what to do with her position,* Dahlia thought. She didn't even bother to speak to Liberty. Tension had been thick since Trixie's death. Only a few weeks had passed, and Liberty made it clear that she didn't believe Dahlia's story. The line had been drawn in the sand. Liberty was on one side and Dahlia was on the other. Po labeled Dahlia loyal and respected her even more since Trixie's shooting. In his eyes, she had proved her worth and would forever have a friend in him, but Liberty was beginning to see through her cousin and made no attempt to hide her contempt.

Liberty spotted Dahlia across the room and immediately felt torn between family and common sense. Dahlia was her last living blood relative. *Why don't I trust her?* She asked herself. Po came to her side, interrupting her thoughts.

"Let me introduce you to my people," Po said. He held her hand lovingly, and they took a step forward.

It was important for her to know the names and faces of his crew. That way, she would be able to decipher friend from foe. Anyone who had the privilege of being in Po's home was trusted, but for added assurance, he had security tucked discreetly throughout the party. Even Liberty had no idea that the armed men were there for her protection. Before Liberty could even get across the room, a sharp pain erupted in her lower abdomen. She stopped abruptly, and her hand tightened around Po's bicep.

"Are you okay?" he asked, concerned.

Liberty felt another sharp pain shoot through her, and this time it caused her to double over slightly.

"Something's not right," she whispered. "I need to go to the bathroom."

Liberty's eyes watered as Po carefully rushed her through the crowd and into the half bath.

"What's happening? Talk to me, Liberty," Po said.

Her heart raced as she sat down on the toilet. She pulled down her panties and gasped in horror at the blood that filled her underwear.

"No! No! No!" she screamed as Po's heart went numb. He sprang into action and picked her up as he carried her out of the house.

"Yo, Rocko! Get the car!" he yelled, his voice alarming the guests and causing everyone to look their way.

Rocko sprang to action, and Dahlia hopped from her seat as they followed Liberty and Po out of the house with a worried crowd behind them.

"What's happening?" Dahlia screamed in fake concern, but she already knew that her master plan was in full swing. She had been waiting for the Plan-B pills to take their toll on Liberty's pregnancy, and she had a feeling that it had finally happened.

"She's bleeding!" Po shouted urgently.

"I'll handle everything here! Don't worry, Liberty. Everything will be okay," Dahlia said as she turned to usher everyone back inside.

Po got in the backseat with Liberty as Rocko burnt rubber out of the driveway.

Liberty's insides felt as if they were being wrung out with an iron grip. She cringed as cramps hit her lower abdomen like a prized boxer. The intense pain ripped through her body as she felt blood leaking between her legs. She tried to clench her thighs tightly, locking them in place as if it could keep her baby trapped inside. "Hurry!" she cried out. Her intuition was telling her that something was seriously wrong. This wasn't normal, and she feared the worst.

Liberty was doubled over, clenching her stomach as the car swerved in and out of traffic. Every bump they hit seemed to rattle her insides. Rocko raced into the hospital parking lot and illegally whipped right to the front door, pulling onto the sidewalk, barely missing bystanders that stood outside. Commotion erupted as Po carried Liberty out.

"I'ma park and meet you inside!" Rocko shouted. Liberty clung to Po, grimacing over his shoulder as he rushed her through the double doors.

A woman dressed in nurse's scrubs rushed to meet the distressed couple.

"Help us. She's pregnant, and she's bleeding," Po said. The woman sprang into action, retrieving a wheelchair for Liberty to sit in and whisked her off, leaving Po standing in the lobby watching in frustration.

Liberty stared at the hospital ceiling as the sterile smell of the room made her stomach turn. She cried because before the doctor even told her the diagnosis, she knew what had occurred. She had seen it too many times before during her days of working the ho stroll not to remember. Po held onto her hand the entire time trying to appear strong. He knew that he couldn't break. She needed him right now, and although his stomach was hollow from grief, he maintained his composure for Liberty's sake. They had been at the hospital for hours, and it felt as though a million nurses had conducted a million tests. As they waited for answers they didn't speak. Neither of them knew exactly what to say. No words could express what they were feeling. Suffering in silent agony they retreated inside of themselves, both pondering the "what-nows" and "what-ifs." A slim, tall woman entered the room carrying Liberty's chart in her hands.

"My name is Dr. Miscka, and after reviewing all of your tests' results, I'm sorry to say that you have suffered a miscarriage."

The doctor's voice was so technical, as if her words hadn't just destroyed Liberty.

"We'll keep you overnight and release you in the morning. I can prescribe something for the pain. You'll have menstrual-like cramps for the next few days, but you should be fine," Dr. Miscka informed them.

"What caused this?" Po asked, his voice steady and even, as if he had taken all of the emotion out simply so that it wouldn't crack.

"Miscarriages are very common. It's an unfortunate event, but most women go on to have successful pregnancies in the future. Sometimes things in the body just don't support a healthy pregnancy and miscarriages occur. It's no one's fault. These things just happen," the doctor replied. She gave Po a sympathetic pat on the back and said, "Please page the nurses if you need anything."

She left the room, and as soon as Liberty heard the door click closed her hard front caved. She cried long and hard as Po stood nearby, gripping her hand. There wasn't much he could do to ease her pain. He was going through his own, and all they could do was lean on each other in hope that they made it through. Liberty held his hand tightly and closed her eyes. She wasn't sure that she had a future with Po without a baby bonding them, and she feared what was to come now that their love was being put to the test.

* * *

Two months had passed, and Liberty withdrew inside of herself as she processed her loss in silence. No one, not even Po, could understand how it felt to have life inside of her one moment and leaking out of her the next. She was angry, bitter, and confused. Wondering why her life had been filled with such bad events she grew resentful at God for dealing her a shitty hand. Liberty grew cold, and although her body had healed in no time, her spirit felt permanently injured. She barely spoke to Po, and when he tried to initiate a conversation with her she showed no interest. Liberty was dry with him, and it was almost as if she took her anger out on him, despite Po being the only other person in the world that mourned with her.

Po understood, even if she didn't think he did. To love a woman like Liberty was difficult. She didn't come with an instruction manual. Her soul was like an onion, and there were so many layers to peel back to see the true Liberty. Her past had done a number on her, and the one time she had gotten her hopes up for the future, she had been let down.

I don't deserve this, she thought. *Why do I lose everything that I love?* she wondered. A piece of her didn't want to care for Po because she was positive that he would be next to exit her life. He made her too happy, and the blueprint of her life was one of sadness. He just didn't fit. She had no idea that she was pushing him away.

The silence in his home had become maddening. Po couldn't think clearly because he was distracted by the conflict that was brewing between him and Liberty. He entered the bedroom that Liberty had confined herself to and stormed over to the picturesque window and suddenly pulled open the drapes, allowing the bright sun to spill into the depressing room.

"Po, close the curtains," Liberty moaned. He looked back at her. Her hair was all over her head; her eyes were swollen and red. She looked like shit.

He took a deep breath and walked over to her bedside, taking a seat on the edge as he grabbed her hand.

"We're going to be okay, ma. I love you, and I'm sorry about the baby. I wanted that baby too, more than you know. You have to get up, Liberty. What you're doing ain't healthy, ma. You can't just shut down because one bad thing happened," Po reasoned.

"*One* bad thing?" she replied sarcastically, feeling sorry for herself. She sat up and snatched her hand away from him. "Try a lifetime of bad things, Po! I lose everything and everyone I love. The baby, A'shai!"

Po's jaws clenched in anger. "Don't mention his name in the same sentence as my baby! You still on that nigga?" he shouted in frustration. No matter how much they grew together, there was always a ghost keeping them apart. "I'm real tired of hearing the nigga's name, Liberty. I was understanding at first because I can respect what you shared with him, but now I'm questioning if you're my bitch or his." He stood up.

"You don't understand," she replied with tears in her eyes.

"I don't? I lost somebody before you too, Liberty! In fact, you just might have her heart in your chest! But you don't ever hear me throw her name in your face!" Po answered.

Liberty shook her head and got out of bed. Standing directly in his face she said, "You don't have to say her name, Po! I see the way you drift off into the past when you look at me. You don't even see me. You see her! Let's stop pretending like this is about us. This is about them. The baby just gave us an excuse to stay together." She stormed past him, headed to the master bathroom, and waited until she heard him slam the door before she burst into tears. She knew that she didn't mean what she said. Of course she missed A'shai, but Po had found a place in her heart as well. There was room for him, and she wanted him, but the toll that life had taken on her was causing her to push him away. She didn't know that her distance only made him grow closer to someone else.

Po stormed out of the room before he said something that he couldn't take back. "I've got to get the fuck out of here," he whispered as he grabbed the keys to his Porsche Cayenne and exited the house. Dahlia pulled up just as he locked the door and greeted him with a smile. Her pleasant face was a welcome relief from the stressful argument he had just had.

"Hey, handsome," she said.

"What up, ma?" he replied.

Dahlia could hear the tension in his voice, and she frowned. "You okay?" She had witnessed the divide that had occurred between Liberty and Po. In fact, she reveled in the fact that it wouldn't be long before their relationship imploded.

She grabbed his collar and stepped close to Po flirtatiously. "You want to take a ride with me?" she asked. "I'll make you feel better."

Po stepped back slightly and looked back at the house to make sure no one was watching.

"Come on, Po. Liberty won't even know you're missing," Dahlia urged as she walked back to her car. She opened her door and tapped her fingernails on the hood. "You coming or what?"

Po wiped his hand over his mouth, and then got into Dahlia's car, looking for a temporary escape.

Liberty's nostrils flared as she watched the taillights of Dahlia's car disappear out of the estate gates. *What the fuck is she doing?* Liberty thought angrily. She cut her eyes as her chest heaved up and down. *She's supposed to be my family!*

Liberty didn't like how close Dahlia and Po were becoming, and she hadn't noticed Dahlia's flirtatious ways until now. *First she claims Trixie tried to rob Po, now she's flirting with my man like he's hers. What the fuck is this bitch up to?* Liberty asked. She picked up her cell and dialed Po's number, anxiously tapping her foot as it rang in her ear. To her dismay it went to voice mail. Liberty sat down on the cold, marble floor and put her face in her hands, defeated. She didn't know what to think, but her eyes didn't lie. Something wasn't right with Dahlia, and if Liberty didn't get her life together she just might lose it all.

* * *

"These the kind of joints you hang out at in your spare time?" Po asked as he looked around the dilapidated dive bar where Dahlia had taken him. He put his hand near his hip, so that his pistol was nearby. He didn't like to frequent spots that he wasn't familiar with, and Dahlia peeped his anxiety as he looked around the room. She grabbed his hand and smiled.

"Relax, Po. Our kind of enemy doesn't frequent establishments like this. That's why it's the perfect place to let your hair down," she said. She knew that the white, working-class citizens in the bar were of no threat to them. It was the most low-key spot in the city. It was anything but fancy, but it was safe and inconspicuous. She led the way to the bar and took a seat on the stool, crossing her legs as she slid her bottom onto it. "Two shots of Patrón," she said to the bartender.

Po looked at Dahlia and smiled slightly. "Since when you hit shots? You're a red wine type of girl."

He had been around Dahlia long enough to know that she did everything with class and expected the best of everything.

"Desperate times call for desperate measures," she replied with a laugh. "Tequila cheers everyone up." The bartender returned with their drinks, and Dahlia lifted the small glass in the air, waiting for Po to pick up his own. Po followed suit, and the two downed the liquor.

Dahlia grimaced from the burn and Po smirked. "Lightweight," he said with a charming smile.

"That I am not, sir," she replied. Dahlia ordered another shot and drank it like water as Po shook his head.

"A'ight, a'ight, ma. You got it," he said. He tried to appear normal, but the cloud that hung over his head rained sorrow all over him.

"Don't beat yourself up, Po. Liberty's going through a hard time right now. You two lost the baby, but just remember that everything happens for a reason. Maybe it just wasn't meant to be," Dahlia said softly as she reached over and gave Po's hand a supportive squeeze.

"She's shutting me out," Po replied as he lifted his second shot to his lips, drinking his worries away.

"Do you want me to be honest with you, Po? Because I can sit here and be a sympathetic ear, or I can put you up on game," Dahlia said.

"Speak freely, ma."

"Liberty never let you in. She's only been in love once in her entire life. She's stuck on A'shai. The only reason she even came back was because she was pregnant. Now that the miscarriage happened, I bet it won't be long before she decides to leave again," Dahlia said with a creased brow.

"Let me ask you something, Dahlia. Fuck is it about this A'shai nigga? He's dead and gone, but it's like he's putting claim on Liberty from the grave. What did they have that was so different?" he asked.

Dahlia shrugged her shoulders and said, "History." She waved her hand in dismissal and continued, "Don't worry about it, Po. I'm just talking, but I'm not in it. You know better than anyone where you and Liberty stand. Don't mind me. As long as she ain't putting up that shoe box money then you're good."

"Shoe box money?" Po questioned.

"Yeah. When a girl starts stashing a few thousand here and there in the back of her closet, she's planning her escape," Dahlia answered, her words running together slightly in intoxication.

Po shook his head and pointed his pinky finger in her direction as he lifted his glass to his lips. He took a long sip and replied, "That's where you're wrong. Liberty don't gotta take from me. She knows if we don't work out she'll be taken care of. That's already understood."

"You sure about that?" Dahlia asked as she raised one eyebrow in a challenge.

Po's mental wheels began to spin as he pondered his situation with Liberty.

Dahlia stood and walked over to the old-school jukebox that sat in the corner of the room.

"This work?" she shouted to the bartender.

"Pop a bill in and see," the guy said back. Dahlia filled the machine with money and an old R&B song filled the room. She didn't know the tune, but she danced to it anyway. She playfully danced over to Po and grabbed his hand.

"Come on, Po. Let's have fun. Get your mind off of things," she said with a smile.

Po shook his head and laughed, grateful for the relief that Dahlia provided. He turned his chair toward the dance floor and replied, "I don't dance, ma, but I like to watch. Do your thing."

Dahlia danced all night for Po as they indulged in liquor and drank the problems of yesterday away. Po appreciated Dahlia. She was always so attentive to his needs, and she vibed with his mood effortlessly. He didn't understand why everything with Liberty was always so forced. Life wasn't supposed to be this hard, especially when you were on top.

As day turned to night and night eventually transformed to dawn Liberty lay in bed furious at the thought of Po and Dahlia out together. All of a sudden she no longer trusted her own family, and she wasn't quite sure if she trusted Po. The laughter that filled the walls of her mini-mansion sent chills up her spine as she listened to Dahlia and Po finally came home. She looked at the clock. It was five in the morning. *Where could they have possibly been all night?* she asked herself. Jealousy was an ugly monster when it creeped into one's head. It started off so small, but the smallest seed of doubt could quickly grow into a tree of accusations and resentment. Liberty sat up in bed with her back against the headboard. She stared Po directly in the eyes when he came into the room.

"Where have you been?" she asked softly, her feelings hurt at the thought of Dahlia and Po together. She was sitting there sulking and mourning the loss of their baby while he was out finding comfort with her cousin. *What part of the game is this?* she thought.

"I had to clear my head, Liberty," Po replied.

"From where I'm sitting, Po, it seems more clouded to me," Liberty said. She turned her back to him and clicked off the lamp that sat on the nightstand beside her bed. She had no more words to say to him for fear that she may speak out of anger.

Po was getting real tired of Liberty's slick talk. He needed a chick that knew how to play her position already. He couldn't keep handing out the instruction manual to Liberty on how to keep him satisfied. Some things a woman should just know and comparing him to another nigga, even a dead one, was the quickest way to run him into the arms of the next bitch.

Dahlia peeked outside of her room and listened as she heard voices coming from the first floor. She quietly crept down the hall and entered Po and Liberty's bedroom. She quickly tiptoed through the plush space of the bathroom and entered the walk-in closet. *After Po finds this, Liberty's ass will be out of here,* Dahlia thought. A conniving smile crept across her face as she opened the shoe box that she had in her hands. Inside of it was $100,000 of her own money, neatly bundled in $10k rubber banded knots. Dahlia placed the box on the shelf, then slinked out of the room. She didn't know when Po would find it, but she knew that he would eventually check to see if Liberty had a shoe box stash, and when he found the money hidden inside of the closet, all of his faith in Liberty would dissolve. It was a small price to pay to get Liberty out of her way. The seed of deceit that Dahlia was planting would be enough to destroy any foundation that Po and Liberty had. Their bond would be broken without a doubt. If there was one thing a man like Po despised, it was a woman who couldn't be trusted around his money, and when it came down to it, getting money was his first love.

The tension between Liberty and Po was no longer something that occurred behind closed doors. Everyone began to watch as the couple slowly drifted apart. Too heartbroken over the loss of their child, Liberty withdrew from the world. She wanted to lean on Po, but Po was forever in the streets. She barely saw him, and when she did, he was always preoccupied with other things. Liberty's grief was taking a backseat to Po's operation, making her feel disposable. *Dahlia was right. Po will never be the wife-and-kids-type of man. He's a hustler. The life is all he knows . . . all he wants,* she thought miserably. She looked up from her cup of morning tea and watched him as he sat adjacent to her.

When the doorbell rang it was a relief to Po. Facing Liberty was becoming more and more like a burden each day. He couldn't read her, and Po was fed up with catering to her. She ran hot and cold. There was no in between. One day she was ready to be his lady, and the next she was crying crocodile tears over A'shai. No man wanted a chick with an indecisive heart. Po wanted Liberty to choose him, but it seemed as though she was unable to do it. If it took a child to make Liberty loyal, then he didn't know if he wanted her at all. Love and loyalty should be effortless with the right person. With Liberty, the shit was just too hard. Po rose from the table.

"Are you expecting someone?" Liberty asked.

All of a sudden Dahlia walked into the kitchen. She

touched Po's shoulder, squeezing it gently, signaling for him to sit back down. "Enjoy your meal, Po. I'll get it," she said. Po relaxed, and Dahlia headed to the door. "Hey, Lib."

Liberty nodded her head but didn't speak as a twinge of jealousy shot through her. Her nostrils flared. She didn't like how Dahlia was all of a sudden so helpful and available to Po. She raised her eyebrows in suspicion and cleared her throat. "I don't like her living here anymore," she said.

Po looked up in surprise and replied, "She's your cousin. You invited her."

They spoke in low, tense whispers so that Dahlia would not overhear them. "Well, now I'm disinviting her," Liberty shot back. Her light skin was flushed with red. "The bitch is too comfortable. She walks around here like this is her house."

Po shook his head and replied, "You're tripping, ma. I know you're emotional from the miscarriage, but you need to snap out of it. You're taking it out on everybody. Dahlia hasn't done anything to you, and I need her here for business."

"Why are you defending her? You're supposed to be on my side," Liberty hissed.

"I'm not defending anybody. I'm just stating facts. I need her here. End of discussion," Po said. As soon as he finished his sentence Dahlia entered the room with Rocko behind her.

"Look who I found," she said cheerfully.

Po and Liberty instantly ended their conversation, and Liberty turned her head to hide her watery eyes.

Po stood. "You ready, fam?" he asked.

Rocko nodded.

"Let me just get dressed real quick. Sit down and have some breakfast. Dahlia cooked," Po said.

"I'll fix him a plate," Dahlia offered.

Liberty abruptly stood up. "I'll fix him a plate," she said, her voice coming out more harshly than she intended. Dahlia paused and looked at Liberty innocently, then raised her hands in defense.

"Be my guest, Lib," Dahlia said. "I have to get dressed anyway. I've got some things to take care of today."

Rocko and Po looked at Liberty in shock. She wasn't acting like herself.

"I'm good, fam. Thanks for the offer. I'm going to wait inside the car," Rocko said.

When everybody had left the room, Po stared at Liberty. "Where is your head at, Liberty? You're suddenly so worried about Dahlia. I don't want her. You're competing with yourself, but you've got me competing with a ghost. I've got no wins with that," Po said.

Liberty was speechless as she stood in front of him. She wasn't oblivious to the fact that she was falling apart at the seams. There just wasn't anything that she could do to shake the funk that she was in. Feeling sorry for herself and reminiscing on A'shai seemed to be all that she could do. She wanted Po to be more like A'shai. To covet her the way that he did, to anticipate her needs, her wants, the way that A'shai had done. She was making the cardinal mistake of comparing the two men when they couldn't be more different. They loved her differently, and she didn't realize that she was taking Po's love for granted.

Po wasn't feeling being a second choice, and if things didn't change soon his interest would wane. He hopped into the shower and washed his frustrations away. It had been too long since Liberty had pleased him. Sexually, mentally, and even emotionally she didn't tend to her man, and Po was beginning to feel the effects of it. A woman who had once mesmerized him was now making him miserable. Po wasn't sloppy. He didn't like his life being in disarray. His home wasn't in order, which made it hard for him to focus on business, and that was a problem. He was tense, his entire body needed attention, and his hard dick stuck straight out. He was sexually deprived and had so much frustration built up that he felt like he would explode. He wrapped his hand around his pole and began to stroke himself as the steam from the hot shower water massaged his broad shoulders. His head fell back as he slowly masturbated. Then Po heard the bathroom door open.

"Lib, that you, ma?" he asked. "Come handle something for me."

He opened the shower curtain and was shocked to find Dahlia standing in front of him with her short silk, kimono robe open, displaying her nude body underneath. One leg was lifted on the toilet and two fingers massaged her stiff clit as she eyed him seductively. "Don't stop," she whispered.

The sight of Po's large dick instantly made Dahlia wet, and she fingered herself as her dark nipples hardened, poking through the fabric of her robe. Po's eyes shot to the door, and Dahlia eased his concern.

"She's downstairs."

Po mentally weighed his options. Briefly he thought about Liberty, of her jealousy, of her sudden suspicion, but when he thought of how she shut him out and how she had left him once before all guilt went out the window. A beautiful woman was standing before him, ready and willing to please him in every way. Po needed it.

Dahlia sensed his hesitation and before he could tell her to leave she moved over to him and stepped into the shower. She pulled the curtain closed and got onto her knees as the water from the shower soaked her body. She opened her mouth and took his thick, pulsing, manhood into her mouth. Po's knees almost buckled as the suction from her mouth engulfed his tool. He grabbed the sides of her face, knowing that Dahlia would take him without complaint. He began to fuck her mouth as if it were her pussy, grinding into her as she took it all, deep throating him as she stared up into his eyes. Dahlia was the perfect woman for Po. She was smart and calculating in business, loyal to her man, and fucked like a porn star. She was fit for a king and understood what it took to maintain control at the top. She wasn't needy; she was needed. That was the difference between her and Liberty, and Po was beginning to take notice.

He pulled her up by her shoulders and pinned her against the shower wall, opening her legs and sticking himself inside of her warm, wanting honey pot. She gasped and arched her back as he fucked her slowly, making her back slide up and down the slippery tiled wall.

"Ooh, baby," she whispered. Po leaned back and looked in Dahlia's face. She rubbed his head and face gently with her hands. She knew just what to do to make him feel her . . . to make him feel like a man, and Po was intoxicated by her at the moment. He and Dahlia had never been intimate until that moment. Yes, they had been physical plenty of times before, but the way their eyes connected and the way they moved their bodies to an unheard beat was more than sex. It wasn't love, but it was definitely an understood infatuation. Po gripped the back of her neck and kissed her deeply, their tongues slow dancing as their bodies grinded into each other.

"Ooh, Po, you deserve to be happy, baby. I can make you happy," Dahlia whispered.

"I know, ma," he moaned back as he pushed his pelvis into her so deep that she was stuck between undeniable pleasure and slight pain.

"Po . . ." Liberty's voice was like a bomb that exploded in his ear and caused Po and Dahlia to pause immediately, breathing hard, as Po's eyes widened from being caught off guard. He put his hand over Dahlia's mouth and put one finger to his lips.

"What up?" he shouted back, knowing that Liberty would enter the bathroom.

Dahlia smiled wickedly as she slowly winded her waist, still fucking Po as Liberty stepped inside.

Po's entire body shook from the pleasure that Dahlia

was giving him. The threat of being caught made his dick even harder.

"Can we talk?" she asked as she stood outside of the shower.

Dahlia snapped her pussy on Po mercilessly. Tightening her pelvic floor, doing Kegels around his shaft as she grinded slowly, her body moving like a snake. Po put his hand on the shower wall to brace himself as he responded, "It's not the time. Rocko's waiting outside. We can talk when I get back. Do me a favor and go tell him to come inside for a second."

"Okay," Liberty replied.

As soon as Po heard the bathroom door shut he put his hand around Dahlia's throat, pinning her roughly against the wall as he fucked her ferociously.

"You're dangerous," he growled in her ear.

"And you love it," she answered. Po exploded inside of her, then rested his forehead against Dahlia's as they panted from exhaustion.

"I want you for myself, Po," Dahlia whispered. She kissed him deeply, then stepped out of the shower and discreetly crept back to her room.

Po put both of his hands on the shower wall and lowered his head to his chest as he gulped in air. The water pounded over him, and he closed his eyes. Liberty wasn't keeping her place locked, and Dahlia had crept into her home and was slowly beginning to take her spot. Po knew that eventually the situation would come to a head. He only hoped that he was man enough to let Liberty go before he broke her heart.

Po quickly washed himself, then turned off the water and wrapped a towel around his waist as he went into the walk-in closet. Dressed in Polo boots, True Religion jeans, and a YSL V-neck, he was ready to hit the streets.

Just as he was about to leave he noticed the row of shoe boxes that Liberty had perfectly aligned on the shelves. *"As long as she ain't putting up that shoe box money then you're good."* Dahlia's words played on repeat in his head as he stared at the boxes. Po wanted to trust Liberty, but it was obvious that they were past the point of the benefit of the doubt. He pulled a Fendi box down and lifted the top and a pair of six-inch heels lay inside. The anxiety in his chest immediately deflated, and he began to feel like a fool. *What are you doing? She would never betray you,* he thought, feeling guilt from the attraction he was starting with Dahlia. He went to put the box back in its place and knocked down the one that sat beside it. Hundred dollar bills fell out and spilled out onto the floor. Po's temper flared immediately, and he didn't even bother picking up the cash before storming out of the room. *She knows that she doesn't have to hide money. I'ma look out for her. She wants to go? Then she can fucking go. I made that clear from the beginning.*

Po was too angry to confront her. Anyone else would have had the hit squad at their front door without hesitation, but Po had a soft spot for Liberty. He was vulnerable with her and didn't know how to confront the issue. When he saw her standing at the bottom of the steps it took everything in him not to slap fire from her. He walked past her.

"Po," she called, trying to get him to speak to her. She

didn't know how much longer they would last in their current state. She grabbed at his arm, but he snatched it away, harder than he meant.

She frowned and looked at him sadly. "Po, we need to—"

Po turned to her and stared in her face. In another lifetime they would be perfect for each other, but today, in this reality, they were tearing each other apart. He wanted things to work with her. He felt that their hearts were connected in a much deeper way than with Dahlia. Walking into that hospital and saving her from Samad's flying bullets was destiny. He couldn't understand why it was so hard to make it work. Money was plentiful in Po's camp. Liberty should have known better than to steal from him. Her actions were unforgiveable. *If you can't trust a bitch with your paper, that's it*, he thought. Liberty could see the hurt in his eyes, but she had no idea where it was coming from.

"Not now, ma. This isn't the time for us," he said. That one statement meant so much more than what was said. Knowing that no sin was greater than the next, he was speaking not only about her betrayal but also his own. He shook his head and walked out the door, leaving Liberty standing there wondering what had just occurred between them.

Dahlia watched from her bedroom window as Po entered Rocko's black Escalade. As if he knew she was watching he turned around and peered up at her. Their eyes locked for a brief moment, and then he hopped inside, riding away.

"What was all that about?" Rocko asked.

Po slumped in his seat, obviously stressed as he ran his hand over his face. "Women problems, fam," Po admitted.

Rocko shook his head and said, "Better get like my nigga, Jay-Z. 99 problems, you feel me? Don't let no pussy get in between this money."

Po shook his head. "Never that. The money is priority number one. Always," Po assured. "I'll figure this shit out with Liberty."

Rocko's lips curled up into a smile. "That wasn't who I was talking about. The bitch you fucking with is in a whole different league, fam."

Po knew there wasn't any point in lying to Rocko. That was his man. "It's that obvious?" Po asked. He had thought he and Dahlia had been careful; that he had been respectful and had kept Dahlia at a comfortable distance, but somewhere he had slipped. Somewhere, Dahlia had crept close to him, and unfortunately, he liked it.

"Only nigga that can't see you hitting that is a blind one," Rocko said truthfully.

Rocko was right. Po had to clean up the mess he had made before it exploded in his face.

Liberty stormed up the steps and into Dahlia's room. She wasn't a fool. She was beginning to sense snake in Dahlia, and she was about to mow her lawn.

"Knock much?" Dahlia asked as she stood in the full-length mirror, applying her makeup.

"Not in my own house. That's what you seem to be forgetting, Dahlia. This is MY house, and Po is MY man," Liberty said blatantly, putting it out on the table. She was tired of holding her cards and biting her tongue.

Dahlia chuckled but didn't even turn around to face Liberty. Liberty wasn't a factor and was barely competition. *This bitch couldn't keep her man away from me if she tried,* Dahlia thought.

"I haven't forgotten anything, Liberty. I know exactly where I am and who I'm dealing with. Do you?" she asked calmly.

Liberty crossed her arms and began going to Dahlia's closet pulling out her clothes. She tossed them on the floor, pulling every piece of fabric she saw off of the racks. "Get your shit and get out!"

"We both know that Po won't have that," Dahlia said arrogantly as she continued to cater to herself in the mirror. There was no part of her that was threatened by Liberty. It was only a matter of time before Po figured out that Liberty was a liability. He didn't need her when he had a woman like Dahlia who was well versed in the life. She knew how to play her role to a tee.

"He'll never choose you over me," Liberty seethed. She wanted to slap the smug expression off of Dahlia's face, but instead, she retreated knowing that Po would handle the problem for her.

TWENTY-FIVE

PO WAS KNEE-DEEP IN THE GAME AND moving more diamonds than any other supplier in the Western Hemisphere. By graduating from bricks to stones, he had become one of the most notorious businessmen in the world. His name rang bells among society's elite, and the underground network of buyers that he had assembled was unlike anything that anyone had ever seen. Po brought his street smarts to a different arena and dominated in the diamond exchange. It was at a point where Zulu needed him just as much as Po needed Zulu. Po was no longer a small distributor for Zulu. They were partners, and it was time that Zulu acknowledged him as such.

"It's about time to take that trip overseas," Po stated. "With the amount of diamonds I'm moving it's time to renegotiate. The nigga Zulu only works through Dahlia, and that's a problem. It's time he came through me. I move more diamonds than Omega ever could. If he don't want to come through me, then we'll pull out."

"As much as we moving he need to lower the price," Rocko stated as he guided his car through the city.

"It's not about the price, fam. I want a stake in the mines," Po said.

Rocko's eyes widened knowing that if Po got a percentage of the diamond mines then they could go legit. Washing the dirty money they had accumulated would be simple once ownership of an African mine was confirmed.

"When are you going?" Rocko asked.

"When are *we* going?" Po replied. "I'm thinking the sooner the better. Like in the A.M. It's time you meet the connect."

The silence that filled the walls of Po's home was maddeningly loud as he entered. Po knew that a storm was brewing before he even saw Liberty sitting in the dark kitchen, sipping hot tea at the table. Deep in thought, Liberty didn't speak. Her eyes were downcast and sorrow filled her as she thought of Po. She wondered what had made Dahlia so cocky. Her cousin seemed too confident that Po would come to her defense. Liberty was vexed at the thought of Po choosing Dahlia over her. Po turned on the light and jumped when he finally noticed Liberty sitting there.

"Why are you sitting in the dark?" he asked.

"I've been sitting here all day. Trying to figure out why and when you and I went left. The only thing that I can blame it on is Dahlia," Liberty said as she squinted as if she were contemplating the issue. "Ever since she's been here, me and you have been distant. While we're growing apart, you and Dahlia are growing closer together. What type of shit is that?"

Po knew that it was a conversation worth having, but now was not the time. He needed Dahlia for the Africa trip, and he didn't want Liberty clouding his judgment right now.

"I told you earlier, ma. Now is not the time. I'm making this trip tomorrow to Africa, and I need my head clear for that," Po said.

"Dahlia's going?" Liberty asked dryly, already knowing the answer to her question.

"You know she's going, ma. We do business together," Po replied, full of guilt that he had to lie to her. He hated himself at that moment. This was not the type of man that he had ever intended to be. The last thing that he wanted to do was hurt Liberty, but he was beginning to think that they just weren't built the same.

"It seems like you doing a lot more than business with her," Liberty snapped sarcastically. Her voice shook as she thought of Po and Dahlia together. She waited for his response, but his silence confirmed his guilt.

"How long have you been fucking her?" Liberty asked.

"How long have you been stealing from me?" Po shot back. His question caught her off guard and gave her no answers. He neither confirmed nor denied her suspicions, but admitted that he had some of his own.

Liberty looked at him in confusion, but before she could respond Dahlia's presence interrupted them.

Liberty was irate as she lunged at her. "You fucking bitch!" she shouted.

Surprised by Liberty's sudden moxie Po didn't grab her quick enough. Liberty snuffed Dahlia, catching her off guard, getting one good hit in before Po snatched her up.

"I want her gone!" Liberty shouted as she looked up at him with tears flooding her gaze.

Dahlia scoffed and licked the corner of her mouth where Liberty had caused her lip to bust. "You got that one, but you won't get another one," Dahlia said calmly as she stormed to the sink to grab a paper towel to blot her lip.

"Put her out of this house!" Liberty demanded. "You either do business with her or you be with me! You can't have both! I want her out of my life! I want you out of the game!"

Dahlia remained silent as she leaned against the sink. She knew how to let a man be a man. Liberty was playing her cards all wrong by giving Po an ultimatum. No man wanted to feel as though he was forced into submission. Dahlia had already put in the work she needed. There was no doubt in her mind that Po would choose her. Liberty was the one who hadn't done her all to keep her man.

Had Po not found money stashed in Liberty's closet he may have had a harder time with what he was about to do. The way he saw it, Liberty had chosen for him the day she had started plotting her getaway. She had left him once. Who was to say that she wouldn't leave him again? Dahlia was there, by his side, strengthening his empire. On top of that, she was willing to please him in any way he required.

"She's not going anywhere, ma. I need her here. You of all people know that, but if you want to leave I'm not stopping you," Po said. He turned and began to walk out of the room, but stopped abruptly. "Oh yeah, and you never had to steal money from me. I'm a man of my word. I'll have Rocko hit you off with some paper and make sure you're straight. You'll never want for anything."

"So the baby never meant anything? How can you just toss me away after what we've been through?" Liberty asked, pleading for Po's loyalty.

"The baby meant everything!" Po shouted. His voice was so loud that it vibrated Liberty's heart. He turned toward her in fury and stood two inches from her face. "What? Just because I didn't mourn the way you wanted me to didn't mean that I wasn't hurt! That baby was the glue that was holding us together. Now we have nothing. There's no trust."

Liberty was so hurt that she couldn't even defend herself. She watched in horror as he turned away from her and left the room with Dahlia following behind him. Dahlia stopped and looked at Liberty. She smiled slightly then said, "Checkmate, bitch."

Liberty's entire world crumbled beneath her feet.

Dahlia arranged the meeting between Zulu and Po, then stayed behind as Po and Rocko made the early-morning flight to Sierra Leone. As Po sat on the plane next to his right-hand man, he couldn't help but think of how far he had come in the game. He had reached a status that most hood niggas only conjured up in rap songs. He was getting it. But he couldn't suppress the guilt that he felt over losing Liberty. Every time he closed his eyes he saw her crying face. There was no doubt in his mind that he loved her, but he didn't trust her, and that was recipe for disaster. He wasn't in a position to forgive and forget, but he had a mind full of regrets. At the end of the day Liberty didn't assimilate to his lifestyle and Dahlia was a convenient, not to mention stunning, replacement.

"When we get back to L.A. I need you to drop off a package to Liberty," Po said.

Rocko looked at Po, taken aback, because he knew what that meant. "You sure about that?" he asked.

Po nodded his head and replied, "We're done. Just set her up for me. Make sure she's good."

Po retreated to his thoughts for the remainder of the flight. When they finally made it to Africa they were exhausted, but Po was eager to get down to business. As personal guests of Zulu they were escorted to his private estate in luxury whips.

"This shit is crazy, fam," Rocko said as he looked around in amazement. The beautiful setting of the motherland had that same affect on Po his first time visiting. The city was well established, and its tall skyscrapers and buildings were much like any major city in the States, but once you got out into the outskirts of town, the thick bush took over the land. It all seemed so isolated, so serene, as nature and man coexisted.

"How far out does this mu'fucka live?" Rocko asked as he stared out the window.

They had been driving for two hours, and Rocko was slightly uncomfortable at the fact that he couldn't get his bearings. If anything popped off he would be at the mercy of Zulu. He couldn't get himself out of Africa if he wanted to. Finally a magnificent home appeared in the distance.

"That's where we're headed," Po said as he pointed his finger at the massive estate.

As they pulled up to the mansion, they were greeted by beautiful women wearing expensive fabric that was draped around their slender bodies. They resembled chocolate Grecian goddesses. They were so beautiful that it seemed as though they had fallen from the heavens. The women in Africa were different from the women Po and Rocko were used to seeing. They had a natural beauty that emanated from them. Ass for days, ample breasts, wide hips, slim waists . . . they had all the characteristics that women paid thousands to emulate. Po surmised that this is where beauty was birthed. He had never seen anything or any place or anyone who could compare. Africa was exquisite.

Zulu stood directly in front of his door, waiting for his guests to arrive. To his right were his house servants, to his left were his bodyguards. Directly behind him stood his trusted associates. All of the people around him were strapped so Zulu didn't need to be. He was the most protected man in the nation of Sierra Leone. The car stopped, and Po and Rocko stepped out.

"Welcome, my guests," Zulu said as he held his hands out in greeting.

Po and Rocko ascended the steps side by side. Po extended his hand, and Zulu accepted it.

"It's about time we sat down and spoke. Settle this beef once and for all. Omega wanted you cut out before his death, but I think it is time to let bygones be bygones. You must be hungry after such long travels. I've had a late dinner prepared for you in your rooms. In the morning we will discuss business," Zulu said. "The women are here for your entertainment. They will make your stay more than comfortable."

Rocko and Po separated as they made their way to their rooms.

"Get some sleep, fam. I need you on point tomorrow," Po said. They slapped hands, and Po followed the beautiful woman that Zulu had assigned to him. She led him into a room that was the size of an apartment.

"Is there anything that I can get you?" she asked as she stood at his door watching him kick off his shoes.

"No, I'm good. Thank you," Po replied graciously. His cell rang, and he saw Dahlia's name pop onto the screen. He answered. "What up?"

"So you made it safely?" she asked.

"Yeah, we're here. We just got in," Po replied.

"Well, I just want you to know that I'm here waiting for you to come home. You're a king, Po. Now turn around and enjoy the spoils of your position, baby. Tell me if she does something that you like so I can learn how to do it too. I told you, I know how to play my position, and I play it very well. Enjoy your trip," Dahlia said.

She hung up the phone, and Po turned around to see the woman standing in front of him as naked as the day she was born. Dahlia knew Zulu well and knew how he catered to his guests. She had blown Po's mind by giving him the go-ahead and had endeared herself to him even more. Dahlia would ride with him as long as he was on top. It was the descent that he would have to watch out for. When she felt he was falling off she would dispose of him and move on to the next, the same way she had done with Omega.

The woman walked over to him and pressed her D-cup breasts against his chest. "Are you sure there isn't *anything* you want from me?" she asked softly.

Pussy that was handed to him on a platter wasn't Po's taste. Although the woman before him was the definition of perfection, he still declined. He wasn't a fool. He knew that distraction was a part of the art of war, and he wanted to keep his head in the game. Zulu wasn't his friend. Po was swimming with sharks.

Po had never seen anything as beautiful as an African sunrise. He felt worlds away from busy California as he stood out on his private veranda appreciating the nature around him. The knock at the door announced Rocko's presence, but Po didn't move. He knew that his friend would walk in uninvited anyway. The knock was more out of habit than courtesy. Just as suspected, Rocko entered and joined him. The two men stood side by side, overlooking Sierra Leone.

"How was your night?" Po asked with a slight smirk. He knew Rocko too well to think that he hadn't taken advantage of the free pussy that had been laid out for him.

"Night was good! Real good, my nigga," Rocko said. The two shared a laugh, but quickly became serious again. There was little time for horseplay when they were up for negotiating a deal worth millions. "You ready to rock and roll, my baby?" Rocko asked.

"Indeed, fam. Indeed. Everything's riding on this. If Zulu refuses to cut me in, then I'm murking him. I've killed niggas for much less. He don't want to step into my crosshairs. I'd much rather be allies than enemies," Po said.

Po's personal concierge stepped out onto the veranda. "Breakfast is ready," she said.

The men joined Zulu on the yard where they sat thirty feet from wild zebras and giraffes. The property was from another world and proved just how long Zulu's money truly was.

"I hope your accommodations are fitting," Zulu said as the men sat around the circle table with him.

"They're fine. Thank you for having us. I'm not one to hold my tongue so I would like to get to business, if you don't mind," Po said.

"Spoken like a true American. Your people are always in such a rush," Zulu replied.

"I can sleep when I die. There's a difference between moving too fast and moving efficiently. I move those diamonds at the same pace I do everything else. It's about the fast life," Po replied with a charming grin.

"Nothing wrong with that," Zulu said as he raised his glass of cognac in respect.

"This is my good friend, Rocko. I felt that it was important to make the introduction. You will no longer be dealing with Dahlia. She plays a different position in my life now."

Zulu smiled and nodded knowingly. "You fell for her. Dahlia is a very beautiful woman. You were smart to pull her out of the field and put her into your bed."

"Rocko will be taking her place," Po finished.

"And how do I know I can trust this Rocko?" Zulu asked. "I know Dahlia. Rocko could be a piece of shit fed."

Rocko cleared his throat and leaned into the table, staring Zulu directly in the eyes. "There nothing federal about me. Those diamonds that you ship to America . . . I move half of 'em easily. That should be proof enough that I am who I say I am."

"I vouch for him," Po finished. "He's thorough. I'd put my life on it."

Zulu raised his fork and pointed at Po with a smile. "Good. One day you may have to."

"Besides. The way we are about to move into the future the feds won't be a factor," Po said.

"How so?" Zulu asked.

"I want a percentage of the diamond mines," Po stated.

Zulu laughed hysterically and put one hand on his gut as he sat back as if Po had told a hilarious joke.

"You must be kidding, Po."

"I am not. I want 50 percent," Po said seriously. "Or I

pull out completely, and I go to Uganda. I'm sure my business with them will be better appreciated. We both know that I am your biggest distributor. I move more diamonds than all of your other clients combined. I've earned a stake in the mines."

Zulu's nostrils flared because he had underestimated the young hustler. Po was smarter than the average.

"You are making millions, Po. Greed destroys the best of them," Zulu warned.

"You should heed those words. Don't let your greed lead to your demise," Po said slickly, putting an indirect threat on the table.

"Ten percent," Zulu countered. The sour look on his face revealed his anger from having to comply at all, but he couldn't afford to lose Po's business.

"Forty percent," Po shot back.

"Thirty percent," Zulu said. "That's my final offer. I cannot go any higher than that."

Po's poker face was phenomenal. He could hardly contain his excitement, but he kept his exterior collected. "Deal," he said.

Bothered that he had just split his empire, Zulu stood to his feet. "You gentlemen enjoy. Walk the grounds, keep time with the ladies. I have other business to attend to. I look forward to our new partnership, Po."

"As do I, Zulu," Po replied.

Zulu walked away from the table swallowing a bitter pill of defeat.

Rocko sat back and shook his head. "Damn, fam, he

took you all the way down to 30 percent. The nigga could have come off the fifty/fifty split."

Po shook his head and said, "Actually, he came up by 10 percent. Fifty was always unrealistic. The number in my head was 20 percent. I went high so that he didn't go low. I just brokered a deal that will keep us rich forever, my nigga."

TWENTY-SIX

LIBERTY SAT OUTSIDE OF PO'S HOUSE AND felt like an outsider. Her castle had been usurped by another woman, and Liberty didn't even feel comfortable enough to knock on the door. She sat in her luxury car a few houses down, lurking, waiting impatiently for Dahlia to leave. Liberty didn't want to run into her. She was too embarrassed, angry, and hurt to even face her right now. Although Po never confirmed that he was fucking Dahlia, Liberty's intuition told her that he had. The average woman would have sought revenge, but Liberty just wanted peace.

The night before had been turbulent, and she had rushed out of the house without thinking. Driving the streets of L.A. all night had given her time to think. She didn't want anything from Po except the original money that they had come upon when they had robbed Samad. She would take her cut and nothing more. He owed her that, but he could keep the rest. She couldn't believe that Po would think she was stealing from him, but she didn't feel the need to explain herself. The relationship had run its course, and Liberty was left heartbroken for the third time in her life. Her first heartbreak had come from watching her father be murdered, the second time had committed suicide in order to join her in death; a death that she had yet to see. Now Po had pushed her out of his life and deserted her when she needed him the most. Finally she saw Dahlia's car pull out of Po's estate. She waited a few moments to make sure that the coast was clear before she slid through the gate.

She entered the house and rushed upstairs, moving with haste as she pulled her luggage out from under the bed. She just wanted to get in and out of there as quickly as possible. When she entered the closet she immediately noticed the rolls of money lying on the floor. She knelt down and flipped through the bills.

This isn't mine. What the fuck? she thought. Liberty picked the money up off the floor, scooping it into the shoe box and placed it back on the shelf. *Does he think that I took this from him? This money isn't even worth taking. I have ten times that of my own. Why would I risk our relationship for chump change?* She turned the box to the side and noticed that it was a size seven. She saw red as the number jumped out at her because she wore a size ten. She stormed out of the bedroom and waltzed into Dahlia's room, heading straight for her closet. A shoe whore at heart, Dahlia's closet was lined with boxes and boxes of designer footwear. Liberty read the size on one of them and sure enough, size seven was on the boxes.

"Ahem!"

The sound of someone clearing her throat caused Liberty to drop the shoe box in her hands. She turned around quickly to see Dahlia standing behind her, arms folded across her chest as she looked at Liberty challengingly.

"I thought Po made himself clear yesterday," Dahlia said. "You need to leave."

"You bitch. You set me up. You planted this money inside of my closet so that Po would think I was stealing from him!" Liberty accused.

"So you know," Dahlia said with a shoulder shrug. "What are you going to do about it, Liberty?"

Dahlia walked toward Liberty and began to walk around her, circling her as she spoke. "You gonna tell him? You gonna force me to leave and reclaim your throne?" Dahlia was so close to Liberty that the scent of her perfume made Liberty's stomach churn in disgust. "You have no idea who you're fucking with. I already took your man, dear cousin. Don't make me take your life. Your best bet is to stay out of my way before I put you in the dirt the same way I did Omega," Dahlia threatened.

Liberty's eyes widened in surprise. She couldn't believe that Dahlia had murdered Omega. She brushed past her cousin, realizing that she never really knew Dahlia. This could not be the same little girl who she played with, bathed with, and slept with as a child. Dahlia was the devil's seed. Disgusted, Liberty quickly grabbed the key to her safe deposit box and rushed out of the house. A part of her wanted to call Po and warn him about who he was dealing with, but the other part said fuck it. He had chosen Dahlia, and there was nothing he could ever say to take away the painful sting of that decision. *He has no idea who he has invited into his bed,* she thought as she reached her car. This time she refused to go back.

TWENTY-SEVEN

JUST AS LIBERTY WAS GETTING INTO HER car, she saw Rocko walking up to the house.

"Rocko! Where's Po! I need to see him!" she said in frustration and pain.

"I don't know. We just got back to the States this morning. He had to go handle some other business," he said as he noticed the pained look on her face. "Why? Is everything okay?" he asked.

"It's nothing," Liberty said as she turned her head trying to disguise her true feelings. Rocko gently grabbed her by the shoulders and looked into her eyes.

"What's wrong? You look crazy right now," he asked, knowing that Liberty wasn't being completely honest with him.

"Po is not the same, Rocko. That bitch is controlling his mind and fucking up my life," Liberty said as her voice began to crack. She felt her knees begin to buckle and Rocko held her up and hugged her.

"Whoa, I got you, Liberty," he said as he held her up. "Don't worry about it. I'm going to have a talk with Po. He's too smart to let this bullshit take place. I feel it in my heart that something isn't right with Dahlia. She has evil eyes. She has a bad soul," Rocko expressed honestly. He looked toward the house and saw Dahlia standing in the window looking down on them with an evil stare.

Dahlia watched as Rocko embraced Liberty and smiled devilishly as she stepped away from the window and began to put her plan into motion. "So, you're the next one to go, huh?" Dahlia said to herself as she saw that Rocko had picked sides. *Too bad, I actually liked you, Rocko,* she thought as she folded her arms and watched them from afar. In her twisted mind, anybody who stood next to her enemy would be caught in her crosshairs. So, therefore, Rocko had to get forced out of the picture as well.

Dahlia had begun to become addicted to power. She loved that she had one of the most powerful men in the drug game under her thumb. She understood that pillow talk controlled the world, and when you are pillow talking with a boss . . . you run his world. She was meticulously establishing her position of power and was at the point of no return. Omega had kept her dormant for so many years, but now with him out of the way . . . she was transforming into what was meant to be: the Queen Bee.

Rocko looked up at her, and they locked eyes. It seemed as if a beamed laser of Rocko's nasty stare shot directly to Dahlia. She smiled sinisterly and turned away. She knew at that moment that Rocko was her enemy and a potential wedge between her and Po. She had to do something about that situation. She peeked out once again and watched as Rocko and Liberty got into their cars and pulled off. She thought it was odd that Rocko followed Liberty in his car as she pulled away, so she quickly grabbed her keys and rushed out. She wanted to see where they were going and what they were doing.

Liberty walked into the hotel room she had been staying at with Rocko close behind her. They agreed to talk about how to approach Po. They both knew that Dahlia had played a big part in his sudden change of character.

"I have been trying to call him. I want him to meet us here, so we can all talk and get this shit together. We have to keep our core strong and tight, and I don't believe we can do that with this bitch Dahlia in the picture," Rocko preached as he stood by the door, attempting to call Po again.

"I'm glad you noticed it to. Something's not right with her. She is crazy, and she has Po moving very sloppy." Liberty added.

"Everything is going to be smooth. I just have to pull my man's coattail on this one. Po is a gangster, and he's going to step back and respect it. He'll make everything right. Trust me. I just can't get in contact with him. His line is going straight to voicemail."

Dahlia quickly pulled back to the house as she began to put her plan together in her head. She smiled, seeing that she had beat Po home. He had a meeting with a coke connect earlier that day, and she expected him any minute now. She quickly rushed into the house with her camera in hand. She had taken photos of Liberty and Rocko entering the hotel room just minutes ago, and she knew how she could work it in her favor.

She walked past the hall mirror. It seemed as if her reflection made her stop in her tracks. She looked at her herself. She looked into her deep brown eyes and glanced at her cocoa skin. A smile formed on her face, and she didn't know why. As she looked deeper she finally realized that she was smiling. She actually liked being conniving and deceitful. It gave her a rush, and it was slightly becoming an obsession. She had always been attracted to powerful men, but she was coming to realize that it wasn't an attraction; instead, it was a desire to be in their position. She hurried to the bedroom so that she could prepare for Po's arrival.

TWENTY-EIGHT

PO PULLED INTO HIS DRIVEWAY AND TOOK a deep breath. He had a long week and just wanted to lie back and relax. The thought of Liberty filled his mind, but when he started to think about how she deceived him, rage overpowered the love. He approached the door and Dahlia stood in the doorway waiting for him . . . naked. The only thing she wore was black lipstick and black six-inch heels. Her fat vagina seemed to be sitting up, and it was shaven bald so Po could see every crease. His eyes scanned her body as he approached the door. He was speechless. His manhood instantly began to rise as she opened the glass screen door and grabbed him by his belt buckle.

Dahlia pulled him in as she walked backward. His hands instantly gripped her perky breasts, and he began to massage them. A small moan escaped her lips as she closed her eyes and ran her tongue across her top lip. Once Po got completely into the house, she dropped to her knees and unbuckled his pants. She quickly pulled Po's rock-hard tool from his jeans and took him into her mouth. She was about to put down another plot, but first, she needed to have Po at his weakest state. She, being a master manipulator, knew that weakness came after a man had been well sexed.

She dropped his pants and began sucking him off as she grabbed his sack with eager hands and began massaging it gently, all while deep throating him. His phone began to ring. Using one hand, she grabbed the phone, still giving him head, and turned it off. She was doing what she did so well that Po threw his head back and was in a sexual trance. He felt an orgasm fast approaching, and his legs stiffened up as he gripped the back of Dahlia's head, forcing his length deep inside of her throat. Dahlia quickly stopped and stood up.

"What's wrong? Why did you stop?" Po asked as he frowned up in disappointment. He pipe was sticking straight out with veins forming all through it. He was just about ready to explode before he was cut short. She turned around and headed toward the stairs. She smiled, knowing that Po's eyes were on her juicy, round, black assets. She swished harder making her cheeks jiggle with each step. Just as expected, he followed her up the stairs.

After she sexed his brains out . . . she would plant the seeds to make her the new Queen Pen and X out all and everyone who could stop that. She had to separate Po from Rocko and Liberty . . . and that's exactly what she planned on doing. This was only the beginning of the takeover; a takeover for the ages. Heads were about to roll, and Dahlia would be at the forefront orchestrating it.

An hour later, Po was laying on the bed breathing heavily, watching the ceiling fan slowly spin round and round. Dahlia had just put the best sex known to mankind on him, and he was basking in the aftermath. As Dahlia, completely naked, walked from the bathroom and joined Po in the bed, she placed a camera on his chest.

"What's this?" Po asked as he looked down at the gadget that was on his chest.

"Just take a look at it, my king. You know I always look out for my man, right? I saw some things that maybe you were too busy to see, and I wanted to put you on to it," she said as she lay beside him and lovingly stroked his limp pole while talking to him.

Po slowly picked up the camera and began to click through the pictures. Dahlia had snapped pictures of Liberty and Rocko entering a hotel room, putting her plan down precisely.

"What is this supposed to mean?" Po asked as he gently tossed the camera on the bed as if it didn't matter to him.

"I just thought you should know. I thought Rocko was your brethren. He shouldn't be stepping out with your ex, should he?" she asked as she smiled on the inside, but had a concerned look plastered on her face.

"Look, ma, I could care less. Rocko is my man, a hundred grand. We don't trip over a piece of pussy, believe that," he stated as he closed his eyes and leaned his head back. Although he didn't show it to Dahlia, he was steaming on the inside. He didn't want to show his real feelings to her, but his clenched jaws told it all.

Dahlia smiled just as she grabbed the vial of coke from the nightstand and placed a small pile between her thumb and fingers. She took a bump, and then prepared one for Po. He quickly snorted the coke off her hand and rested his head on the bed. He smiled as his rod instantly began to grow. He discovered sex with coke and Dahlia was the next best thing to heaven. It got to the point that every time they had sex, he had to have coke in his system. What he thought was having a good time was actually Dahlia's deceitful web that she was spinning. She controlled his mind while he was high and horny.

She smiled as she saw the coke taking effect on Po and lowered her head, putting her juicy and warm mouth on his now-growing rod. Her seed had been planted. Now, the only thing she would have to do is water it, and Rocko would eventually get pushed out of the circle like she had planned. In her twisted mind, Rocko was on Liberty's side and that made him her enemy. She knew to fully control Po's thoughts, she had to separate him from any and everyone he loved. Then she would eventually call all the shots . . . through him.

Two weeks had passed, and Po had completely cut Rocko off. He never told him the reason behind their sudden disassociation, but honestly, Po's ego was bruised. Dahlia had consistently drilled that Rocko was jealous of him and would eventually come for his spot. She was highly intelligent and had managed to break a bond that was once so strong. With the sex and drugs, Po had no chance against Dahlia's game of mental chess.

Rocko, on the other end, had been trying to catch up with Po, but his calls went unreturned and the door was never answered. Po's business in the streets was going unhandled, and Rocko knew something was up. He intuitively knew that Dahlia was behind his man's change of character. He kept in contact with Liberty and checked up on her frequently, trying to be the bridge between her and Po, but with no contact with his man . . . things didn't look good. He let Liberty borrow his car for the week because her car had been "mysteriously" vandalized and all her tires had been sliced. She put the car in the shop, and Rocko let her used his tinted Range Rover for the weekend.

Rocko drove on the highway, heading to Po's house, hoping to catch him there. He had to see what the deal was. He had no idea that Dahlia had cunningly turned Po against him. Just the one hug that he gave Liberty, which was seen by Dahlia, changed their whole relationship.

The sun's beams shined down on the massive blue ocean. There wasn't a cloud in the sky. With an open lined shirt, Po stood at the dock and looked at Dahlia who stood on the boat, applying suntan lotion to her arms and neck. Her voluptuous body filled out the two-piece Burberry swimsuit nicely. Po looked down at his watch, and then slid his hands into his pocket. Dahlia looked over at Po and smiled as the boatmen pulled up the anchor and prepared for their weekend at sea. It was Dahlia's idea to take a weekend getaway, and Po felt it was needed.

He yelled over to Dahlia. "I'll be right back. I have to talk to my man," he said as he walked down the boardwalk toward the parking area. A tinted Range Rover was waiting for him. Po looked around, and then got into the vehicle, where Li'l Mikey waited on him.

"What's up, big homie?" Li'l Mikey said as he gripped the steering wheel and checked the rearview mirror.

"What's good, li'l man?" Po asked as he looked over at the live wire from his old trap spot.

"Thanks for coping me this nice-ass whip," Li'l Mikey said as he smiled and rubbed the wood grain on the steering wheel.

"No doubt. That's what you get when you move up in the ranks, li'l homie," Po said as he reached into his pocket and pulled out a small vial of coke. He emptied a small pile onto the dashboard, and then used his nose as a vacuum to snort it up. He passed the vial to Li'l Mikey, who poured a small amount between his thumb and his finger. He snorted it like a pro and threw his head back to prevent his nose from running.

"I got you. I'ma hold you down," Li'l Mikey said as he nodded his head up and down with a cold stare.

Po really did not trust Li'l Mikey, but he loved his coldness and live-wire attitude. He felt he needed a crazy nigga on his team to take the place of Rocko. The heavy coke snorting began to cloud his judgment, and he began to move sloppy. He didn't realize it, but Dahlia had begun to call the shots.

"Remember what I said. Make it clean and quick." Po

stated as he reached into his pocket and pulled out a roll of money. He placed it in Li'l Mikey's lap, whose eyes lit up like a Christmas tree.

"I got you! Rocko will be out of here before you get back from your trip. It's a new era," Li'l Mikey said as he wiped his nose and nodded his head up and down.

Li'l Mikey had spotted Rocko's car earlier that day and was just waiting on the confirmation from Po. Po was about to knock off his best friend because of Dahlia's manipulation. She had somehow convinced him that if he didn't get Rocko, that Rock would eventually get him. With the coke in his system, Po was a different person. He was about to commit the ultimate betrayal. He slapped hands with Li'l Mikey and exited the car, heading back to the boat where Dahlia awaited. Their voyage was about to begin as someone else's was about to end.

Rocko pulled up to Po's house and hopped out of the car. He tried calling Po's number again, but this time he got a disconnection message. "What the fuck?" Rocko said to himself as he looked at the phone's screen to see if he had the right number. He was totally in the dark of what was about to unfold. He walked to the front door and noticed that the door was slightly ajar.

"Yo, Po!" he yelled as he put his hand on the doorknob. He slowly pushed the door open and stepped in with caution. "Yo, Po!" he yelled again.

Rocko stopped in his tracks when he saw about ten Africans standing with guns pointed at him. He quickly tried to reach for his gun, but a single shot rang out hitting him in the knee, causing him to crumble. A tall chocolate man with a model's physique stepped over him . . . It was Zulu. He came over to the States to end the burden that was over his shoulders. Dahlia had to die. The itch of killing her was far too difficult to ignore. He came over for one reason and one reason only. His secret would die with Dahlia, and he wasn't settling for anything less. He wanted Dahlia's head. Zulu looked down and pointed a gun at Rocko's head.

"I'm going to ask you this one time and one time only. Where . . . is . . . Dahlia?"

Sitting in the parking lot of her hotel, Liberty had a heavy heart. She wiped the single tear that dropped from her face as she sat in the truck and rested her head on the steering wheel. She missed Po and wanted things to be normal, but she realized that she would never be able to make things right. She was ready to leave town and Po for good. She just was waiting until her car was repaired, and then she would leave. As she sat in Rocko's tinted Rover she thought about the current day's date. It was a date that was close to her heart and dear to her soul. It was the anniversary of A'shai's death. She knew that Po would never give her the love that A'shai once had. Maybe that was why she chased love so quickly with Po. She was merely trying to fill a void that A'shai had left vacant with his death.

Liberty was ready for a new beginning . . . a new life. She took a deep breath and started up the car. She was headed to get a bite to eat. That's when a vehicle pulled alongside of her. She didn't even notice the sinister scowl that the young boy had on his face as things unfolded. "I love you always, A'shai," she whispered as she closed her eyes and imagined his face. Liberty never saw it coming . . .

As Li'l Mikey extended his arm out the window, shots rang out from his gun as he Swiss cheesed the truck. He thought Rocko was in the truck, but the tint didn't reveal that it was Liberty that he was shooting. *Rat tat tat tat tat tat tat* . . .

MURDERVILLE 3

THE BLACK DAHLIA

Coming Soon

This book is dedicated to the fans.

Without you, there would be no us.

We love you all.

True story.

ALSO BY ASHLEY AND JAQUAVIS
Murderville
Dirty Money
Diary of a Street Diva
Supreme Clientele
The Trophy Wife
The Cartel
The Cartel 2
The Cartel 3
Girls from da Hood 4
Girls from da Hood 6
Kiss Kiss Bang Bang
Black Friday
Prada Plan 1
Prada Plan 2
The Dopeman's Wife
The Dopefiend
Dopeman
Moth to a Flame

For sneak peeks and an excerpt of our next novel visit:
WWW.READORDIEONLINE.COM and
WWW.ASHLEYJAQUAVIS.COM

Next comes *Carter Diamond* (an e-book short story):
Before there was the Cartel . . . he stood alone
(September 1, 2012).

Also look out for *Cartel 4* due out this fall
(October 31, 2012).

Follow us on Twitter @RealJaQuavis *&* @Novelista
Web site: www.ashleyjaquavis.com

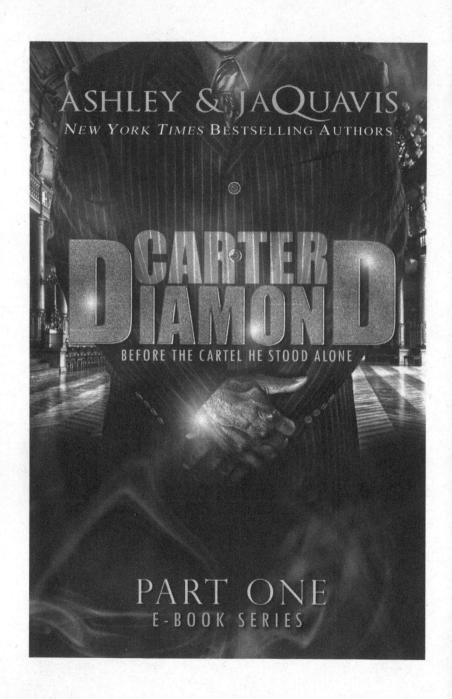